BRIMSTONE NIGHTMARES

DAMNED MAGIC AND DIVINE FATES 4

KEL CARPENTER

Brimstone Nightmares

Kel Carpenter

Published by Kel Carpenter

Copyright © 2019, Kel Carpenter

Edited by Analisa Denny

Cover Art by Yocla Designs

Exclusive Stock from Lindee Robinson Photography

Models Featured: Kailey Marie & Dimi Bozinovski

 Created with Vellum

To the people who stand with you through the hard times...
because the best is yet to come.

Pride goeth before destruction, and an haughty spirit before a fall.

Proverbs 16:18

PART I

CHAPTER ONE

WHO WOULD HAVE THOUGHT THAT HELL'S GATE was inside a donut shop?

Okay, not a donut shop, per se. The infamous French café was much classier than that. Still, the powdered sugar things on my plate were really deep-fried donuts if we were all being honest. While it wasn't Martha's, I wasn't turning down donuts and black coffee for my last meal on Earth.

"So, how's this going to work?" I bit into a sugary sweet piece of dough. "We just walk through the portal and bam—we're in?" Bandit reached over my shoulder and swiped a beignet off my plate, stuffing it in his mouth before I could try to steal it back. I gave him a sideways look that he pretended not to notice as he dove off of me, onto the table, and flung himself at Laran. I shook my head as Laran nuzzled him behind the ears. Sucker.

"Pretty much." Rysten nodded, picking at his own breakfast. "There's typically a queue to get through the portal, but you being who you are and us being the Horsemen, they're going to make an exception." I nodded along, trying to take it all in.

"Not to mention my badass wings," Moira piped up. She stroked the tip of her marbled blue wing and tucked them in tight. While she wasn't completely back to her usual self after being trapped in the underground of Le Ban Dia, she was better. It would take time for her to work through what happened. I would respect her choice if she chose to never say what went down in that dark place—as long as she got better.

"They can't see your wings," I reminded her, taking a sip of coffee. Hot and bitter. Just the way I liked it.

"Such a pity." Her dismissive tone had Rysten rolling his eyes and she left it at that. We lapsed into a comfortable silence for a few minutes, finishing off our breakfast while I decided how to phrase my next question.

"So, when we get to Hell..." I paused, nibbling on the edge of a beignet. The anxiety of it all had my stomach in knots. "How exactly is this going to go down?" Another sip. I cocked an eyebrow, looking around the table from Julian—who sat stoic at my left—all the way to Moira who placed herself on my right.

"Don't look at me." She raised her hands. "You know as much as I do."

Point taken. I switched to staring at Rysten. He

sighed and became very interested in his donuts, as if grappling for words. It was Laran that spoke.

"When we left Hell, our mission was to retrieve you as fast as possible. Return, so that the Sins could judge you. It should have been less than a week."

I frowned. "But I had a life..." Laran nodded, understanding.

"You did," he agreed. "But you are Lucifer's heir. Neither the Sins nor your father took whatever life you would build in their absence into account while planning. They didn't take *you* into account. You were born to rule and it's as simple as that for them. Just as they are the chosen stewardesses, we all assumed that you would accept your role without too much...trouble." Bandit moved around his shoulder, perching perilously close to a tray a server was holding. One swipe of his paw as the server walked by and a beignet went missing without anyone else noticing. Bandit stuffed it in his mouth and turned around. His cheeks were comically packed when he looked at me.

"What are you saying exactly?"

"He's saying," Julian said, settling back, the dark green of his eyes weighing on me, "that we were supposed to return with you in under a week and it's been almost two months." I took another swig of coffee, swallowing hard.

"Well, yeah...but I had to transition and there was the whole thing with the imp—"

"The Sins aren't known for their patience," Allistair said. "One day on Earth is a week in Hell. It's been over a year for them since Lucifer died. They probably think we either didn't want to bring you...."

"...or I didn't want to go," I finished for him. Allistair gave me a tight smile and nodded once. "Well, it could be worse. I could be dead." Laran choked on his beignet.

"That won't happen," Julian said with great assurance. I wanted to spout some nonsense about 'pride goeth before the fall,' but after all the near-death experiences it wasn't nearly as funny as it once might have been.

"Either way," Moira interrupted, running a hand through her dark green tresses, "she's not dead and we're here now. What was the original plan?"

"The Sins intend to test you. Test whether you are worthy to rule," Allistair answered. I didn't miss the way Julian fell pensive beside me, seeming to be out of it, but the nerve in his jaw twitched, giving me the impression it wasn't that simple. "When we cross through the portal, we'll land in Lust. Then you'll meet with the current Sin of Lust and be asked to complete a challenge to prove that you are capable of ruling her province should she fall, if another has not already taken her brand to replace her. Once you pass, we will move to the next Sin, and the next, until you pass every test."

"Honestly, love, you're half-succubus. You should be fine," Rysten said with a wink. Somehow that didn't ease the slow tightening creeping through my chest. Worry. That I wouldn't be up to par. That I would fail. That the beautiful illusion of what they've told me is just that. A dream that will never come to pass.

"Should be." I had to work to keep the bite out of my tone. "That doesn't mean I will. What happens if I fail?" I asked them. No one answered me. They were too busy mentally communicating with each other, and unfortunately—thanks to Sin and her rune of silence—I could no longer hear it.

"We have a backup plan," Julian eventually said. My eyes narrowed.

"What is that supposed to mean?"

"It means"—Rysten leaned back and dug through his pocket—"that we won't let anything happen to you." He pulled out something and extended his hand. When his fingers unfurled, I frowned.

In the center of his palm sat a silver ring flecked with gold.

"Um..." I was at a loss for words. "If that was meant to be some kind of proposal, you're a little late." Laran threw his head back and laughed. The sound was followed by the booming of thunder and the wind picked up outside. It would be strange to be an elemental, where something as simple as a laugh could trigger a change in the atmosphere. In New Orleans, so many of them gathered in one place and it didn't often make for sunny skies.

"It's not a proposal, love. It's our get out of jail free

7

card." Rysten dropped the ring into my palm and dug through his pocket, pulling out another and handing it over to Moira. She slipped it on her right-hand ring finger, and we both watched as it shrunk to fit her perfectly. "Have you ever heard of *The Divine Comedy?*"

I snorted. "Is that a question?" Moira snickered into her coffee cup.

"So, you know all about the rings of Hell?" Allistair asked. *Well, now, I didn't say that...*

I slid my eyes sideways, chewing on my lip. I paused, and my lip slipped free of my teeth at the twinkling amusement in his eyes.

"There's nine of them," I replied, fairly certain of myself until the four of them all started laughing and I remembered that was the human version. "Um... seven?" Julian's large arm fell around my shoulders as his foot hooked around my chair and jerked it closer to his.

"First, there's six provinces," Julian said. "It's only because of that damned poem that everyone refers to them as rings." His free hand reached around and grabbed the small silver piece out of my hand, holding it up. I realized my own mistake just before he said it. "Second, the rings he referenced were *these.*" I could feel his sharp green eyes on my face, and the proximity between us in public should be a lot larger if they wanted me to think clearly.

"I think she gets the point," Allistair said. The corner of Julian's lips turned up as he dropped the ring back in my hand but made no move to put more distance between us. "Dante was the only known human to be taken into Hell that also found his way back, but by then his mind was utterly broken. *The Divine Comedy* is closer to the hazy remnants after a vivid dream than it is to Hell itself. The rings are how you get from one province to another. Hell is so large, and only a very small percentage possess a form of teleportation, so the Unseelie created rings with blood magic and brimstone. For most demons their ring will take them to anywhere within the province they were born. Yours will take you to any of the six provinces that the Deadly Sins watch over."

"Six? That doesn't make sense. But I thought there were sev—wait, did you just say that demons can't normally just go wherever they want in Hell?" Moira asked, and the tone of her voice clearly suggested how put off she was with that thought.

"No," Rysten answered after taking a sip of his café au lait. "Most demons are born and die in the same province. Unless they have the money or power to do otherwise."

"Harsh," Moira whistled.

"There are worse things," Rysten shrugged noncommittally.

"Such as?" she fired back.

9

"Being born on Earth," Allistair replied. A noise of spluttered disagreement.

"What's so bad about Earth? I'd rather be born here than be a born a slave," Moira said acidly.

"Earth robs you of your magic. While Hell is overflowing with it," Allistair said. "Only the strongest of demons or Fae can truly thrive here because the very ground itself leaches away your power."

"We are stronger in Hell," Laran said and nodded in agreement. They continued discussing the advantages of being in Hell compared to the barren planet that was the only home I'd ever known. I vaguely wondered if my own abilities would be stronger in Hell and shuddered at the thought. The flames were destructive enough as it was.

I turned the ring over between my fingers, feeling the slightest sliver of power emitting from it, not completely different than my own. Almost familiar in a way...

"How does it work?" I asked, angling the silver in the light so that the etchings on the inside revealed themselves.

"Think of where you want to go and twist the band once," Allistair rattled off. A knowing smirk lit up his lips as Moira twisted her ring and nothing happened.

"Mine's broken," she complained. Bandit let out a raucous laugh.

"No, it's not," Rysten said.

"Yes, it is."

"They don't work on Earth."

"That's a dumb design," Moira said sharply.

I rolled my eyes, thinking on what he'd said. Most demons were born and died in the same province, but I'd been born in Hell and came to a new world. I may as well be an entirely different kind of demon because I couldn't fathom a world where I didn't even have the choice of where to live.

These were my final moments on Earth, the place I grew up, the world I was raised in, and it struck me that I had very little clue of what truly waited for me on the other side. Sure, the Horsemen could tell me about it, but in the end, I wouldn't know until I got there. It was almost surreal to sit in this rickety wooden chair, simultaneously knowing and not knowing what was to come.

Not two months ago these four males walked into my life, and I knew then it would never be the same. If someone had told me I'd literally be sitting in front of Hell's Gates, drinking coffee and eating donuts with the Four Horsemen—who I'd branded as my mates— well, I'd have asked what they were smoking and where I could get some. Never in my wildest dreams had I imagined this would be what became of my life, but I wouldn't change it.

In these four that I still knew so little about, I found happiness. That's not to say I wasn't happy before, living with Moira and Bandit...but it was a different kind. This ache in my chest felt so wholly different from the kind of pure emotions I felt for my familiars. Where they were a gentle breeze on a summer day, my four mates were a disaster. A beautiful, natural, reckless disaster that left me gasping for air and wondering how I could possibly survive.

Maybe I wouldn't. I turned the ring over, letting my thoughts wander. They'd called this tiny piece of metal a get out of jail free card, like it would somehow save me from the wrath of the Sins should I fail. As I angled it under the light, something caught my attention.

"When did you have these made?" I asked. That strand of blue was too familiar to be anything other than my own hair. Moira's probably had her hair as well.

"How did you know we had them made?" Laran asked. I glanced up, only then noticing the way all five pairs of eyes were on me.

"Well there aren't exactly factories cranking these things out, and even if you made this when I was a baby"—I thrust my thumb in Moira's direction—"you didn't plan for her. So, you had to have these made after coming to Earth. Yes?"

Laran nodded slowly, watching me curiously.

"We had them made yesterday," Rysten answered. "After your transition. Once we knew that neither of you had any form of teleportation." The very mention of my transition had my blood heating a little. I plowed on, choosing to focus on the need to know instead of the need that was never sated with me.

"Blood magic," I mused, still trying to lock down on that niggling feeling inside. It was just a ring. Moira also had one...so why did I feel like there was something strange about mine? "I'm guessing you didn't make them yourselves?" I phrased it like a question, hoping for some sort of confirmation one way or the other. Allistair watched me closely.

"No. An old friend of mine made them," he said slowly. "Is there something wrong?" he asked, his gaze flicking between the ring I still hadn't put on my hand and the strange path my line of questioning had taken.

"Just curious is all," I answered with a smile.

"You should try it on," Julian said suddenly.

I swallowed hard, not sure why I was so nervous to begin with. None of them would do anything to harm me. Well, nothing to truly harm me. A little bruising or blood otherwise...I held up the ring with one hand, positioning it just over my right ring finger. Allistair's deep golden gaze drilled into me, watching me slowly slip it on.

It settled at the base of my finger and shrunk to size. Holding my breath, I waited, but nothing happened. The faintest trace of magic touched me, but it was so slight compared to what was already within me that I didn't even shudder. Both foreign and familiar, I knew the magic in this ring just as I knew who made it, but it seemed my fears—at least in this—were for nothing.

My response to it was the reason she had spelled

me in the first place, and now they thought I was acting strange for nothing. I moved my hands to my lap, forcing myself to be at ease.

Julian rubbed my shoulder, softly kneading the tissue. I froze, forgetting myself for a moment because the gesture was so strange coming from him. Julian paused. "Something wrong?" His lips skimmed the hollow of my ear and my eyes fluttered. I fought the urge to sink into him. The only thing that stopped me was the narrowed eyes of my other three mates.

"No—"

"Ready?" The voice carried on a heavy note. A subtle thrum of the old south to it. Standing with his right arm crooked in a proper motion of a server, the demon had dark skin, long dreadlocks woven with gold, and bright purple Cheshire eyes.

Enigma. Chaos demons.

Their kind weren't common on Earth, partially because their inability to blend as well as most other species. Enigmas were incapable of glamoring themselves because of the chaos that lived within. It leaked out into the atmosphere causing misfortune wherever they went—usually in the form of breaking things. Two tables over, a waiter stumbled. Three cups of coffee tipped off the tray, straight into a rubrum's lap. It was only seconds before a fist went flying and the cafe descended into madness.

I swallowed hard and Julian's arm dropped away from my shoulders.

"We should be going while they are distracted," the enigma said. My eyes drifted over the scene as multiple demons had to move on the rubrum in an attempt to subdue him. Most other demons didn't even bat an eye at the outburst.

As if sensing my hesitation, cool fingers brushed across my cheek. I turned into Julian as he captured my chin between his forefinger and thumb. "We will keep you safe." His dark eyes trailed over my face for a fraction of a second longer before he dropped my chin and pushed back in his chair. He got to his feet and extended his hand, waiting for me to follow him and take it.

Ordinarily I would have gotten to my feet and stalked off, but I wasn't feeling all that sassy or brave today.

I took his hand and he pulled me to my feet. Without another word, the enigma turned and led the way through the cafe. My palms started to sweat as we came to pause before a black metal door that was scraped in spots. The paint had faded to leave a silver sheen beneath the claw marks. The enigma shot us a grin over his shoulder before pushing the door open.

My feet stalled as my mouth fell ajar.

I wasn't sure what I was expecting, but a ten-foot-wide hole that plunged straight down with no end in sight wasn't it. The weathered concrete floor gave way to some sort of craggy black stone as it neared the abyss.

"What the fuck are you doing here, Jax—"

"I'm on an assignment," the enigma cut in. His purple eyes flashed with something mischievous.

"No can do," the same guard who'd called at him stepped up. "We're under strict orders. No one is supposed to go through that portal." He thrust his chin towards the portal and came to stand toe-to-toe with Jax. The enigma smiled at the other demon, clearly not all that concerned.

"If that's the case, you can be the one that tells the Sins why I couldn't escort Lucifer's heir and the Four Horsemen back to Hell," Jax said. The pale demon raised his eyebrows and flicked his gaze towards me. The beast pushed forward to smile callously at the demon, and he flushed.

"See something you like?" she asked in a flat, dead voice. Rysten stepped in front of me, blocking the male's line of sight. A low growl reverberated from him. That seemed to please her. I shoved forward, rolling my eyes as she receded with a smirk on her face.

"That's his daughter?" the guard asked in a hushed voice. "I thought it was just a rumor that she'd been in NOLA..."

"Are you going to let us through or stand there ogling at my mate?" Rysten asked softly. It wasn't the caress that woke me from my nightmares, but the whisper of death and decay. "If it's the latter, you won't be standing long."

Moira snorted and the glamor around her

dropped. The other guards surrounding the portal cast her wary glances as she smiled ruthlessly, flexing her wings like a proud stallion might strut. The very tip of one whacked into the back of Rysten's head, and she snapped them in tight, whistling to herself as he looked over at her. What I would've given to see his face.

"Who is she?" The same guard that had been staring at me only a moment before now watched Moira with interest. She lifted a dark green eyebrow and ran a hand through her hair, pushing it back so that the brand on her forehead glowed. The horned helmet with black wings.

"No one," Rysten growled.

"Out of your league," Moira said at the same time. She twisted her lips in a smirk at Rysten's expression, not even noticing the way the guards watched her.

"Doesn't matter," Jax answered, crossing his arms over his chest. He nodded toward the portal and said, "What'll it be, Levi?"

The guard looked over all of us, seeming to weigh his decision back and forth. The Horsemen seemed utterly at ease, and I got the feeling if he denied us entry it might not matter. He likely wouldn't live to see that decision through. Levi must have realized this as well because he took a few steps back and swept his arm towards the pit to motion us forward. An uneasy knot twisted in my stomach as we approached the chasm.

"Out of curiosity," Levi mused, "which Sin sent you?"

The enigma paused at the edge of the rock. His bright purple eyes shining faintly in the low light as he stared down into the seemingly never-ending hole. "Which one do you think?" He let out a dark chuckle. "The only one I was dumb enough to make a deal with."

He stepped off the ledge without a shred of fear. I wish I could say the same, but even the beast couldn't make me that brave. A warm hand wrapped around mine and I looked up at Moira.

"It's going to be okay, Rubes."

"You say that about everything," I scoffed. Inside me the panic was slowly rising. This was it. My last moment on Earth. And I was quickly becoming paralyzed with fear. Sharp claws pricked my leg as Bandit tried to get ahold on my jeans to pull himself up. I bent at the waist and scooped him up with one arm. He clung to me as his tiny paws wrapped around my neck, like he understood what was happening.

"I say that because I know it." She tapped her temple with her free hand and flicked her eyes towards the abyss. "We're going to get through this, and you're going to pass the trials and get your crown. It's what you were born for."

I shuddered. *If only it could be that simple.*

My arms broke out in goosebumps at the subtle

heat emanating from the portal. The energy felt familiar. Almost like...home.

Without giving myself the chance to rethink it, I gripped Moira's hand and held Bandit tighter—and then I stepped over the ledge and into my future.

My life on Earth was done.

My life in Hell...it was only beginning.

CHAPTER TWO

THE RUSH OF THE WIND RATTLED MY BONES AS A scream ripped from my throat.

The time Allistair pushed me off a cliff felt like a lifetime ago, and I thought that was bad. Little did I realize how much worse it could get. At least the lake beneath had stars to look at as I thought I was hurdling towards my death. The abyss was simply nothing.

There was no light. No stars. No end.

We could be freefalling to our deaths for all I knew. Not that I believed that. Jax had stepped off without fear like he'd done this a hundred times, and while I couldn't turn to look, I did sense that the Horsemen were falling behind us.

A light touch to my back made me twitch as a warm hand grasped the back of my shirt. I craned my neck to the side as flames sparked in my hands. Golden blonde hair tinted blue shined in the low light, and my terror thawed just a smidge. Rysten's comforting darkness wrapped around me, settling like a security blanket. Moira squeezed the hand she held tight, her palm growing slick from the smothering heat of the portal.

Tiny beads of sweat flew behind her as whatever force pulled us downward grew hotter. Moira opened her mouth and yelled in carefree abandon like she was having the time of her life, oblivious to the power I sensed and ignoring the stifling temperature.

Pressure built, making my ears hurt. Rysten yelled something that was lost in the chamber as it echoed off the stony rockface around us. Bandit followed it up with a savage growl, his claws hooking into my back like devil-damned talons just as the swelter and strain became unbearable.

Like breaking through a sound barrier, a pop filled my ears and suddenly we weren't hurdling down anymore—but up. It started as a tiny flicker of blue in an endless darkness. A light where there wasn't. And that spot continued to grow. A hole appeared above us, one that was an impossible azure, almost like the sky, but somehow brighter. I squinted my eyes to discern what it was as droplets of water splattered against my face. My mouth fell ajar. Only as we were cresting the edge did I realize that the speck of blue was actually the other end of the portal. We shot twenty feet straight through a spray of rushing water and into the open air.

A cool breeze filled with the scent of smoke and

ash hit me. I reached a peak in my ascent, becoming weightless for a split second before gravity rushed in. Rysten's fingers slipped from my loose t-shirt as a sudden force kept me from falling, and he was jerked away. I swung my gaze wildly, breathing out an uneasy sigh at the sight of flaming wings. Moira hovered above me, gripping my hand with a strength I didn't know she had while she pumped her wings to slow our descent.

Hell, I thought to myself. This is Hell.

The skies were a jewel tone of sapphire blue, intense amethysts, and the deepest of reds. Ruby. grey wispy clouds hung overhead, luring my gaze to the mountain range and dark plumes of smoke in the distance. That was far off, though, and between here and there was a stretch of burning forest. Trees so tall they had to be a hundred feet from the ground, reaching their spindly branches for the sky. Ones that hadn't yet been eaten by the flames had lost any of their original color, glittering black ash dusting every inch from trunk to the furthest tip of a branch. Flames so dark and devastating flickered in patches where only those ashes remained, encroaching on the hauntingly beautiful trees.

My feet had only barely touched the ash covered stretch of beach when I asked, "What happened here?"

"You left," Jax answered before Rysten could. "Lucifer died, and without power to hold the barriers, our world started crumbling."

"It's not exactly like I had a choice in the matter," I

said tersely. The beast's ire rose at what he implied. Like it was our fault. It was Lola, Lucifer, and the Horsemen that took us from our home world. They were the ones that left us on Earth for twenty-three years.

"You asked what happened. If you don't like the truth, then change it."

"She can't go back in time, asshole," Moira snapped. Her wings spread wide as she stepped up beside me and bared her teeth at the chaos demon with a fierceness not even a hellhound could muster.

"That's not what I meant." He swept his hand all around, referencing the burning patches of Hell. If not on fire, I imagine it might have been beautiful. It still was, in a way. "She's the only one that can stop the borders from continuing to collapse inward on Hell itself. If she doesn't like how our world looks, then she's the one that can change that."

"What do you think I'm doing here?"

Jax eyed me shrewdly. "It takes balls to enter Hell when the Sins aren't happy with you. I'll give you that. Whether or not you fix this remains to be seen." I swallowed hard, biting back my words. There was no point in arguing with him when he wasn't the one I needed to convince. Jax was just an errand boy. The real people calling the shots were somewhere out there—in the fiery depths of Hell.

I turned my back on the burning landscape to look at the sandy shores we'd landed on. The beach stretched on for miles in the opposite direction. Sand mixed with ash, giving it a marbled effect of black on white. The tide reached for my boots as it pushed in and out, but never got closer than six inches away.

"What's that?" I pointed to a mass of rocks. Water crashed against them, giving off a misty spray that reflected rainbows a good thirty feet out at sea. This ocean had some of the clearest water I'd ever seen, which made it all the more troubling at the way it glittered in the sun as particles of ash danced within.

"The portal," Rysten answered as Julian appeared out of the rocks. A blowhole, I realized, as he shot into the sky looking like some god of legend. His white hair sparkled with the same ash that permeated the air and sea and every part of this devilforsaken land. As he crested mid-leap, his legs swept forward, and he hit the ground running, far more graceful than the tumble and roll Rysten took in the sand.

"Already forgotten how to stick the landing, brother?" Julian asked as he came to a stop. Rysten rolled his eyes as both Allistair and Laran burst from the portal, sending a shower of glittering water several tens of feet high and landing a few feet over from us. Bandit chose that moment to fling himself from my arms and into the crystalline waves, if you could call them that. This close to land the water didn't get higher than a few inches, but that didn't stop Bandit from rolling around in it, coating his fur with sand and salt.

"I'd be wary of letting your familiar get too far," Jax

said behind us. Bandit waddled a few feet farther to where the tide came all the way up to his chest.

"Why is that?" I asked, debating taking my shoes off and joining him. No sooner did the thought occur did a dark tentacle snake around Bandit's entire body and pull him under. I lurched forward to grab him as Bandit let out a garbled cry of dismay that was abruptly cut off by the waves.

"The Kraken."

"What?" I screeched. "You mean to tell me a motherfucking kraken just—"

I didn't get through my sentence. A large mass rose up from the water, pouring gallon upon gallon of sea water off its sides. Tentacles—all eight of them—were as long as any bus and the undersides dotted with massive suckers the size of my head. And one of them held Bandit by the foot.

I grit my teeth against screaming for him and instead reached for the flames of Hell. That squid was about to become calamari.

A burning orb of blue appeared in my hand when Moira grabbed my wrist.

"What are you doing—"

"That thing is massive, and the waves are rough. If you kill it, it could land on Bandit and he could drown," Moira said.

"If I don't kill it, he could be its dinner!" Bandit let out a mewling wail as the sea monster's mouth opened and let out a roar. A tongue as fat and thick as any tentacle twisted crudely in the air, pointed teeth as large as my raccoon covered every inch of it. I tore my arm away from Moira, adrenaline making me desperate. Fire licked up my right arm as I hurled a ball of blue fire. It put a hole straight through the fleshy part of the tentacle holding Bandit. The monster thrashed in pain as the fire spread, eating away its skin. Bandit went falling. A gust of wind from the rapid thrust of Moira's wings slammed into me as she jumped into the sky and darted forward to catch him. Another tentacle took a swipe at her, and the split second it took for her to dive and recover her balance sent Bandit careening into the depths of the sparkling black ocean below.

"No!" I shouted, but just as my voice broke across the waves, something crazy happened.

A second mass rose from the water where Bandit had just fallen. One with teeth and claws of its own. He stood over thirty feet tall, water cascading over his body as his black and blue-ringed tail twitched side to side.

"What in Satan's name—" Rysten started to curse. The growl coming from Bandit's chest cut him off as my raccoon stood on two back legs and lifted his arms in the air, letting out a roar that pierced the fear coiled around my heart. Fire shot from his mouth, only missing Moira by inches as she dove to the side, the muscles in her wings strained against the battering winds as she tried to get out of the way of Bandit's raging as fast as possible. Fire rained down on the

kraken, blasting it to pieces as claws slashed fero-
ciously. The kraken tried to wrap a thick tentacle
around Bandit's short snout in an attempt to close his
mouth and stop the spewing flames he breathed.

It was a bad move for the monster. Bandit lunged,
his jaws snapping shut over the meaty appendage. He
bit clean through it and the flames ate at the moist
flesh, leaving the air smelling fishy and charred as the
tentacles dropped off the body, one by one.

Within moments, the only remains of the great sea
monster were ashes in the waves.

Moira swooped around and landed on the beach
beside me, looking as shocked as I felt.

"Remind me next time I call him a trash panda that
he can eat me," she muttered. I took off at a dead sprint
into the water.

"Wait, Ruby!" Rysten called.

"Damnit!" Julian growled.

Water splashed behind me, but I didn't pay it any
mind as Bandit reached out and grabbed me. He let out
a purr, setting me on his shoulder as he walked us back
to land. Oh, how the tables have turned. I wrapped
both my hands in his wet fur, clinging tightly as my
body swayed back and forth from the wind and his
scampering. He still lumbered around like he weighed
thirty pounds and not thirty thousand.

"Now look what he's done—" Rysten started.
Moira elbowed him hard and crossed her arms over her
chest.

"You don't get to speak. He might never give her back just to spite you," she said pointedly. Rysten shut his mouth, glaring to the side at my best friend.

"Ruby, get him to put you down," Julian demanded.

"Why? I can just ride him to the first Deadly Sin like this." I wasn't being serious, but the dark look in his eyes made me snicker. Bandit's massive shoulders shook as he let out this booming noise and fell to the side. I realized too late that he was laughing and I lost my balance. Airborne for only a second, my butt smacked hard against the wet sand, six inches from the incoming tide. "Ugh," I groaned.

"You saw that! The vermin almost got her hurt," Rysten said. He reached out to help me up. I ignored the gesture, pushing myself up with my own hands and feet.

"Pussy," Moira said under her breath, making me choke on a laugh.

"You guys are ridiculous sometimes," I said, brushing my hands together to get the clumps of sand off. Bandit threw himself sideways and the ground shook for a second as he started rolling in the sand again, his thirty-foot form steadily shrinking. I shook my head, muttering, "Completely ridiculous."

"You would do well to heed the warnings of your mates, child," another voice carried from behind them. Jax came strolling up to the water's edge, hands in pockets with a bored expression.

"Bandit literally just killed the kraken. I think it's alright to say I'm safe with him," I replied rather pointedly. Bandit preened under my praise, sitting up nicely as he shrank the rest of the way to his regular size. I smiled and scooped him up in my arms while he chortled happily. "And if for some reason I wasn't, I can take care of myself. But thanks for the input."

"Careful of that pride, Baby Morningstar. The Sins aren't the biggest fans of that particular vice." My lips fell open and then my jaw snapped shut.

"Speaking of the Sins, aren't you supposed to be taking us to one of them?" Moira asked sharply. He smiled bitterly and motioned to the burning forest.

"You want to lead the way?" Judging by his expression, he didn't know Moira was immune to the flames.

Nevertheless, she said, "I don't like this guy's attitude. Can we get rid of him?"

Jax glanced over his shoulder and let out a raucous laugh.

"Why are you laughing?" I asked, completely exasperated and we'd only just arrived.

"You think I wanted to do this? I was sent by one of the Six Sins. It's not like I get a choice," Jax said. I looked over at the Horsemen who seemed to be weighing the enigma's worth.

"Which Sin sent you?" Allistair asked eventually.

"Lust."

My mother's sin.

"Fuck," Allistair said. Yeah, that about sums it up.

29

"You don't turn down a present from Lust. She's not one to take kindly to it," Rysten explained.

"Of course, not," Moira grumbled. "Because that'd be convenient or something."

"I owe Lust a debt and this is what she asked from me to pay it. Escorting you to Inferna is about as easy as it will get with her—"

"Inferna?" Laran asked with a frown.

"Did I stutter?" the enigma retorted, drawing a laugh from Moira.

"Lust may have sent you, demon, but you forget who you're speaking with," Laran growled.

"Inferna wasn't where we were supposed to start, was it?" I asked, a lead weight settling in my stomach.

"No," Julian said, brushing a hand over his jaw. "It wasn't. Then again, Hell shouldn't have started burning either."

"Then why did it?" I asked.

No one seemed to have an answer for that either.

"Is there a way to test the chaos demon and see if Lust really sent him?" Moira piped up.

"We could peel his fingernails one at a time—" Laran started, completely serious.

"Or we could not," I cut in, because I was clearly the only voice of reason around here.

Laran shrugged.

"I can hear you," Jax called loudly.

"Good!" Moira shouted back. "Maybe you'll be less of a dick since she's the only thing stopping them from peeling your nails." She turned away and let out a little huff. "Asshole." I ignored them entirely.

"Can we not just pyroport into Inferna and be done?" I asked, looking at Laran.

"No," Julian said. He faced the forest looking at something far away that none of us could see. "If Hell is on fire, it means the borders are destabilizing and the landscape itself is moving. From here on out we can't use teleportation to get around."

I wrapped my fingers in a tight fist and pressed my lips against it in frustration, the cold metal of the ring bit into my chin. "I'm assuming the rings also won't work?" It was a long shot, but one I needed to ask either way.

Rysten shook his head. "Those can't take you anywhere they haven't physically gone before, and since we had them made on Earth, they can't go anywhere here yet."

"Even if they did, we could be entering any number of places with the current state of things, including the belly of a monster," Laran answered.

"This is shit," Moira declared. She wasn't wrong. Any form of magical teleportation was off the table, which meant we were going to have to do this the old-fashioned way.

"Sounds like we're hiking to Inferna, then." I rolled my shoulders, rocking back on my heels and into the squishy sand. Julian continued to stare off into the distance, but the other three all exchanged various looks of unease. "Unless you guys have a better idea..." I trailed off, raising an eyebrow expectantly.

"It's not that," Allistair sighed. "Ignoring the many things we might come across traveling over land, the only way into Inferna is through the coliseum."

"Coliseum?" Moira stepped forward, sounding far too interested by this. Allistair nodded.

"Hela's idea of *population control*," Rysten said. His fingers curled into air quotes while his cheeks were pulled taut in distaste.

"Is there another option?" I asked.

No one spoke. No one wanted to say it, but the truth was—no—there wasn't. If we couldn't get there magically, we had to find other means, which meant trekking through the forest.

"Do you really think I'd be here if there was?" Jax asked us, his voice dripping with sarcasm.

"Not the point," I said, focusing on the Horsemen. A warm wind blew down the coast, whipping my hair away from my face. Bandit let out a squeal of delight, his tiny paws scrabbling to grab the strands as they danced in the air.

"I think..." Rysten started, "that we don't have another choice. Lust will have already evacuated her province if she sent him to escort you."

"I don't understand that," Moira said suddenly. "You four are like a bajillion years old. You should know how to get there just as well as this guy." She waved her hand in Jax's direction.

"Not if we're dead, we can't," Laran said quietly. My muscles locked up at the very idea. "Hell is very dangerous, and Lucifer had a great many enemies. The Sins won't want to take any chances on her making it back, with or without us." He looked away, and there was something hidden in that gaze of his. A worry he did not want me to see.

"No one is going to die," I said sternly. Not that my heart listened to me. My pulse quickened and my palms heated at the very thought of losing any of them...fire arced across the sky and I stilled. "What was that?"

Jax looked directly upward, narrowing his eyes. "If I had to guess: you."

"Me?" I pressed a hand to my chest as Bandit wrapped his tiny arms tightly around me.

"Likely," Allistair nodded. "If the fire is eating away at Hell it's because the magic that maintained the borders has failed, and it's the same magic that runs in your veins. I wouldn't be surprised if all of this was connected to you." He swept his arm wide, toward the forest.

"Do you think I could put the fire out?" I asked.

"Possibly. Though it would take a great amount of control to put it out and not spread it faster," he answered. I swallowed hard.

"If it's happening because I took too long coming, it's really my responsibility to at least try." Allistair cocked his head.

"It's worth an attempt," Laran said, his axe appearing out of nowhere. He swung it with ease.

"It's not like we actually have another choice," Rysten added. "The forest is burning and we have to go through it to get there."

"So, are we agreed? We're walking to Inferna?" The four of them busted out laughing.

"Walking?" Julian turned toward me, only a fraction of his expression visible. "You do know we are called the Horsemen for a reason, don't you?"

"Well, yeah," I laughed nervously. "I figured it's because, you know...never mind."

I broke off as four massive stallions appeared out of thin air. Moira let out a small shriek that had the forest quivering. "Are those what I think they are?" she asked, out of breath.

"You see them too?" She nodded. "Thank the devil it's not just me. The transition was enough crazy for one lifetime, thank you very much."

One of the horses, a dark chestnut red color, strutted forward, flicking its tail affectionately. Without waiting for me to put out my hand, it leaned in and bumped me with its nose.

"Well, hello there," I murmured, securing Bandit in one hand and patting the horse with my other. I expected my raccoon to lunge and bite, but he was being surprisingly docile for once.

"Oh, of course, it's War's familiar that approaches

her and the trash panda without a bloody reservation," Rysten grumbled.

"Familiar?" I asked. Rysten nodded and Laran beamed like he was damn proud. "You four have horses for familiars?" I repeated. Allistair shrugged, but it was Julian that caught my eye. His horse was ginormous. The thing had to be standing over eight feet tall. With a dappled grey body and silver mane, it was beautiful. Julian patted its side affectionately, not saying a word while I watched the private exchange between them.

"Technically, they're manifested familiars," Rysten said.

"Huh?" I asked, swinging my gaze around to him. His was pure white with a mane that practically glowed. "What do you mean manifested familiars?"

"We were born with them," Allistair answered, patting his pure black beast. It lifted its head and snorted, proud as the man who'd bonded to it. "They're technically a part of us, which is how we can go into your world without them, and when we're here we can communicate with them across great distances."

"Can they teleport?" I asked, looking down at Bandit. Could he?

"Aye," Laran answered, sidling next to the red one still nosing me. "Ours can teleport to us, but yours are a different type of familiar. They won't be the same."

Bummer. That would have been cool if Bandit could have.

"What's your horse's name?" I asked him as it tried to munch on my hair. I jerked back.

"Epona," he answered warmly, running the back of his knuckles along her side.

"It's a girl?" War had a horse for a familiar and it was a chick? I had a raccoon. Who was I to judge?

"She is, as is Death's familiar, Rhiannon." Hearing her name, the silver mare walked forward and lowered her head. Instead of poking me like Laran's, she waited for me to pet her. Expectant and intense, just like Julian. I reached out and touched her face.

"I hate to break up this little reunion," Jax snapped and didn't sound like he was all that sad about it, "but we're wasting daylight if we plan to ride."

Laran let out a dark chuckle. "Who said anything about you riding, enigma?"

CHAPTER THREE

Turns out, he wasn't joking. While the Horsemen's familiars may have liked me and tolerated Moira, it wasn't happening for the enigma. Jax couldn't get within five feet of one without it snorting and rearing up to bash his head in.

"There has to be a way to do this," I groaned. We didn't make it all this way to be thwarted by an asshole and some reluctant horses .

"Anybody have a bottle?" Moira asked.

I cocked an eyebrow. "Why?"

"He's an enigma," Moira said, like that meant anything.

"So..." I drawled out, waiting for an explanation. Moira sighed, running her palm over one of her horns. Her flaming wings fluttered almost irritably.

"They can travel in hollow objects. Which means he can hitch a ride without the horses flipping their shit." She hiked her thumb over her shoulder, pointing at the large male with amethyst eyes.

"You can't be serious," Jax started.

"How else are we going to bring you with?" she snapped. Her stomach rumbled even though we'd just had breakfast. A hungry Moira was a dangerous one.

"No one has a bottle or lamp that I can 'hitch a ride in,' so—"

"Actually," Allistair paused. He rubbed his hands together, his lips twitching in a sensuous grin. "We have everything we need." He waved his hand wide again, and this time saddles appeared on the horses, and in Moira's hand was a small glass vial.

"You mean you could do that this entire time?" I asked him.

"When I'm in hell, I can."

"But not Earth?" I asked curiously.

"My magic isn't as strong on Earth. Here, I can make my glamors real." He waved a hand to the world around us dispassionately. "Rather convenient, if I do say so myself." He grinned.

"Can you change clothes?" I asked. His lips curved up.

"Yours, I can. What do you want me to take off?" My cheeks flamed under his golden stare.

"Can we *not* do this whole foreplay-not foreplay-dirty talk-thing when I can still hear you?" Moira groaned. "Her transition was bad enough and I wasn't even there."

That sobered me up instantly.

"I'm sorry, Rubes, I just—"

"No, it's alright," I said and waved her off. My slightly hurt feelings weren't her responsibility, and certainly not over that. I turned my attention to Allistair. The heat in his gaze hadn't cooled a fraction, though I was downright chilly in my wet clothes and squishy shoes. "Can you dry my clothes and give me better shoes if I'm going to be riding a horse?"

With a wave of his hand it was done. Not only were my clothes dry, but they smelled clean as well, and the boots fit me perfectly.

"Alright," I said, hiking farther up the beach. "We ready to go?" I turned back, putting my hands on my hips. Jax and Moira were staring each other down as she held out the bottle. "You two alright?"

"No," Jax answered.

"Yes," Moira said at the same time.

"Okay, then," I drawled. "The sooner you get in the bottle, the sooner we can be to Inferna and you can be done with us." That only made him glower more.

"You have to let me out as soon as we stop," he told her.

"Yeah, yeah, I won't keep you locked in the bottle like a sadistic bitch. I am one—but that's not my style." She continued telling him all the things she would do instead, and it really wasn't helping our case.

"Moira, just promise to let him out so we can get going. When that's done, we're out of here and we can find food." At that she obliged, and with her genie in a bottle we mounted the deadly steeds and set off for the forest like this was some sort of fairytale and not a fucking nightmare.

WHILE BETTER AND faster than walking, riding on horseback wasn't all it's cracked up to be when you've never ridden a horse and are suddenly sitting astride a moving creature while attempting to put out the flames of Hell. We started a slow walk to give Moira and I time to adjust on Nessus, Allistair's familiar. After several hours of gripping Moira's waist rather awkwardly—thanks to her wings—I was over the novelty of it. She steered us as smoothly as possible, occasionally adjusting her grip at Laran's quiet instruction. I focused on the forest, and more importantly, the flames.

While in New Orleans, the beast had taken to teaching me how to finally control the cursed fire that only answered my call. I hadn't thought this particular gift was a blessing apart from when I was in a stabbing mood. Fire was destruction. Death. The ultimate form of ending and becoming something else entirely.

But it also gave me the power to stop the destruction.

Hell was burning, but I could end it.

I reached for the flames, lifting my hand towards

them to act as a guide. Pressing my lips together and closing my eyes, I sent out a lick of magic—simply tasting what power sat in the forest, drifting lazily through the undergrowth like a heady fog—and Hell answered.

My eyes flew open as magic shot from the very ground itself and fire erupted around us. The horses let out a sound of dismay and Nessus reared back. I clamped my thighs tighter to his sides, gripping Moira with all my strength as she held tight to the reins.

Black flames only glinting with blue towered around us as I looked every which way.

"Easy!" Allistair's voice cut across the six-foot gap between his familiar and Laran's. Nessus stilled under his person's command, his hooves dropping back to the ground.

"Uh, Ruby," Moira called over her shoulder. "I don't know if you've noticed this, but you made the fire worse—"

"I'm well aware, thanks," I ground out between clenched teeth. On Earth, it had been difficult to control magic because there was none in the atmosphere around me. It taught me to draw it out and use it as an extension of myself, but here...here my power was already *everywhere*.

I didn't need to send even a sliver of myself out to find it.

"Hurry it up, babe," Moira breathed. Nessus, while not actively attempting to throw us off after Allistair's rebuke, wasn't exactly happy either. His dark head thrashed back and forth, making his body jerk and my concentration slipped.

"Almost there," I replied, not wanting to waste more time when the dark tendrils of flame were already nearing Rhiannon's beautiful hooves just ahead of us.

Instead of flinging my own power out to search, I pulled it in, and even when every drop of my own magic was locked so tight it was stifling—I continued pulling. My hands clenched as if gripping the slippery whips of flame in my bare fists and I drew them into myself, even when there was nowhere to put it.

"You good?" Moira asked as the horse lurched forward. His hooves hit the ground with a thud that rattled my bones and threatened to upend me despite the death grip I kept on Moira's waist.

"Fine," I answered, not wanting to say much more when the magic writhed just beneath my skin, still searching for a way out. They'd said I might be able to control it, and they were right, but the power that was now restless within me wasn't my own. Just familiar, like an imprint of a memory felt long ago.

Unlike my own power, it didn't settle and linger, but instead fought savagely like an animal trying to tear its way out of a cage, seeking out any weakness inside me. I grit my teeth against the intrusion, hoping, praying to an already dead devil that I'd taken enough out of the forest to get wherever we were going.

That prayer went unanswered when some time later we stumbled across more fire and I had to repeat the same trick. This time it came easier, but holding it was getting more difficult.

Instead of wrapping my arms around Moira's waist, I rested my hands on my knees, fists closed and nails digging into my palms hard enough to pierce the skin.

A copper tang hit my nose, making me grimace, but it was working.

Pain brought clarity. It eased the churning power in my veins that pushed against my skin and threatened to unleash the deadly force.

Taking slow, steady breaths, the muscle straining in my ribcage let up as the sun began to descend on the horizon.

"Hey, are we going to stop sometime soon? My thighs are killing me," I lied. Well, not completely. My thighs were killing me, but the pressure trapped just beneath the skin was far worse and I feared I couldn't take any more fire if we came across it before stopping for the night.

"Soon," Julian said from up ahead. I clenched my teeth shut and focused on breathing through my nose. It was getting better, but not fast enough. The constant jostling wasn't helping.

It felt like forever when I asked, "Are we there yet?"

Moira pulled Nessus to a stop and turned to look at

me over her shoulder. "Are you alright?" she asked, point blank.

"Yeah, yeah, I'm fine..." My words trailed off as dark spots appeared in my vision.

Too much pressure...

"You don't look fine." She squinted in the setting sun as the horse gently rocked side to side. All the twisting and writhing in me had finally died down, leaving me heavy when the flames finally settled.

"Sure...I am," I said. My voice came out distorted, sounding far away. It echoed in the space between my words, widening the gaps of silence as it repeated over and over in my mind.

"Ruby?" a voice asked. I tried to place it. To connect it to the face before me.

To tell the green-skinned girl that I was *not* alright, because I didn't realize until too late why the darkness was swarming in.

But there it sat on the tip of my tongue as night finally took me and the sun slipped below the horizon.

CHAPTER FOUR

An uncomfortable crick in my side had me groaning. I rolled on my side and rubbed the sleep from my eyes, blinking hard to discern what happened. Then the thoughts came tumbling into my mind so fast and vivid that I lay there panting for a moment before asking, "Where am I?"

I blindly patted around me for something to get a grip on. Rough edges pricked my palms and my hands came away dirty. *Devil-damnit, what happened now?*

I placed my hands back on the rocks beneath me and pushed up, ignoring the pinching pain.

"Whoa there, Rubes—"

"What's going on?" I breathed. My head swam as gravity worked to pull me back again and strong hands grasped my upper arms.

"Easy, love," a voice murmured behind me. "You

fainted. If Moira hadn't been watching you would have fallen right off Nessus."

I swallowed, tasting nothing but salty air and dirt. "I fainted?"

"Yup," Moira said, exaggerating the 'p.' She turned back for something and held up a bottle of water. I reached for it, nodding in thanks.

The top cracked as I roughly turned it and drained the bottle in several long gulps. The plastic crinkled when it hit the ground. I wiped my mouth with the back of my hand.

"I really gotta stop doing that," I said.

"Littering?" Moira asked pointedly with a twist of her lips.

"Fainting," I snorted. Moira scowled.

"My job would certainly be a lot easier if you did. As it is, I'm the one in charge of making sure the enigma doesn't get up to anything...shady." Two booms echoed behind her and Moira rolled her eyes.

"What was that?" Not sure I wanted to ask.

"Trouble."

Moira let out a small sigh as she looked at something over my shoulder. A silent conversation seemed to pass between her and the person on the other end of that gaze. The fingers at my forearms tightened, and I had a pretty good idea who that might be.

"I need to go check on Jax and make sure he's not asking for a death wish." I quirked an eyebrow and she smirked dubiously before getting to her feet and walking out of the—

"Are we in a cave?" I said, trying to turn so I could see behind me. Not that it would have mattered because it was all darkness. A cavern ceiling spanned one side to the other, not smooth, but rocky and uneven. Ahead of me, the low light of a fire lit the shadows under a moonlit sky.

"Not quite," said a second voice. Honey, seduction, and a hint of scotch permeated the air. I blinked up at Allistair. His dark hair seemed to absorb the night as it framed his pale skin with an unruly wildness that was unlike him. Instead of the standard suit that I'd come to know and love, he donned the same low-slung jeans and tight t-shirt I'd gotten a peak at just before we set off for Inferna.

"What's that supposed to mean?" My voice came out huskier than I intended. Hungrier than before.

"We're in a tunnel on the edge of Lust's province," Rysten answered behind me. His fingers loosened their hold around my forearms and slid across my shoulders. I leaned into him.

"Okay," I answered. "Why are we in a tunnel at the edge of Lust's province?"

"Because this is Hell," Allistair answered like that meant something. I raised my eyebrows and he inclined his head, his sensuous lips looming too close to be so far away. "Bad things happen at nighttime.

Unless you're in a city, you don't want to be caught out in the open when the sun goes down."

My eyebrows drew together and I took a second appraising look of the tunnel because this didn't really seem that much better. "A Kraken tried to eat Bandit ten minutes after coming through the portal. I feel like bad things are implied in the name." My voice had more steel behind it than what I really felt. I was from here. Born here. And after only a single day, it struck me how incredibly out of my depth I was.

I wanted to hang my head in my hands and plead to go home. Tell them that I give up. Keeping Bandit and Moira safe were more important. We could go live on some remote island in the middle of nowhere while this apocalypse business worked itself out...but I didn't get that option. There was no 'working itself out' that didn't involve me and my beast.

And so, while it was scary as fuck and the first day here was more than a little disheartening—I was Ruby Morningstar—Satan's one and only child.

"Perhaps it is implied," Allistair nodded. His lips twisted in a wry grin that did bad things to my libido. "But there are many good things too...if you look for them."

"Uh huh," I said slowly, fighting the smirk threatening to break through. "What kind of good things are we talking about?" I asked, more than a little breathless. Allistair leaned forward, stealing a kiss with the briefest brush of his lips before pulling back with a chuckle.

"You'll see."

"What kind of answer is that?" I groaned, remembering the pressure in my head when it suddenly throbbed to life. I pulled away from Rysten and got to my feet. Oddly enough, I didn't feel very weak after that—all things considered. I stretched my arms high and my joints popped like a kid shooting a coke can with an air gun. I shook my limbs free and turned to wink at the two Horsemen standing behind me, clearly enjoying the show.

"See something you like?" I purred, not the least bit ashamed. I certainly liked the view from where I stood.

It wasn't Allistair's sexy smirk that did me in, though, but Rysten's soft eyes. "Always," he whispered with conviction. I smiled softly, emotion swelling in my chest.

Unnamable, just the way it would stay.

Behind them something stirred in the shadows. I froze, my eyes narrowing on the lumbering movements —not at all stealthy. Remembering Allistair's warning, my hand came up to summon fire...when I saw Laran.

"What were you doing back there? I almost set you on fire—"

"You can't burn me."

"Well, no..." I paused, running my thumb over my bottom lip before crossing my arms. "But I could set fire to the cavern, which would compromise the rock's

49

structural integrity and weaken it enough that it could potentially collapse on you..." I trailed off when they started snickering. "What?"

"Well, it's just..." Rysten paused when I raised an eyebrow.

"We don't typically see your more...calculating side," Allistair said quickly. I snorted. "Sometimes I forget you're the girl that kept a tank of chloroform in her office."

"Ah." I smiled fondly at the memory of tattooing Kendall's face. "You really shouldn't forget that. If anything, I've evolved." I lifted a hand, letting a sliver of flame dance over my fingers.

"Where'd you learn that?" Laran asked as he slowly advanced toward me. His dark hair was pulled back into a low ponytail at the nape of his neck, revealing the slight scar that nicked the arch of his right eyebrow.

"Moira," I murmured, putting the fire away. "When she started college, she was going to school for civil engineering. She'd listen to her videos while I built a client base tattooing people in the studio apartment we shared before I bought the house that was blown up."

"And you learned that just from listening?" Laran asked. I nodded, scratching the back of my head.

"I wasn't much for school because I found the environment stifling. Some people can learn while being packed in a room and told to read from a textbook, but

I'm not one of them." I shrugged and picked at a leaf that was stuck to my flannel. "I learned a lot while she was in school."

Ironic as it was, I probably learned more during her four years than I did the past eighteen, between her videos and my ex's. I'd seen a variety of men with very different professions while passing the time, some more helpful than others.

"Why'd she switch to business?" Allistair asked. His eyes flicked behind me to look at Moira. I felt her change in emotion the minute she walked in. The erratic excitement and swaggering bitchiness she wore with pride.

"Have you ever studied civil engineering?" she asked, her voice on the very brink of a screech. Ever since she'd transitioned, she seemed to stray the razor edge of screaming like a—well, banshee—and speaking like a normal person.

"She got bored," I answered in short. He blinked, reassessing Moira.

"Bored? Studying engineering?" he asked skeptically.

"Bored studying *civil* engineering. It's fucking droll. Also, the other students were all pricks that had a pine tree up their asses." I choked on a laugh as she sauntered up beside me.

"She did *very* well and the guys in her classes were intimidated," I explained as she flicked her dark green hair over one shoulder.

"I switched to business because I could start my own company with Ruby. I had it all laid out and we were just getting started. With my brain and her fingers, we'd retire as millionaires," Moira huffed. The three of them seemed more than a little surprised.

"I don't know why you're all shocked. I may have a birthright, but she's a fucking genius." I rested my arm on Moira's shoulder as she put one around my waist. Behind us a deep baritone let out a cough of derision.

"If you two are done talking about what you wasted your lives doing while Hell's been burning, I'd like to know what War found," the enigma jested. I tensed, debating between saying something and letting it go when Moira shrugged.

"He's kind of an asshole," I whispered to her.

"You have no idea."

Was that a blush creeping up her cheeks? No fucking way. I snapped my jaw shut just as it started to fall open, and I turned to Laran.

"What were you searching for?" I asked. Laran's closed fists drew my attention as he glanced between me and the asshole at the mouth of the tunnel. Anger wafted off him. Aggression and....possession. "Laran," I said lightly, pretending that I didn't notice how he might throttle Jax for talking to me like I was the reason his world was ending. I mean, I was...but it was only half my fault. I wasn't claiming responsibility for being shipped off as a baby no matter who tried to feed me that bullshit. "Laran," I repeated. His attention wasn't on me, and his feet were already moving. I made a split decision and the beast came forward.

"*War.*"

All it took was a single word and he stopped mid-step. Turning to look over his shoulder, the beast stared back at him expectantly. "Your mate has asked you a question. You'd do well to remember what she is capable of when you don't answer." Her words were chilled. Apathetic. The beast receded with ease and I stared up at him not even missing a beat with our shifting. I was getting the hang of this.

"Of course," he answered softly. Laran turned his back on the enigma, giving me his undivided attention. Out of the corner of my eye I didn't miss the assessing gaze of the chaos demon, or Julian standing behind him —Bandit riding on his shoulder. "Did they tell you why we came here?" he asked.

"Allistair said the boogeyman comes out at night—"

"I did not," he growled.

"I'm paraphrasing."

"Can we get on with this—" Jax started, and like that he went one step too far. Laran's eyes darkened, blotting out any white as his savage fury and territorial urges finally got the better of him. He lifted his hand without turning, and the enigma lifted off the ground.

He clawed at his throat but there was no one there.

"Dude, I already saved your ass once. You really don't learn, do you?" I started, crossing my arms over my chest.

"He's slow," Moira said, not sounding the least bit concerned as she toed a rock with her boot. In her nonchalance, she missed the way Jax's panicked gaze flicked to her.

I sighed. "Put him down, Laran. As much as he's an asshole, Jax isn't exactly here because he wants to be." There was once a time that such a show of brutality would have sent me running for the hills, but not anymore. While I didn't revel in the violence, I also didn't shy from it when need be. This just wasn't one of those cases.

"He doesn't treat you with respect," Laran answered.

"Yeah, he's not the first jackass to and he won't be the last. While rude, it doesn't warrant death, so let's dial it down. It's awfully dark outside and we're standing next to the entrance of the tunnel. I would like to know what the hell the next step is here." At this, he appeared to see reason. His fist unclenched as his hand dropped and with it, the enigma did too. Ignoring his spluttering coughs and furious gaze, I focused on Laran.

"I was searching to see where it let out. The vast majority of the tunnels in Hell lead to the Garden—Sloth's province. I was hoping that this one did, but it's collapsed," Laran said. "We'll have to find another way."

I frowned. "Another way?"

"Another way to Inferna," Julian answered.

"What's wrong with the way we're going? We'll get there eventually."

Utter silence.

Laran looked at the ceiling while Julian looked on with...pity? I whipped my head around to Moira who was picking at the dirt under her nails with a dagger. I didn't even bother to spin around on the two behind me, because they'd all come to a decision already. Without me.

And here I was letting them distract me because I didn't know any better—no, that's not right—because I expected better. I expected honesty.

Shame on me for holding these demons to the same standards they tried to hold me to.

"You fainted today," Julian said slowly. Softly. Hesitantly. "When you absorbed the fire, you were taking in too much power, weren't you?" I said nothing. They didn't get my answers when they withheld their own. "It's okay, Ruby. We're not mad at you because you took too much, but we didn't notice in time when you started to shut down."

Emotion clogged my throat making it hard to breath. I swallowed down the hardness and infused my spine with steel.

"We're looking for alternative route to Inferna so that you don't feel like you need to extinguish the fire. Once we get there—if the Sins have all truly gathered—then we can work to find a solution once you take the throne." He continued, but I wasn't listening. I brushed past Laran and strutted towards the mouth of the tunnel. I stepped around Jax, who finally had the good sense to not say shit, and I didn't even look at Julian as I walked by.

A hand snaked out to wrap around my wrist, pulling me up short.

"Let go of me," I snapped, rounding on him with a fierceness he didn't expect.

"No."

"Damnit, Julian," I growled. Fire started in my hands, burning dark and deadly.

"Put it out," he ordered.

"Fuck you," I spat back. "You don't get to order me around." I tensed, recalling my transition, though hazy as some parts were. "You have five seconds to let me go."

"You're not walking off into the woods—"

"One," I said simply. His eyes turned cold. Feral.

"I would listen to her, Julian," Moira warned.

"Two." Julian tightened his grip on me.

"She's going to get herself killed—" Laran started. He knew I would bolt if Julian didn't back down.

"Three," I said. My arms began to shake, my legs trembling with the urge to run.

"Damn you, Death. You do not want to see her temper—" Moira spoke faster now, trying to plead with him. Trying to reach me.

"Four," I snarled, baring my teeth.

Power was building. It flowed through me and

clashed together with a thunderous crack. All of the pressure from before...I realized it didn't simply leave me while I slept. It *integrated*.

Somehow. Someway—I absorbed it and made myself *stronger*.

The same as I had done with Sin's blood magic.

I inhaled deeply, preparing myself for the line I did not want to cross when—

"Please."

I stilled. His grip dropped away.

Then he said the only thing that could make the power leave me cold.

"I'm sorry, but *please* don't walk away." His eyes still burned, and his breath tasted of winter. His emotions were an ice storm: turbulent and brutal.

But he was trying.

"Tonight, we camp here and tomorrow, we ride. Those are my conditions." I kept it simple. I wasn't in the business of playing games. We were mates, for fuck's sake. He wore my brand and I wore his. If he couldn't run decisions by me before taking it upon himself—if none of them could—I would find a way to rule Hell on my own.

He didn't have to be perfect. He had to realize who he fucking branded.

"Ruby..." He gritted his teeth.

"No, Julian. I'm not mad that you're concerned. I pushed it too hard today, I get that, and I'll work on it— but you don't get to make decisions for me." I turned to look at the rest of them pointedly. "None of you do. How can you expect anyone to take me seriously as a queen when the four of you can't even seem to do it?"

To that, they said nothing.

But that's okay. I didn't want pretty words. I wanted actions.

"Take it or I walk, Julian. Trust me or let me walk away now." His jaw ticked and I was completely aware of just how much this took from him, but I was going to win this particular battle before it started. All of them needed to nip this shit in the bud, especially him.

In the end, he did. "Tonight, we camp. Tomorrow, we ride," he agreed. "But that isn't the last of this conversation. Understood?"

I bit back the grin that wanted to break through. "Understood."

"Good," he growled. "Tonight, you're sleeping with *me*."

My toes curled in my boots with anticipation. This was a compromise I was more than willing to make.

CHAPTER FIVE

Bleary-eyed and in desperate need of a shower, I climbed onto Rysten's familiar, Arion, and settled in for the journey. After riding a horse all day and Julian all night, it was only my immortality that kept me from not crying like a wimp every time my mount shifted impatiently.

He smacked my ass raw more times than I could count. I loved every second of it at the time. Now? Not so much.

"Can we get moving already?" I grumbled, only barely covering my wince as Rysten climbed up behind me. His large thighs pressed into mine as he settled his arms loosely around me, one hand resting on my stomach.

"Just waiting on your familiar and her genie, love," he rumbled in my ear, drawing a screeching from Moira in return.

"He is not *my genie!*" she yelled.

"I'm no one's genie, thank you very much," Jax muttered. She crossed her arms over her chest and glared at him.

"Get in the fucking bottle," she seethed.

"Not if you're keeping it between your tits again," he replied, standing firm.

"Oh, for fuck's sake," I groaned. "You're the one who's been complaining about us not getting a move on, enigma. Get in the devil-damned bottle." Moira lifted her chin to smirk at him. "He's not going between your tits. Put him in the fucking saddle bag. I have a headache and Bandit's being an asshole because I'm out of sardines."

We all turned and looked over at the raccoon-turned-hellcoon sitting proudly on Laran's shoulder. He looked more than a little hellish with the branded eyes and blue fur. He lifted his head and let out a loud chittering while grabbing at Laran's hair. The demon had to be a fucking saint because I would have walloped him for that shit, but War took it in stride.

"She has a point. The trash panda is being a little shit this morning. But I don't have to deal with it anymore. So, in the bottle you go." Moira uncapped the bottle, extending it to Jax.

"In the saddle bag?" he asked, waiting for her to say it. Moira rolled her eyes, but obliged.

"You'll go in my saddle bag, right next to the condo —" Before she could finish, he evaporated in a cloud of

60

smoke that was instantly sucked into the bottle. When not a trace of his essence was left, Moira capped it and looked at me with a smirk.

"Saddle bag." I pointed to the one hanging off of Rhiannon. After my little fainting fiasco the day before, I would now be riding with Rysten and she'd be with Julian.

"Do I have to?" she groaned. I gave her the *don't fuck with me* look. I was without coffee and bacon. She sighed and slipped the bottle in the bag without any more shenanigans. I had to look away when Julian grasped her by the waist, albeit clinically, and helped her onto the saddle.

She's your familiar. Get it together! I chided myself. It was only because of that she could even be that close to him without me losing my shit. I knew that after Julian and I had fully mated, it would never be the same again. Being a shade, Rysten's magic was able to sense if I would faint again, so I had to ride with him. Which left Julian as the only other fully branded mate Moira could ride with, despite the beast's mild annoyance that a female—even our familiar—was riding with any of them. He was the only one she would allow as neither of the other two had given her their brands yet. As far as she was concerned, it was still an uneasy time until we were fully branded.

Which meant I was even bitchier.

Sore thighs...and other bits. No coffee. No bacon. My best friend was riding all pressed up against *my mate* and to make matter's even worse, I needed a shower.

Turning forward I forced myself to relax into the saddle as we started out for Greed's province.

We only made it twenty minutes before Moira started her own version of *are we there yet?*

"So..." she started. "We're still in Lust's province, yes?"

"Yes," Rysten answered behind me.

"That's ruled by the Deadly Sin of Lust?"

"Yes," he repeated, his lips brushing against my temple, drawing a small grin out of me despite my dour mood.

"That used to be Ruby's mom?"

"Yes..." Rysten was slower to answer her this time.

"Shouldn't that mean Ruby's the new Sin of Lust and this is her province now?" Moira asked, like it made perfect sense.

"No." Rysten shook his head and pulled on the reins making Arion sidle up to Rhiannon's side. "The Six Sins, while also Lucifer's harem, were *chosen* to rule within Hell. In the event that one of them were to fall, it was that Sin's duty to appoint someone before-hand. If she couldn't, the remaining Sins or the ruler of Hell would, but Lola chose someone," he explained.

"Alright," Moira said. "So, this new chick, did she just join the harem after the original Lust died?" If I had anything other than curiosity about my mom, this conversation might have hurt, but after thinking my egg donor gave me up because she didn't care only to find out she *died* hiding me was quite a change. I no longer hated the idea of her, but I also didn't know how to love someone I didn't know.

"Doubtful," Julian said. "Lucifer and the Sins formed their relationship at the dawn of Hell. By the time Ruby was born he was very committed to them, especially Lola. Even as her province had gone to another, I would have trouble believing he would mate with any other after her loss."

"You make it sound like he loved her," I found myself saying.

"He did," Julian answered in earnest. I glanced sideways at him, biting the inside of my cheek. "He had a child with her knowing it would mark the end of him. For him, I think there was no greater love than Lola." His eyes focused on me with such a deep connection that I blushed. It didn't take a rocket scientist to figure out who he related to in this story.

"What about Lola?" Moira asked.

"What about her?" I replied, somewhat defensively. Moira shrugged.

"Don't you want to know more about her? I mean, your dad may have been Satan, but your mom was a Deadly Sin—the only other Sin to have kids was Lilith, and she's not even a real demon," Moira said, almost a little envious.

"I mean, I don't know," I said, struggling with

words. "She's a succubus and I'm a succubus. I don't know what else there is to really get to know there."

"She was more than just a succubus," Laran said, coming up closer.

"What do you mean?" I asked, more than a little skeptical.

"In many ways she was the strongest Sin. Certainly, the most compassionate. While her abilities weren't as flashy as Hela—or as terrifying as Saraphine—she held her own among them with her mind. Your mother was a brilliant woman." Laran paused before adding, "Just like you."

"What about the other Sins?" I asked, fully aware I was turning the conversation away from Lola. It was early in the morning and I didn't sign up for a conversation this deep.

"What about them?" Rysten asked.

"Who are they? What are they? Aren't these things I should know about them?" Until coming here it never occurred to me how little I truly knew about Hell, even when jumping through a portal.

"Well," Rysten started, rubbing his lips across my cheekbone. His stubble scraped my skin, making me shiver. "After Lola comes Saraphine, the Sin of Greed. She's a nightmare."

"As a demon or a person?" I asked.

"Both," Laran chuckled.

"It was part of why I was hoping to avoid Greed's province so early," Julian murmured. "She's not likely to be forgiving if her realm has burned as much as Lust's."

"Who's after Greed?" I continued without commenting on his assessment. I already had enough to worry about. No point in stressing over a she-demon I didn't know.

"Depends on how you look at it," Allistair answered. "Sloth's province runs under the whole of Hell. She'd be contesting with Saraphine over it if it weren't for the fact that it's underground and no one wants it."

"Why does no one want it?"

"Because it's underground," he replied like that made sense. I frowned, but didn't ask again. I figured I'd find out soon enough.

"If it's not Ahnika's province, it would be Gluttony. You'll like her," Allistair grinned. "It's nothing but booze, bacon, and blood with Lamia." I wasn't sure whether I should be smiling or grimacing.

"I want to go to her province," Moira muttered.

"Don't we all," Rysten replied, his hand on my stomach sliding lower. I turned to stare at him over my shoulder, calling him out on his brazenness when he started toying idly with the button on my jeans. My face flamed as I spun forward in my seat like nothing was going on. He certainly wasn't—

"Inferna is divided down the middle. Half of it is in Gluttony and half in Wrath—Hela's province," Allistair continued. "Don't let the name fool you, though. She's not as bad as she sounds."

If only I was paying attention to them and not the button that just slipped free and the finger that was slowly teasing at the edge of my panties—

Flickers of blue caught my attention up ahead as we approached the first fire we'd seen today. It wasn't quite as dense or as tall as yesterday's flames, which suited me just fine, but it did put a damper on whatever ideas Rysten had.

"Just when things were getting interesting, eh, love?" He grinned against my temple and I smirked to myself when Moira turned and shouted, "Aye, Ruby, you're up!"

I resisted the urge to groan when Rysten chuckled. "You're the one that asked for this."

"Don't remind me."

By the time Arion pulled to a stop, the sun had dipped to the jewel-toned horizon just above the mountains in the distance. I'd spent the better part of the last eight hours putting out fires, and while it was thinning more and more, the flames of Hell seemed to never end. At least I didn't pass out this time. Small blessings, I supposed; although, who in this world would grant them was beyond me. It's not like God gave a damn.

"How far to Greed's province?" I asked, trying to

keep the strain out of my voice. Between the day of riding and impending exhaustion, I could have stripped right there and slept on a rock. Unfortunately, my Horsemen had other plans.

"We're right on the border, but the capitol of Greed is half a day's ride and we do not want to enter the City of Hoarders at night. If Saraphine has left for Inferna, the city will have descended into chaos by now," Julian said, by way of answer. There was a terseness to him that I really wasn't liking, especially with Moira's mood souring the longer they were in close proximity of each other.

"City of Hoarders?" Moira asked.

"The demons that thrive in Greed are collectors of sorts," Julian answered with a harsh twist of his lips.

"What do they collect?" Moira continued.

"Everything."

"What's that mean for us tonight?" I said, changing topic before a fight broke out. We were all running low on fucks to give at the moment.

"We camp," he replied with a grunt.

"Seriously?" Moira snapped. "After all the bitching and whining about being out in the open at night, we're stopping in the middle of the damn forest?" Julian grit his teeth, pulling Rhiannon to a sudden stop just ahead of us and slipped from the saddle, leaving Moira to figure out her own way down from the unnaturally tall horse.

"Do you see a cave?" He motioned around him.

"How about a tunnel—or better yet, an actual building?" Moira pressed her lips together, glaring at him. "No?" If looks could kill, he'd be dead, but neither of those things were possible. "I guess we'll just have to fucking make do."

"Who shit in your coco puffs—" She didn't even get to finish her sentence before I hopped off Arion, hitting the ground hard on the balls of my feet and stumbling when my legs locked painfully.

"Guys. Both of you take a damn chill pill." To my utter surprise and satisfaction, they both shut their mouths and went separate ways.

"I'm going to scout the area," Julian said without looking at me. A sliver of hurt cut at my heart, but I turned the other way and brushed it off.

"Don't let his piss poor attitude get to you," Rysten said from behind me. That was easier said than done when it came to Julian, but I knew better than to force the topic until he was ready to talk.

"I'm going to deal with Jax," Moira said from across the clearing. She gripped a small glass vial with swirling smoke containing the enigma's essence. She thumbed the lid awkwardly for a moment before a large pop filled the clearing. Smoke drifted lazily out of the vial, reforming as a shadow that came to life as a demon. Violet eyes settled on Moira and a blush crept along her cheeks.

Laran was just slipping from his saddle when Bandit let out a chitter now that dinner was in sight.

He rolled around on Epona's back, falling sideways and into the saddle bag when Laran opened it.

"You going for a walk soon?" I asked, wanting to focus on anything other than the headache forming at the base of my neck, the aching in my thighs, and the heated looks Moira and her new stud were giving each other. Tensions were running high.

"I was," Laran paused. "But you look like you could use more than a walk." I blinked, mostly out of surprise. He was always blunt with words, and while I appreciated it, the blush on my cheeks betrayed me. My Horseman of War let out a deep chuckle. "Not what I had in mind." Laran flashed me a wicked grin and pulled something from his saddle bag. I saw the sleek grey instrument with yellow speckles and realized what he was holding.

"Wait—you're going to let me practice?" I rubbed my hands together, shifting side to side so my stiff legs wouldn't go numb.

Laran nodded. I couldn't help bouncing a little as I followed him deeper into the woods and away from camp. "After the Kraken, I got to thinking that you may need more ways to protect yourself—beside the flames." At my frown, he explained, "The flames are very effective at killing, but sometimes you don't want to risk the collateral damage using them would cause. While a great last effort weapon, I want you to have other methods at your disposal."

"Starting with the crossbow?"

He nodded. "Need help strapping it on?"

"Please," I said, my cheeks aching with how wide my smile was. Laran quickly went through what each strap was for and how to put it on by myself.

"Make sure you curl your fingers over this one—there you go—just like that." I smiled faintly as he assessed my grip. His brows puckered slightly inward as his full lips pressed together while he turned my hand every which way to assess. "I think you have it," he finally said.

I lifted my arm slowly, twisting it both ways.

"How do I fire it?" I asked, careful of the bolt sitting cocked within the bow.

"You see that fig tree?" He motioned with a tilt of his chin. I nodded. "Point your arm towards a piece of fruit. Make sure the bolt is pointed directly at it—" He slapped my arm when I squinted and lost concentration. "Tighten your muscles. You don't need to squeeze so hard you cramp, but another demon shouldn't be able to slap your arm away without trying." At his instruction, I lifted my arm again and held steady. "That's it." He grinned when I grit my teeth, waiting to be told how to fire. "To shoot, all you have to do is flick your wrist."

"Well, why didn't you just say that?"

His only answer was a devilish smile as the last of the sunlight peeked through the branches, highlighting the red streaks in his hair. I blew out a breath and looked at the fig high up in the trees.

"Breath in and hold. As you release your breath, do it slowly, and try not to move your arm too much." I sucked in a quick breath and held it for three seconds before slowly letting it loose. Snapping my wrist down, the arrow went flying and...dropped.

I was so transfixed on the arrow I noticed the moment it stopped mid-air and gravity took over.

I opened my mouth to ask if that was supposed to happen and hesitated at the wicked gleam in his black eyes. My teeth clanked as my mouth snapped shut.

We stared at each other for a hard moment, my irritation and his amusement slowly transforming to something else.

"Try again," he said. The wind rustled, sweeping the edge of my flannel up to send a trail of gooseflesh across my bare midriff. Laran's eyes heated as they flicked to the pale stretch of skin.

I swallowed against the lump in my throat and lifted my arm again. Moving to grab the bolt, warm fingers wrapped around my upper arm as he stilled me.

"I need the bolt..." I trailed off at the gleam of silver already in position and cocked to fly.

Magic. Seelie magic. Taking it in stride, I stopped, took aim, and breathed. Hold. Release. With the snap of my wrist I watched the bolt fly and once again drop out of nowhere.

I frowned. That wasn't normal, but the only consistent part of it was me and the crossbow. So, either the damn thing was broken—or the much more likely option—it was me.

"What am I doing wrong?" My voice came out sultry. Huskier than I expected. I groaned into my hand, wishing for the umpteenth time that I didn't sound like a thirsty bitch. I'd rather be able to shoot a man instead of fucking one. That would show real talent.

One of these took effort.

"Not focusing hard enough," Laran answered. His eyes dipped to my lips and I instinctively ran my tongue along the edges of my teeth before remembering myself and biting down on my lip to hide that devilish tongue away. I swear, some days it had a mind of its own where the Horsemen were concerned.

"Not hard enough?" My voice was all purr as my gaze swept down to his jeans and back up. Laran let out a small growl.

"Focus, Ruby."

A smirk made its way to my lips as I slid my gaze back to my target. *Focus.* I inhaled deeply, closing my eyes. Holding my breath, I opened them again, and breathed—letting the bolt fly.

It soared and my smile split wide as I watched it close in on the target—only to fall. Again.

"Damnit," I swore under my breath.

"Focus on the target, not the arrow," Laran's breath fanned my ear. I gasped, turning my face to look at him. Strong fingers brushed down my jaw as Laran faced my head forward. "Focus," he murmured. My breath stuttered as I lifted my arm, aiming the bolt again.

Calloused fingertips pressed into my hip bones, pulsating warmth into my skin beneath the thick material. Sweat dotted my brow as those same fingers swept down, under my shirt and back up, skating along my ribs to my— "Focus," he growled.

"I'm trying," I snapped back. "Hard to do that when you can't keep your hands to yourself."

The warmth disappeared instantly as he removed his hands and stepped away. Sweeping towards the fruit I was aiming for, he waited expectantly. Pissed at him for moving away and pissed with myself for telling him to, I aimed at the fig and snapped my wrist, but my attention was all on Laran.

The bolt released, shooting through the air in a wide arc and whipping around. It defied all physics as it shot at Laran and landed in the thick muscle of his arm. A strangled noise slipped from my lips as I dropped my hand away and stepped towards him. Laran didn't blink or bat an eyelash as he held my gaze and reached over to grasp the bolt sticking out, ripping it free.

"Laran!" I crowed, diving forward. I whipped my shirt off to press against the bleeding gash in his arm. Meanwhile, War just smiled as if this was all very amusing.

"I'll be fine, Ruby," he said quietly. "It'll heal."

"You don't know that," I replied stubbornly.

"Oh, but I do," he grinned again. "Lift up the shirt."

"No."

"Suit yourself," he growled. Grasping my hips, he pulled me to him as his lips came down on mine. Laran kissed with a wildness that was all fire. His lips parted mine with ease, his tongue tasting me. Not hesitant or challenging, Laran's kiss didn't demand—it gave. Everything and all that he was, he poured into that kiss. Into me.

I arched my back into him, holding the shirt tight to his wound as I reached up to wrap my other arm around the crook of his neck. Laran pulled back with a groan, sucking my bottom lip as he did. With a pop, he released my lip, his hands reaching down to slide over the sides of my breasts that already ached for his touch, across my abdomen, all the way to the 'v' of my hips. His knuckles brushed the sensitive skin, just underneath the hem of my flannel, and I jumped, letting out a gasp.

"What are you doing?" I asked with a shaky breath. My hooded eyes looked both ways, but no one appeared to be around.

"Motivating you." With one arm, Laran held me tight to his chest, my head resting on the curve where his neck met his shoulder. He leaned into me, his lips skimming the column of my throat while his teeth left nibbling bites that sent jolts of pleasure shooting through me. Strong fingers slid between our bodies, pressing into the seam of my jeans. He ran them back and forth, finding my clit through the thick material and twisting his arm to press his palm into me. It only took seconds and I was panting.

"Oh, good god—"

"There's no god here, baby. Only me and you," he rumbled as I rocked into him. A low moan slipped from my lips.

"This is so wrong," I groaned. "You're hurt." Even as I said it, I pressed the shirt harder, but didn't stop. Laran pressed his other hand into my back, urging my rocking as all the tension of the trip settled on me looking for a way out. I chased my release, tilting my head back to part my lips in a plea.

"Laran I'm going to—" He stepped away before I could finish, his bloody t-shirt slipping from my fingers. With his heat gone I was too cold, but also too hot. Needy. I'd have dropped my jeans and bent over right there if he asked me, but he didn't. He stopped, despite the slight taste of his kama on my lips and the red particles floating in the air.

"Focus, baby girl." His eyes blazed despite his steady words and my body ached for him.

"I want you," I breathed.

"Prove to me you can hit your target and I'll take you however you want."

A challenge? Oh man, I hadn't hit a damn thing except his arm.

"And if I don't?" I asked.

"Then you have to find your own release," he answered. His eyes filled with fire. Light and shadows flickered there, existing side by side. I took a deep, steady breath and aimed.

My eyes zeroed in on the fruit and this time when I snapped my wrist, the bolt flew true.

The fig fell from the tree limb, but my attention was on the glorious male kneeling at my feet as he undid the buttons on my jeans with a wolfish grin on his lips.

My pants didn't even hit the floor before his mouth was on me.

Laran spread my folds and pressed his tongue flat against the bundle of nerves. My legs quaked as he licked me, slipping two fingers into the wetness between my thighs. Laran sucked my clit between his lips and bit roughly, a rugged chuckle escaping him as my knees went weak.

"Mmm, I knew you could hit it. I was getting hungry."

He wasn't talking about the fruit.

CHAPTER SIX

HE BROUGHT ME TO CLIMAX TWICE WITH HIS wicked tongue before I straddled him in the grass. I rode him again, relishing in the way he worked me over his cock until we both collapsed in a tangle of sweat-slicked limbs. We finished target practice completely naked before putting clothes on and gathering up the figs for dinner. While Allistair seemed to be able to glamor anything we needed, food and water included, there was something thrilling about sharing the fruits of my labor, quite literally.

We walked back to the campsite, arms full and smiling like a couple of high schoolers and not a Queen and her consort. With Laran it was easy, simple. Our relationship wasn't as disruptive as Julian, or a balance of control like Allistair's, or even a guessing game like Rysten's—because while Pestilence certainly cared for me, he was just as bad as the others when it came to my safety. They were all possessive with me, but more than that, we were still working on building trust. Laran and I were already beyond that. He had proved it to me from the beginning, loving me enough to treat me as an equal and never pulling punches when it came to the truth; in return, I was pretty sure I loved him first.

The thought made me go still.

I...*loved them*.

Like the echo of thunder, my heart almost cracked with the immense realization, because as soon as you loved something it became a weakness. I already had two that my enemies used against me, and now...I swallowed hard and lifted my head. Laran's coal black eyes met mine, silently asking if I was alright.

I smiled despite the lead weight in my stomach, and it poisoned me. The feeling running in my veins, while strong and deep and *sure*—also scared the shit out of me.

So, I stayed silent and fell into step beside him like nothing was wrong and my heart wasn't aching with the sting of resentment against my father's enemies for forcing me to be so cold with my mate. They protected and cared for me. They gave me everything that was them.

But I wouldn't say those words until it was safe.

I wouldn't let my heart bleed all the more, because if they said them back and then something happened...it just might kill me.

So, I tucked those words in close and stuffed them down inside until we were safe. One day, and one day soon, I would say them.

But today wasn't that day.

"What took you so long?" Moira snapped. Her light green arms were crossed over her chest while she leaned back against a log. One of them had already made a log cabin out of wood and started a fire, even though it was hotter than—well, Hell.

A small chuckle slid between my lips as I amused myself, but no one besides Laran seemed to find it all that amusing.

"Is she delirious?" Jax asked, and I couldn't be sure, but I thought he was being serious.

"Do you have a death wish?" Moira asked, turning her ire on him. "Everyone knows only I get to be bitchy and get away with it. Get with the program, genie."

The enigma's lips thinned and his eyes turned luminescent. If I didn't know Moira could hand him his ass, the beast and I might have felt protective where she was concerned. But Moira was a legion now. One who clearly wasn't all that worried about a pissed off enigma with how she liked to goad him.

"I'm not a genie," he growled. His hands clenched into fists at his sides. "I'm an enigma, one of the most powerful of my kind, and you'd do well to remember it." Moira just kept her back turned to him and flipped her hair. No one did condescending quite like her. She exuded this vibe that she was above everyone, especially the one she seemed to delight in taunting. With her back to him, though, I was privy to the smirk on her face as he glowered at her. "Are you listening to me?"

Suddenly, his voice went all rumbly as he started to grow larger, his skin shifting.

"What in the Devil's name is going on here—" I asked, the figs tumbling from my arms as several things happened simultaneously. Frozen to my spot, I watched it all as if it were slow motion.

The trees shifted as soft footsteps surrounded us. Out of nowhere, people—demons—wearing masks made out of wood, carved and crudely painted, stepped out of the forest. They carried long wooden sticks with arrowheads attached to the ends, an archaic form of a spear. Tension rippled across the clearing as they moved swiftly, closing in around us.

Jax bared his teeth at the masked demons. His skin trembled, blurring as it shifted and molded into something else before my eyes. Four legs with clawed feet jutted forward, and hair as dark as his skin sprouted. His teeth grew larger, more pointed, as his face became that of a predator. The transformation complete, a hell-hound stood in his place, and it was only those glowing purple eyes that made him recognizable. He gave Moira a pointed look—as if telling her to stay—as he turned, *protecting* her against the unknown demons now boxing us in.

"Drop the weapon!" someone yelled. It wasn't a voice I recognized.

A blunt force connected with my back.

Wrong. Fucking. Move.

I stumbled a step forward and only Laran's hand grasping my arm kept me from falling. Lightning flashed across the sky. A warning from the Horseman of War.

"Aw, fuck," Moira drawled standing up. "You've really done it now."

"Drop it!" the same voice commanded from behind me. Laran's eyes darkened as he pulled me closer. I stopped him with a pat of my hand against his rough fingers.

"I got this," I murmured. He stepped back a fraction giving me room to react without bearing down on me. I winked at him, and in that blink of an eye, the beast came out to play.

Fire came to life at her call, racing up her arms as she turned on a dime and grabbed the end of the blunted walking stick that had been used to prod me like fucking cattle.

"Now, now," she trilled with a husky laugh that was both seductive and terrifying. "Is that any way to treat your Queen?"

The end of the stick caught fire under her grip and the masked man holding it shuddered. His fingers trembled as the fire slowly ate its way towards him. She reared back, striking him in the head once with the not-yet-flaming end of the stick. He crumpled to the ground easily and she let out a tsk, sending the spear up in flames while she was at it. Black ashes blew in the wind within seconds. They quieted.

"I warned you!" Moira called from behind me. Through our bond I could tell she wasn't all that worried. Not when Jax-turned-hellhound was guarding her hide while the beast was out. No one fucked with our familiars and lived.

"Queen?" one of the faceless demons asked. The new spokesperson for the group walked forward, stepping over the crumbled body of their friend without hesitation.

This she-demon wore brown leather pants and moccasin style shoes with a loose shirt made of a dark indiscernible cloth. Her spear was larger than the others and decorated with a swatch of fabric on the end that swished lightly as she moved.

"Did she fucking stutter?" Moira snapped from behind her. The beast didn't bat an eyelash at the outburst. She preferred to watch the strange woman.

"Who are you?" The voice behind the mask was muffled, making it deeper. More animalistic in its tone than human.

If the she-demon meant to intimidate, the beast wasn't impressed.

"I go by many names," the beast mused. "Take your pick."

Silence extended between them as the masked demons seemed to weigh this. I could almost hear their telepathic conversations, but thanks to Sin, that was no longer one of my abilities.

"I think she's lying!" a voice in the crowd called out. There was a chorus of cheers, both for and against, but they all fell quiet when the strange girl before me lifted two fingers beneath her mask and let out a shrill whistle.

"Her fire is blue. Its ashes are black. If she really is Satan's spawn come to return and put an end to the fire, I—for one—do not wish to die this day." Another chorus both for and against rang out, but this time it seemed in my favor.

"Um, I hate to be the bearer of bad news," Moira piped up behind me, "but you guys kind of lost the power to say what happens here." All heads apart from ours whipped towards the girl now sidling up beside me. "This guy here," she hooked her thumb to the right, "he's War, and he's a lot nicer than your Queen when she's cranky." I would have chuckled, but the beast only stared apathetically, seeing them all as objects in the way instead of living and breathing creatures. Pieces on a board she would take out if needed. "Assuming you somehow could take War out, there's no way you'd get past her other three mates." She swept her hand wide, motioning just behind the crowd where Rysten, Allistair, and Julian now stood. "Also known as the Horsemen: Pestilence, Famine—and the big motherfucker in the middle—that's Death. He really doesn't like other people poking her with sticks."

If they weren't afraid before, they should have been then.

We'd faced worse odds. I'd killed more demons with far less skill than I now possessed. In a fight to the death, they wouldn't win.

Which is why it came as quite the shock when the masked she-demon threw back her head and cackled.

She withdrew the mask, showing off a mane of golden hair that would have been enviable if I were insecure. As it was, the beast withheld all judgement... until she turned and walked right up to Rysten. He stared and stared until she said, "Long time no see, golden boy. It's been a while for us."

Then she kissed him.

CHAPTER SEVEN

I'VE BEEN THROUGH A LOT OF THINGS IN MY LIFE. Seen a lot of things. Done a lot of things. Set a lot of things on fire... and my fingers twitched for her to be next.

Never once have I considered cold-blooded murder when it came to something as simple as kissing, but when she strolled up to Rysten and wrapped her arms around his neck, pulling him to her...red. My vision went red.

A dull roar filled my ears as the world slowed down to the beat of my heart. The only sound was that of the pounding in my head. I longed to move and pull her away, but the smallest thread of sanity kept me grounded to my spot and told me to watch. To listen.

I stared at the back of her head. Waiting for him to respond. Waiting for him to refute what I just saw. To correct her. To push her away. To do something.

I wasn't the girl that stood for this, and after everything we'd been through, he should know that. I also wasn't the woman that let jealousy eat at her like poison. I cared about myself far too much for that, and with his brand on my neck, I'd think he'd know that too.

But still, I waited.

Rysten's silence must have shocked her as well, because she pulled back, just enough for me to see his face. To the see his furrowed brows and his eyes squinting as he looked down at her.

"Iona?" he asked. The confusion in his tone was clear. A cool hand wrapped around my elbow, drawing me closer. I knew it was Moira. That she was pulling me to her, hoping that her touch would soothe me as it often did. I was as numb to her as I was to the vision before me. I simply stood there—and I waited.

Assumptions make an ass out of everyone.

Isn't that what people always say?

It seems that no one thought to mention how much this hurt; how much giving a shit *hurt*. His silence was hard, but his first word? That was harder.

And I was trying really fucking hard not to assume what the fuck this all meant—because his first words weren't a correction. They weren't an apology. They weren't even addressed to me.

They were for her.

A blade twisting through my chest would have been kinder.

My hands curled into fists at my sides, nails biting into the palms. The world seemed to be at a standstill, waiting for them to say something. No one more so than me.

Because I wouldn't believe it. I couldn't. After everything we'd been through...

"Iona, I thought you were dead. I watched you die," he uttered and then he backed away. His golden hair lit up like the dying sun. His eyes sparkled like gems, but there was a dangerous undercurrent within. That dark power he kept locked up tight was straining. The veins beneath his tanned face turned black as he struggled for control over his emotions.

"I'm sorry—" She reached for him again and he recoiled.

"No, I watched you die," he repeated. His head shook. He sounded very sure of this.

"I almost did," she murmured, swallowing hard. I wanted to tear my eyes away because it felt like watching a lover's quarrel. One that didn't involve me.

"Clearly." Rysten's mask snapped into place, hiding his emotion from all except me. Even with the added touch of glamor to keep his true feelings concealed, the bond allowed me to see and feel through it. Inside, he was hurting.

"Aren't you happy to see me, Rys?" she asked, a slight whine to her voice that had me closing my eyes and turning away. I didn't know what I was watching unfold, but I was sure I didn't want to be a part of it.

"See that you're alive after thousands of years?" I felt her reaction. The way her heart echoed mine from moments ago. "I looked for you. I mourned for you, and you've been doing what all this time? Hiding? Working?"

"It's not that simple, baby—"

And that was when I started walking.

"Don't call me that!" he roared. "I'm not your anything anymore. You left me."

A bundle of fur at my feet made me stop. Bandit pulled on my jeans and I bent at the waist to scoop him up. Water pricked my eyes, but I'd be damned if I let myself cry over this. Rysten already owned a piece of my heart. He didn't get my tears too.

"I *lived* because of you," she snapped. "When my body was broken and bleeding out, I thought of you. He tossed what was left of me into the lake, but I survived because of *you*." I clung to Bandit as I walked away. All eyes seemed to be on the arguing couple. All except mine.

I had no desire to see where this was going.

Storming past the makings of another campfire and a snarling enigma in hellhound form, I pushed between the few demons in masks standing at the other side of camp and continued on.

On to where I could no longer hear Rysten's accusations and that woman's excuses. On to where the bond wasn't so sharp between us, and his pain didn't bleed over into me so acutely that it felt as if she'd betrayed me and not him. On to where the last of the setting sun dipped below the horizon and that jewel-toned skyline went grey.

Focusing on the colorless sky was easier than sorting through the pains in my chest and the ache in my heart. A sharp wind rustled the trees around me. Branches whipped, trees swayed, and an unsettling cold slapped me in the face. I touched my cheek and my fingers came away wet from tears I didn't even know I'd shed.

I glared at the liquid on my fingers. Tears mixed with sweat and dirt and heartbreak.

"For fuck's sake," I cursed, wiping my hand on the tight pants I wore. Bandit nestled closer as I lifted the edge of my shirt to clean my face.

What happened back there looked pretty bad, and I reacted on that, but at least I hadn't burned her alive. I was a lot of things, a murderer included, but that didn't mean I had to act like it. Inside me the beast writhed with anger and dark promise. She wanted to punish the blonde for touching Rysten, but the way I saw it—it wasn't the blonde's fault. Iona. That was her name.

She wasn't the one bonded to me. She probably had no idea.

It was on Rysten to set her straight, and while he'd been pretty shocked to see her—reasonably so from what I heard—that didn't excuse him. That didn't place the blame on her.

The beast didn't really fault that logic, but she was far more forgiving towards him if the other she-demon was dead. Something about that snapped me from my own stupor and made me roll my eyes. How very...beast-like of her.

Our bond connected us in ways I wished to escape at this moment. I could feel his emotions spike. Betrayal was prominent. Guilt. I couldn't figure where the emotions came from or why, only that they were there and for some reason, they had hit a staggering frequency despite the greater distance.

Their argument must be cresting just as my head was clearing and the rising bloodlust cooling.

Bandit curled around me tighter and he bared his teeth at the outer forest, but nothing was there. Just dirt and trees and grey. Turning from the far-off horizon still very much out of our reach, I looked back towards the direction of camp.

I sighed. "We should probably get back," I told Bandit. His ears twitched, but other than that he didn't respond. Not that I really expected him to.

As I started walking the strangest feeling crept up on me. Almost...no, that can't be right. I brushed my hands over my arms and against the goosebumps that were rising on my skin beneath my flannel. Then the hairs on my neck stood on end.

It was silent. Far too silent.

My footsteps slowed to a crawl as I approached the tree line. On the other side would be the clearing where the Horsemen, Moira, Jax, the four steeds, and the many masked demons should be.

Why was it that I felt eyes on me then?

I stared straight ahead as the wind whispered across the forest floor.

A twig snapped.

I spun around, but it was the wrong move. A hand clamped over my mouth. I panicked.

Reacting on nothing but instinct and adrenaline, I brought my foot back and down on the foot of my would-be subduer. They held strong, though, and the scent of flowers washed over me.

"Listen carefully because I won't repeat myself," a female voice whispered in my ear. Deep and husky. The scent of blood and lilies settled around me. "You're in great danger here. My master is watching both of us." A chill skittered down my back, leaving me cold. Sin was nearly as tall as I and her slender fingers as calloused as the Horsemen's. The rough pads pressed against the column of my throat as if in warning. "I am trying to help you, but my hands are tied in how much I can do. Your path is set. All that's left is for you to follow it."

The second her hand dropped from my mouth I whirled on her. Mercury eyes watched me with a carefully crafted sort of stillness that wasn't natural. This woman was every bit the predator my beast was, except one of these was born out of nature and the other...I could only guess.

I tampered down the rising anger by reminding myself who I was talking to. Sin wasn't one to fuck around when she wanted something. She didn't understand shit like boundaries. Hell, she stripped my telepathy with a twirl of her fingers. That alone should give the beast pause, though it didn't. It was good the beast wasn't the one in charge here, or Sin might already be burning.

The corner of her lips curved up in a crude sort of smile.

"You're a smart girl. So was your mother."

"What the hell are you talking about, Sin? The path is set? What fucking path?" I threw my head back and closed my eyes, pressing the palm of my hand to my forehead. I took a deep breath and said, "Is it even possible for you to speak plainly? I'm getting tired of the games here."

Her lips twisted into a grimace. "We all are. This world is dying, and we're being forced to leave it in the hands of a child. If I could speak plainly and tell you exactly what to do, I would—but there are things in motion you don't know or understand yet."

I shook my head and my hand fell away. "Why are you here, Sin? You seem to only come when I'm either going to die or already dying. Since I am currently neither, your sudden appearance makes me think those demons in the woods might change that." I raised my eyes to the treetops looking for any sign of eyes watching, but we were alone. As alone as one could possibly be in a forest filled with monsters.

"They are not who they appear." She looked over my shoulder as if seeing something faraway. "They've been...changed by time and desperation."

I rocked back on my heels and wiped my thumb across my bottom lip.

"Great. So, they *are* trying to kill us," I said. My voice was oddly steady for the panic I should be feeling. There was once a time that one full demon would make me scared, but that time was no more. I'd killed men, dozens of men, in the name of destroying evil and avenging my familiars. I'd lit them up without a thought and watched their corpses burn until only black ash remained, all without a single grimace.

The masked demons, while problematic, were not my biggest concern.

"Who isn't?" Sin scoffed, looking to the treetops above us.

"That's the real question," I murmured, more to myself than anything. Sin cocked an eyebrow in my direction and I sighed. "What changed them?"

Sin didn't react, but that in and of itself was a reaction. Her unfettered response was too cool. Too...practiced. The way her eyes didn't avoid me but also didn't drill into my soul. She never shifted or otherwise fidgeted when we met. Sin was far too confident for that sort of thing. That didn't mean she didn't have tells, though.

"Magic." Her eyes flashed, the only warning I'd get about straying too close to questions she can't answer. Her half-answers wouldn't work forever.

"*Who* changed them?" I rephrased.

That cruel smile—the one that danced on the edge of chaos—sat on her lips again.

"I can't tell you."

"Can't or won't?" I pushed. The silver of her eyes darkened a fraction.

"Both," she answered with the slightest growl to the word. I narrowed my gaze, flicking my eyes between her and the tree line.

"Do they have a master?" I asked so quietly I almost wondered if she didn't hear it.

But then came her response, and it wasn't even a sound. Just a silent word on her lips. "Yes."

I nodded slowly, taking that in.

"You know," I said, "your master may prevent you from saying a lot. The rune of silence you placed on me prevents me from doing the same. I can't say anything to the Horsemen. I can't talk to Moira. This whole thing would be a lot easier if I could speak with *someone,* though. Maybe they could help me—"

"No." Her tone was sharp. Short. She didn't leave room for arguing.

"I understand very little about this world and now I'm having to rely solely on you to handle whichever of Lucifer's enemies is after me." I'd been playing this game with her for a little while now, but my patience was running thin after what went down in New Orleans. Now after trekking through Hell, my temper was even thinner. "I know that your hands are tied, but you're giving me breadcrumbs here. One of these times someone is going to be one step ahead of you and it's going to be me that dies because of it."

The silver of her eyes seemed to transform and glow as she watched me, jaw tight and body stiff. She didn't like that I was pushing back, but I didn't have a lot of fucks to give at this point.

"Devil-damnit, Sin," I whispered a curse. "You owe me after all the shit I went through."

Sin continued to watch me as I let out a sigh and moved to step around her. Cool fingers touched my forearm.

"She is going to invite you to the Garden tonight. Go with her. You and your mates will be in great danger, but you will find the answers you seek." Her words were punctuated with strain and inundated with weariness. She was struggling with something. If only I knew what.

"Thank you," I whispered.

"Don't thank me just yet."

I glanced sideways, but her eyelids were shuttered, keeping the hidden truths in her eyes concealed. "I don't understand everything you've done or why. At times it has infuriated me because I wish that this were simple. My life will never be simple again, though, and I have to learn to live with that." I paused, sucking in a deep breath. "I'm going to choose to overlook what happened in New Orleans. Without you I have very few allies. That doesn't mean I trust you. It means that I trust you had a damn good reason for what you did to me and mine." Her eyes opened, zeroing in on me. "I trust that you meant what you said that night, that you want to see me on the throne. Which is why I'm not going to let the beast do what it really wants to you. *This time.* Next time, I make no promises. Your master clearly holds a lot of power here, and I need to find out who they are, with or without you."

"You're threatening me?" she chuckled, not sounding even the slightest bit scared.

"No, I'm warning you that this is your last chance before the beast overrides my forgiveness." She paused, tilting her head to the side. "I'd like us to be true allies. Friends, even, when this is all over. Friends don't stab each other in the back to meet their own needs. Remember that."

Her hand dropped away from my arm, and I didn't need to look to know that she was already gone.

Sin came to deliver a warning and I gave her one instead.

Perhaps if we both listened to each other we'd all make it out of this alive.

Where the fuck had she gone?

I'd been scanning the clearing while Iona and Rysten were at each other's neck, hashing out the details of a history I'd rather forget. While everyone was watching them, I had been watching her. The shock on her face. The flush that crept up her neck and over her cheeks. The bitter tang of betrayal when Rysten made the mistake of letting Iona kiss him and not correcting her. She was like an open book when I could read her body and emotions, and Rysten had hurt her greatly.

But then something happened.

Her eyes went cold and she disappeared, along with any trace of the bond. If I hadn't watched it with my own eyes, I might have thought it was one of the fuckers in a mask toying with us, but that sort of power...no, none of them could have done it. She glamored herself so efficiently that I, nor any of the other Horsemen, could not find her.

"Where is she?" I telepathically shot towards Moira. Her familiar seemed none too troubled in the slightest and was more concerned with analyzing Rysten's every move than helping us find Ruby.

"She needs space," came the chilled reply. It was the same she'd given the last five times and I was losing my patience, but no matter which of us asked, she was unwilling to comply. Her loyalty was to Ruby, and Ruby alone.

"She could be in danger," I thought, changing tactics. The corner of her dark green lips curved up in a cruel sort of smile.

"I pity the idiot that tries her right now."

I clenched my teeth and turned away. She wasn't wrong, and that made this all the more dangerous. The last thing we needed was an all-out fight with Iona's faction before reaching Inferna, which is what it very well could turn into if they were here for her and noticed she was gone. Except fucking Moira was stonewalling me and the damn raccoon had gone with Ruby, which left me with no way to find her until she decided to show herself.

Stretching my fingers to keep from curling them into fists, I headed towards the edge of the forest, opposite from Rysten and Iona. If she was looking to get away from them, it made more sense for her to go that way.

"You're threatening me?" came the hushed chuckle of amusement I knew all too well. I peered out into the trees as I glamored myself to blend in with them.

"No, I'm warning you that this is your last chance before the beast overrides my forgiveness," a second voice said. I squinted my eyes. "I'd like us to be true allies. Friends, even, when this is all over. Friends don't stab each other in the back to meet their own needs. Remember that."

A shadow appeared where I now knew Ruby to be standing. The faint outline of two women and a raccoon. Sin's fingers slipped from Ruby's forearm as she took a step away. In the blink of an eye the white-haired woman was gone and Ruby stood alone.

While my eyes roved over her for signs of distress, my mind was more occupied with what exactly those two were doing with each other. Sin had only met Ruby once in passing...or had she?

I wanted to believe that my little succubus wasn't keeping secrets from us, but the hard edge to her expression as she stared toward the clearing didn't leave me so certain. Half my instincts told me I should go to her now and try to pull the truth from her lips, but the other half told me to wait. Watch. Ruby was loyal to those she considered hers, even if she didn't say everything. Devil knows there are things that we've been reluctant to tell her. After all she's given up for us and for this, the last thing anyone wanted was to bring her more pain. In doing so, though...she may have sought out other answers from people with less reservations. Like Sin.

Torn by indecision, I hesitated as a banshee's screech split the air. Ruby's eyes flashed obsidian and then back to blue as she pulled her shoulders back and walked towards the clearing. Walked, not ran. Which meant either Moira wasn't in trouble, or Ruby trusted her to handle it on her own. I doubled back, instantly assessing the scene before me, just as Ruby did.

What I didn't expect to find was Iona sprawled out on the forest floor, Moira's boot planted on her sternum.

CHAPTER EIGHT

"WHAT PART OF *MATED MALE* DID YOU NOT understand the first time, blondie?" Moira snapped. Iona tried to sit up and Moira's boot pressed down harder. Fire swirled in the depths of her blue pentagram eyes.

"Rys—what is she—" Iona only rasped half her sentence when Moira stomped again, forcing the air from her lungs as she ground her boot into the flimsy homemade shirt.

"Do not look at him. Do not speak to him. He is your *nothing*," she growled in a voice that made the beast proud. "I don't give a shit who you are, but you will not come between my girl and her men—"

"Moira." My voice cut through the crowd like blades against paper. "Get. Off. Her."

"She disrespects you knowing that he's mated—"

"It is not her place to respect that bond. It's *his*, and that is something he and I will deal with later."

I could feel Rysten's eyes on me. Sense his panic as I purposely didn't spare him a glance. They'd turned my life upside down and inside out, but I didn't grovel. I didn't beg. If he wanted me, then it was on him to fix this. That didn't mean I needed to ream him in public. This was no one's business but our own.

Moira lifted her boot from the demon's sternum and crossed her arms over her chest with a huff. Iona scrambled to her feet and dusted off her basic clothing, eyeing me with apprehension. "You have his brand..."

She was confused. Hurt. There was more than a little spite in her voice to cover it up. Envy too. I chose to ignore it.

"And he has mine, but that is neither here nor there." I kept my voice clipped and my expression detached. After all, they weren't here by happenstance. I had to play along, but that didn't mean I had to be friendly. "Who are you and what do you want?" Her lips fell ajar as if surprised by my straightforwardness.

With a heavy sigh she readjusted her stance to a slightly more defensive posture. Her chin lifted and the self-importance of it all had me...bored and annoyed. I was so over the mean girl shit.

"I am Iona LeGrase, the Deadly Sin of Envy's niece."

I blinked as she extended a claw-tipped hand that had Moira stepping in front of me with a growl.

"If you so much as scratch her, goldilocks—"

"I think she gets the point." I squeezed her shoulder causing Moira to turn her chin up. I shook my head once, and she furrowed her brows but stepped away. My best friend's instincts were right not to trust her, but I couldn't tell her that. Not if I wanted to find out the truth about who was after me.

"I'm Ruby Morningstar, and this is my familiar, Moira."

"I'm also a legion and a banshee. I wouldn't try anything if I were you," she said with a purse of her lips.

Iona appraised her distastefully, a tendril of apprehension running through her before she said, "Welcome to the family."

Swallowing down the painful emotions riding me, I lifted my hand to hers and clasped it. She was stronger than me, but for what she had in strength I made up for in fire. My palm grew warm as I let the flames play just beneath my skin. Not enough to burn her, but enough to feel the heat as she tried to crush my fingers.

A bead of sweat dotted her brow when she released me. I kept my expression cool. Civil.

"She's only speaking metaphorically," Rysten said with a piercing look in her direction. I lifted an eyebrow without looking at him and a slight blush darkened his skin. "The Sins, apart from you mother, never had children. Merula formed a very close relationship with Iona's mother."

"They were practically sisters before she died," Iona added bitterly.

"I see..." The words hung there, not hostile, but not exactly friendly. I ignored Rysten's eyes that pleaded with me to understand their complicated histories, just as much as I ignored Iona's calculated gaze. At the end of the day I didn't particularly care if we shared blood or not. Moira and Bandit were my family. The Horsemen were. This girl—she was a stranger trying to kill me. I needed to get closer to her, but I didn't particularly want to understand her. It was easier that way.

"This is all fine and well," Allistair interrupted, "but what are you doing all the way outside Rieka?" His eyes narrowed slightly as he took her in. I didn't miss the way his posture remained stiff.

"Hunting," the girl answered, giving him only half her attention. The other half was on my Horseman. Rysten. The beast growled, warning me that if Iona didn't keep her hands and eyes to herself that the not-so-friendly alter-ego of mine was going to deliver the warning in person. With a punch to the cunt.

"What do you mean by *hunting*?" Moira asked before someone else could cut in. Iona regarded her with enough animosity that I felt the need to step a little closer to my best friend.

"I mean that Hell is on fire and half the planet is in chaos, Rieka included. Lust crumbled first, and Greed wasn't far behind it once the borders destabilized. The Sins went into hiding, leaving the rest of us to fend for ourselves." Iona waved to the group of demons around her. "This is all that's left of Sector Forty-Nine."

I swallowed and refused to look away even as the guilt leaked in. She could be a liar about everything, but I knew first-hand how destructive the flames were when I lost control and destroyed my own tattoo parlor.

"Why didn't you go to Inferna?" Allistair asked.

"It's full," she answered. "Lust was given the order to evacuate first and by the time the fire reached Rieka, it was too late."

"Surely your *aunt* would have made room for you. Since you're close enough to be family," Moira commented. Iona looked like she just drank piss the way her lips twisted, and eyes brightened.

"She's the leader of a province," Iona snapped. "She doesn't get to play favorites. Something you might know if you were from here."

Funny how she didn't seem this snappy about me being Satan's kid until Moira threw her on the ground for kissing Rysten. I wondered how much of her being here was for me and how much was for him. I supposed we'd find out soon enough.

"I didn't grow up with a silver spoon up my ass. Sorry if I don't understand how it works." Moira threw her hands in the air and I groaned.

"Moira, why don't you go sit with Jax and see if you can get him to change back. I don't think they're going to attack us now..." I turned to Iona. "Are you?"

She gave me a flippant look but spoke clearly. "No. We never intended to hurt you. We just needed to make sure you weren't here to mean harm."

"Interesting way of showing it..." Moira muttered. I cleared my throat and she blew out a breath, stalking off towards the shaking enigma-hellhound.

"She's got a point," Laran said. "Holding weapons to us is not the best way to show peace. Even I know that." The corners of my lips turned up as War slipped an arm over my shoulders. Iona looked anything but peaceful in the way she watched Moira leave.

"When Rieka burned, neighbors turned on each other," she said slowly, her voice far calmer than the look in her eyes. "You were just as likely to be stabbed for the shirt on your back while walking down the street as you were to find someone that would help you. I won't apologize for being vigilant when you're this close to one of the two ways in and out of the Garden."

"It's still open?" Julian asked.

"It is. Only path not on fire that leads through to Inferna," she answered, baiting us.

"Funny that, we're headed there right now," I said before anyone else could answer. If she was going to try to lure us, I may as well let her think I was naïve and didn't see through the subterfuge. I'd been feeling out of my depth to a certain extent ever since we arrived in Hell, but bitches certainly made it feel like home.

I wondered how much of this was personal for her

and how much was the unknown face that's been following me since Portland, trying to kill me at every turn.

"I can't guarantee you passage through the Garden, but if you're here to fix this mess, the least I can let you do is stay through the night." The creeping sensation along my spine had me on edge. I already knew not to trust her. I was walking into the viper's nest with eyes wide open.

So why did it feel like there was something I was still missing?

"That would be great," I said before I took the time to reconsider the decision. Sin said if I went along, I'd find my answers. No matter how much I hated the looks she continued to give Rysten, nothing was stopping me from searching for the truth.

Not fear. Not Rysten. Not even love itself.

"If we stay with you, do we have your word that you mean no harm?" Laran asked.

"You do." Her voice resonated with a truth, but as we moved to pack up our camp, a sliver of emotion escaped through her nonchalance. I tilted my head to the side. It felt like...regret?

It was gone so fast I almost thought I imagined it.

Almost.

CHAPTER NINE

EPONA'S SIDE BRUSHED AGAINST ME REASSURINGLY. On her back sat Bandit, gnawing his way through the straps. He wasn't the biggest fan of the other demons and given that he wore the devil's mark, they weren't fans of him either.

Not that it stopped him from snapping at anyone that stepped a little too close to me or the horse. He seemed to be growing an attachment to her, one that I hadn't expected given her massive size. She was a gentle soul, though, which was strange given whose familiar she was.

A cool hand pressed against my elbow as a slim arm hooked around it. The scent of peppermint floated over me as Moira leaned in to whisper, "I don't trust her."

"Me neither," I muttered, trying not to pay too much attention to how closely Iona walked beside

Rysten. Jealousy. Territorialism. Call it what you want, but the green-eyed monster was not a pleasant feeling when it chose to visit.

It helped that every time Iona got close to touching him, Rysten stepped a good three feet to the side to dodge her.

"Something's off about that one," Moira continued. "She didn't lie earlier, but I don't think she was telling the full truth." I stumbled when my boot hit a rock and Moira caught me easily. I grinned at the way her small frame held the brunt of my weight without breaking a sweat. She'd always been strong-willed, but now she had the body to match it.

"What makes you say she wasn't lying?"

"I can tell," Moira said evasively. My eyebrows inched up my forehead and she chuckled under her breath. "Ever since I transitioned, things have been...different. There's power in words, and I can taste it. Lies taste bad."

"You never talk about what happened," I said. It was my way of prodding, but just a little. If she wanted to talk, that was her choice; the same as if she chose to be silent.

"It's still happening," she murmured. I paused, the eerie tone of her voice had my skin prickling.

"What do you mean?" I said slowly. Moira stopped, and because we were at the back of the group, no one minded one bit. She looked up at the night sky. On Earth it would have been a hazy blue-grey that was too murky to discern much of anything. Here, it was more saturated, and the sky shone like navy paint splashed across a canvas. The stars popped like glittering gems against the darkened atmosphere.

"Our lives changed the day Allistair paid your bail. We've had a lot of ups and some pretty low downs. I've been kidnapped, drugged, tortured, imprisoned, and starved to a certain extent when Bandit and I had to share any food we found." My mouth went dry and I wished I'd never asked now, but I opened up the door for her to speak. I needed to hear what she had to say. "I think if we only looked at the bad things, people would wonder why I'm still with you. Why I chose to stand by you all these years. Why I chose to follow you into Hell. But you know what? The same thing could be said about you with me.

"I remember the day you stood up to Brayden Patterson for me. He wouldn't stop throwing rocks and you slugged him in the face so hard his nose was never straight again. Neither was your right index finger." My hands flexed as I remembered the impact. "You've fought people for me. You've risked yourself time and time again. You've been teased and tormented, and if we're both being honest, that night in Pandora's Box never would have happened if I hadn't insisted on taking you out alone because I don't like to share." I opened my mouth to refute it, but a slight finger rested on my lips telling me to shush. "We've hurt each other by association, but we've also completed each other in ways that no one else understands. You wanted to know why I don't talk about what happened? About my time with Le Dan Bia, about my transition, about being branded—the thing is, I'm still living it. Every day with you, I am preparing for the next horror I might face. I'm terrified that one day these close calls will be just a little too close, and I'll lose you like *that*." She snapped her fingers, and it reverberated in my bones. "So, I don't talk about it. I prepare. I practice when no one is watching. I listen to the things people don't say. I watch the world around us. Because our lives are still changing, and until it stops, I have no intention of pausing to think about what has happened and letting it distract me. The second I do might be the second someone strikes and then all the talking in the world won't matter if you're gone. Being angry won't matter if you're gone, because all I'll have is myself and my own resentments. And that's the worst place to be."

I stared at her and couldn't find words.

Certainly not one's like hers. Moira didn't talk because she existed in an eternal state of fight or flight. Our lives were dangerous, and she was absolutely right that we hurt each other by association, but she was also right in that I wouldn't change the pain if it meant not knowing her. She didn't talk about it or let herself feel it because we were still living it.

And to her, not feeling it meant that she was better equipped to keep it that way.

Bottling emotions was never my thing. I was the

kind that let it all out and got over it, but not Moira. She held it close and locked it up tight, turning it into fuel to do and be better, and in the end...she exploded.

Today wasn't that explosion, but the building of it.

She gave herself a foundation built on spite and hope and guilt and love. She crafted herself into the perfect disaster. Wild. Passionate. Disruptive.

I wrapped my arms around her shoulders and pulled her close, knowing that one day soon, in the right collision of events, she would go *bang*—and nothing would hold her together then.

"I love you, Moira," I muttered into her shoulder.

"I love you too. That's why I don't like this." It didn't take a genius to know what she was talking about. "Her timing is too convenient. Rysten thought she died like three thousand years ago, and now all of a sudden she makes an appearance?" Moira scoffed. "Puh-lease. This bitch is here to drive a wedge. Which is why I lost my shit when she tried to kiss him, again."

I froze and both my eyebrows shot to my hairline. "Again?"

"He pushed her away the second time," Moira said. "But the fact that he told her he was mated and she still tried that shit...I just couldn't stop myself. I'm tired of all these petty bitches. You won't go beast mode on them, but there's nothing stopping me. I'm no one." She shrugged her shoulders with a wicked smile on her lips.

"You're not no one—" I argued. She threw her head

back and let out a loud, obnoxious laugh that had half the masked demons turning to look at us.

"Oh, babe, I'm no one, but that's fine by me. Being your familiar is more than enough responsibility." She patted my back. "Means I get to do all the fun things, like pick on the Horsemen because they can't do shit about it."

I snorted. Of course, that would be a perk to her.

"They're not the only ones you've been picking on lately…" I started, letting my voice trail off while tilting my chin towards Jax.

"That's because he's a dick." Her forehead went tense as she purposely stared straight ahead.

"Uh huh." I threw my arm around her shoulder. "So are you. Your point?"

She spluttered for a second, grasping for a response. I cocked an eyebrow, fighting a smile and her cheeks blushed pistachio. "I choose to be a dick, thank you very much. He wouldn't know how to be nice if it bit him in the ass."

I snorted. "You keep telling yourself that."

"I'm serious—" Moira said loudly, elbowing me in the ribs for cracking up so hard. A heavy arm landed around my shoulder, edging between us. "What the hell?" She jumped away from the intrusion. "Famine, I'm not all about your incubus cooties, man. Save that shit for Ruby and a closed door."

"Mind if I cut in here?" Allistair asked, his lips brushing over the tip of my ear as he leaned into me.

113

"Just help yourself." Moira rolled her eyes and he flashed her a wink as she moved up ahead to give us room to talk.

"You handled yourself better than I expected," he said quietly, the overt flirtatiousness slipping from his tone.

"Oh?" I asked. "And how did you think I would handle myself?"

"I wasn't completely sure Iona was going to make it out of that alive."

Was that a ghost of a smile?

"I'm not that petty," I snorted, blowing a sweaty strand of hair away from my face. "Besides, I meant what I said. This is between me and Rysten. How Iona acts isn't my business."

He nodded silently, watching them up ahead of us, the same as I did.

"You're wise for one so young."

"She's not the first bitchy ex I've dealt with. I doubt she'll be the last." But I wished she was. I wished it more than anything. Ever since puberty I'd been dealing with women like this. It's a devil-damned miracle that I had Moira.

"She's not an ex," Allistair said. I frowned.

"But she kissed him. Moira said she tried to again—"

"When you are close with someone it's not uncommon to kiss them here. She took it a step too far, though, and I didn't see the second time. I was too busy looking for you." My breath hitched and I tried to smother it with a cough, but the look in his eyes said it all.

"How much did you see?" He seamlessly missed the roots and underbrush as we walked, even while watching every expression that crossed my face.

"I saw you threaten Sin. Care to tell me how long you've known her?" My teeth sank into my bottom lip as I looked away. Two fingers grasped my chin turning my face back to him.

"A while," I found myself saying. "She came to me in Portland."

His lips slipped ajar as an understanding settled over him. "She's the one that saved you from the Seelie." It wasn't a question, so I didn't treat it as one.

"Amongst other things." I wasn't trying to be purposely evasive, but I wasn't sure where the rune would come into play and prevent me from speaking. It was better to be vague than have him stumble upon something I couldn't tell him about and have another one of those damn coughing spells.

"She's dangerous, Ruby—"

"You think I don't know that?" I snapped, harsher than I intended. My mouth closed as his fingers slipped from my chin. Running a hand down my face, I sighed deeply. "I'm sorry. I'm not trying to be an asshole here."

"You're under a lot of pressure. I get it, and I even get why you might have kept this to yourself. Julian is prone to jumping the gun when it comes to you." We both looked to where the Horseman of Death rode atop Rhiannon. "Just be careful with Sinumpa. Nothing with her is easy, or free."

"Speaking from personal experience?" I asked him.

"Yes," he answered, turning his gaze to the ground in front of us. Avoiding mine.

"She was the girl, wasn't she?" I asked softly. His muscles went tense. "The one you loved?"

"*Thought* I loved. It wasn't the same." I wanted to ask him the same as what, but I wasn't ready for the answer to that yet. If he said what I thought he was implying, it would be awkward when I didn't say it back. Not until this was all over.

"But that was her?"

"Yes."

We fell silent as I thought about that. Sin was the only woman in all of his life that he felt anything for besides me. I suppose that was when I ought to feel jealous, or at least territorial. But unlike Iona—who was playing with fire—Sin wasn't driving wedges. On the contrary, I wouldn't have known at all if he hadn't seen us together.

When it came to whatever happened between them, I didn't really feel any which way about it. They'd both clearly moved on and his straight forward-ness left me at ease.

"I'll be careful. I promise."

He nodded. "I trust you, Ruby. I just don't trust her."

"Will you keep this between me and you?" I rolled my shoulder back and slipped one arm around his waist as we walked.

"For now." His knuckles brushed softly down my side in an intimate gesture. My blood heated, and not because of the exertion. "Julian would lose his shit if he knew you two were in contact, but there's not exactly anything we can do. You're your own person, and even if we wanted to keep you from Sin, she would find a way." He sighed, sounding far closer to his age than usual. "Just know that if you get in too deep with her that I'm here."

My eyes closed as I turned and placed a soft kiss against his chest. "Thank you."

"Always, little succubus."

I smiled, feeling truly content despite where we were headed.

Even going into Hell could be a pleasant experience if you had your people with you.

Then the excited cries rang out into the night as Moira came doubling back into view. "We're here," she said as she projected her voice to me through the crowd.

I looked beyond her and the thin slip of trees to the mouth of the tunnel that led underground. The warm fuzzy feeling in my chest dissipated.

This was it.

"Ready to find out why no one wants to live in the Garden?" Allistair chuckled.

No, I couldn't say that I did. But unfortunately for me, Iona had the answers I needed. "Let's go," I said with more enthusiasm than I felt.

My gut had kept me alive this long, maybe it would keep us alive a little longer.

CHAPTER TEN

NEVER HAD I BEEN SO WRONG.

The very rockface itself seemed to be acting as an oven trying to broil me alive. While Allistair insisted it was always this way, Laran and Julian were speculating that it was worse than usual, but at least underground no one had to fear that they'd burn from the flames. In some ways, it was similar to the portal since it was made of the same stone, and like the portal—it was downright uncomfortable. With millions of pounds of rock surrounding me, not even the slightest breeze giving relief, and Bandit's god-awful whining—I understood why no one wanted to live here and no Sin contended for this province. It sucked. No two ways about it.

After walking for what felt like hours, I was ready to faint or cry when the tunnel finally opened up into what everyone had been calling the Garden. A sprawling underground city filled with a million tiny flickering lights that centered around a clear luminescent lake. Towers of black stone rose up from the water, each individual floor appeared like a pavilion with columns instead of true walls acting as the structure. Within them demons laughed and dined, they fucked, they fought, just as they would anywhere else.

Children high above us, on the upmost floors, ran out to the edge and looked down ten stories without fear. One of them, a boy not so far out, reached up and wrapped his hand around a gleaming cable—the place was filled with them. They spanned from one tower to the next, going up and down and straight across. Some even led off into the rock wall, seeming to disappear, which made me think they were actually caves.

The boy's cable led straight to the rock beach where I stood. I frowned as he whipped up a length of rope dangling from his belt; on the end, a metal hook reflected the water's low fluorescence. He slipped that end over the cable and without any hesitation, he jumped.

My mouth fell ajar from shock, but before I could even say anything the boy rocked himself forward and detached his clip, somersaulting in midair to land like an Olympic gymnast. No one around me took notice as he went to work helping load people onto the boats and then pushing them off the edge of the lake. "Did you see that?" I asked the Horsemen around me, pointedly focusing on everything else but how Iona continued trying to use her persuasion to get Rysten to join her boat—like she was strong enough for that to work on him. A look of disgust came over his features as he regarded her once before storming off to the side of the shore.

"See what?" Laran asked, coming to stand beside me. I pulled my attention back and pointed to the boy in a half-mask, wearing cinched baggy pants with layers of fabric and rope around his waist. Only a single white brand spanned half his back.

It gave off the same light as the water.

"That kid. He just rode one of those cables from across the lake." Laran nodded, brushing a hand over his stubbled jaw.

"Ahnika came up with those. It's the fastest and easiest way to get around here."

For the Sin of Sloth, I imagined her to be a little less...ingenious. Guess that's what I got for assuming. "It's a clever idea," I said.

"And it sure as Hell beats the climb up." Allistair pointed to the tower and motioned vertically. I squinted, trying to pick out how you got from one floor to the next when I saw— "Are those ladders?" My voice sounded a little breathy and shrill at the mild panic of having to climb hundreds of feet after already being this exhausted...

"Yes, but we won't be staying in a tower while we're here," Allistair answered, guiding me towards the shore.

"We won't?" I breathed out a sigh of relief and muttered, "Thank the Devil." Laran and Allistair chuckled, both offering me a hand to help me into the surprisingly stable boat.

"We'll be staying in a cave closer to the other side of the lake," Allistair said. I moved to the far end and waited patiently as they loaded Rhiannon. Epona followed, carrying Bandit as he slept and snored obnoxiously loud. "I'm surprised the boat can hold their weight," I said as Allistair and Julian joined me.

"These boats can't sink, flip, or otherwise be destroyed," Allistair said by way of answer. He reached out and clasped a paddle before War pushed us off. A pang of sadness hit me as I realized Laran was staying with Rysten. I saw him gather up Moira, Jax, and the final two familiars before loading themselves on a boat that trailed behind us.

"Must be magic," I breathed, taking the chance to absorb my reality.

I was in Hell—underground—sharing a boat with two horses and two of my mates.

Shit didn't get any crazier than this. It really didn't.

In such a short period of time, my life had changed so drastically, I don't even know if the old me would recognize what I'd become. Sure, on the outside we looked the same, but inside I was different. Changed in ways I couldn't even fathom then. I had powers. Dangerous. Deadly powers. I had brands. I had familiars. I had enemies that weren't just jealous women anymore— and more than anything—I had responsibilities.

To myself. To my family. To my mates. To an entire world.

If I wasn't still riding the wave of shock and incredulity, suffering a caffeine withdrawal induced headache accompanied by mild exhaustion ...well, I'd probably have either fainted or panicked by now, but I didn't have time for that anymore.

In a matter of months, life as I had known it crumbled around me and served as kindling. Up in flames it went and where the glittering black ash settled, my new life grew. I'd reoriented my entire spectrum of being, and here underneath a caverned ceiling that glittered like the ash of my flames, I'd never felt more afraid, but I'd also never felt stronger.

The stalactites loomed hundreds of feet in the air, glowing water dripping like rain from the ends of them. I thought of the old Bible verse about a man in Hell begging God for only a drop of water. It never came.

Maybe he'd have had better luck begging Satan.

"Penny for your thoughts?" Allistair asked, sidling up beside me as he guided the boat.

I wasn't exactly in the mood for a heart-to-heart before I talked to Rysten, so I settled for something a little simpler. "It's beautiful," I whispered, waving my hand to the ceiling high above us.

Allistair chuckled. "Until one falls and kills someone."

"That happens?" I asked, unable to judge how truly large they were without much light.

"Yeah, about once a century or so. It's Ahnika's preferred execution method." I blinked slowly, thinking about that.

Not only was she a genius, she was also vicious.

Yet another reason for me to *stop assuming*. Even as I thought it, I kept my eyes and attention glued to the ceiling instead of turning to the darker thoughts and feelings that settled in the back of my mind.

"I'm sorry—hold up for a second—did you just say *execution method?*"

He grinned up at the cavern canopy. "Yeah. Even in Sloth there is the occasional execution, although, it's far better here than Greed. Saraphine is a sadist that makes even Julian look like a choir boy at times."

I blew out a low whistle. "Damn. How do you even use a stalactite to execute someone? That's gotta be over three hundred feet high…"

"Six hundred," a gravelly voice said behind me. I could feel a blush creeping up on my cheeks after Allistair's sadist comment, but what did I have to be embarrassed about? They all knew each other even better than they knew me.

"Like I said, I don't see how that's even possible."

"Sound waves, believe it or not," Allistair said, dropping his hand to my lower back to guide me forward. "Ahnika is the strongest banshee in the world.

One scream from her and she can direct it to split one of those straight from the ceiling."

"That's insane."

"Moira could probably do the same if she tried," Julian said. He was trying to be nonchalant, but I didn't miss the very calculated way he glanced behind him and up at the stalactites. I only needed to think about that for half a second to know how much of a bad idea it was.

"Don't give her any ideas," I muttered. She would practice trying to drop them on Rysten just to see him dodging out of the way, all the while cackling something about whack-a-mole.

"Wouldn't dream of it. She's already a big enough pain in the ass," Allistair replied, but Julian stayed silent. I turned my slight frown to the front of the boat just as we hit land. The stop jolted me, and it took all my balance and Allistair's fingers gripping the material of my shirt to keep me from being tossed out of the boat.

What it didn't do was keep Bandit sleeping. My raccoon woke with a damn vengeance, jumping to his feet with a growl and reaching for me.

"You good?" Allistair asked. I nodded and he released me, stepping out to offer his hand as I wrapped one arm around Bandit and gave him the other.

Something cool and wet whacked against my arm. I dropped my gaze to glance over my shoulder at

Rhiannon as she tried to nudge me along. Pushy horse. She was definitely Julian's familiar.

"I think she's giving you a hint," Allistair smirked. I pursed my lips at him but held his hand tightly, more out of necessity than anything. These rocks were slippery, and I was just as likely to bust my ass as I was to fall out of the boat and drown. While my pride didn't like it, my body was sore and shaking.

Fingers trembling, I gripped him as I stepped onto dry land. The second he released me my body swayed, but a sturdy side was there to catch me as I stumbled. Epona turned her head to nuzzle Bandit and I smiled faintly, petting her forehead while I waited for the dizziness to fade.

Winter and pine invaded my space as a cool arm wrapped around my ribcage, pulling me back into a hard chest. "You're dehydrated from riding and walking. Let's go find you somewhere you can rest for a little bit." Those wicked fingers toyed with the hem of my shirt, briefly brushing against the skin of my stomach, and just like that, resting was the last thing I wanted. But Julian—like his horse—was stubborn as a damn mule.

Without asking, he swept me up in his arms and walked farther into the cave while the others were busy unloading. Bathed in the red and yellow firelight of torches placed in rungs bolted to the craggy rock side, the cave was...homier than I expected. Chaise longues lined the walls with plush cushions and a fur rug that had enough room for ten people.

"This place looks like the get-up for some ancient king out of a history book," I said, my eyes trailing over every lush fabric and vibrant hue. The blue and green pillows had swaths of purple material pinned and sewn in beautiful designs with beads hanging from threads on the corners.

"It was," he grinned. I frowned, noting the smaller things then. The things that weren't immediately obvious. Like the lack of boats apart from ours, the lack of footprints, and even the thin layer of dust on the otherwise gleaming pleasure chamber.

"Lucifer?" I asked softly, already knowing but needing to hear it anyway. He nodded.

Once upon a time Lucifer shared this place, probably with Ahnika—the Sin of Sloth—but possibly with others too. Maybe even my own mother.

Laying on these pillows was a lot less appealing all the sudden.

"Iona thought you deserved to have your father's chamber..." Julian said quietly, trailing off at something he saw on my face.

"I feel disgusting after the last few days. Is there anywhere I can wash off first?" I was stalling and we both knew it, but it also didn't hurt anyone. Part of me wondered if Iona had planned this or if it was the master pulling her strings. If they knew just how out of place I felt sleeping in a king's nest while crowds of people holed up in the towers, sleeping in hammocks stacked on one another...

The rest of me was selfish and didn't mind the distance from Iona one bit. It gave me a chance to get my bearings without her sly smile and tanned hands trying to worm their way around Rysten. He could handle himself, but I wasn't comfortable putting him in the position to begin with when I knew there was something there and still, I agreed to come down here.

I needed answers, though. We all did.

"There are some pools around the back of the cave where you could bathe..." he trailed off, lifting an eyebrow in a silent question. My cheeks heated because that sounded like a great way to get my mind off whatever Iona was planning.

Until someone cleared their throat. Instead of desire, a cloud of dark emotions that weren't mine fell over me.

"I can take her," Rysten said. His usual playfulness was non-existent today. Where my Horseman of Pestilence loved to tease and get under his brother's skin, today there was nothing. Only loneliness and a well of betrayal so deep he was using every fiber of his being to not feel it.

The snarky asshole in me wanted to brush him off, but I couldn't do that. He wasn't Josh— who I caught pants down stumbling out of a broom closet. He was Rysten: the demon that made Josh bleed from the eyes for touching me without consent after slipping me a demonic roofie. He was the man that watched *How to Get Away with Murder* with me and brought me pad Thai when I was upset. He came to Earth for me and learned our customs, just so he could be there for me in ways the others couldn't when the day came for me to be called home.

Rysten wasn't like any other man that came before him, or even like my other three mates. He was sweet and sensitive. He was the guy that let Moira throw an eggplant at his dick, and if that wasn't caring I didn't know what was.

"I can walk," I said to Julian. He looked between the two of us, his gaze oscillating back and forth before he put me down, sliding me across his body in a seductive manner. Part of me thought he might be trying to get a rise out of Rysten, but with a quick peck to my lips and a warning look over his shoulder, Julian went back to the mouth of the cave, leaving the two of us alone.

"Thank you," Rysten said in a hoarse whisper.

"For what?" I folded my arms over my chest, drawing on that core of strength that fueled both me and the beast. She sat back, looking on with approval at how I chose to handle him.

"Not berating me in the middle of a crowd. Not tossing my ass aside when I deserved it. Not..." He swallowed and the well of hurt coming from him pulsed like a throbbing injury. "...Not dismissing me right now."

I nodded, a little bit of the tension slipping from my shoulders. Angry as I was, I wouldn't kick him when he was already down.

"Let's go find these pools Julian was telling me about," I said, motioning for him to lead the way. He stepped ahead of me and around the love nest that had bile coming up the back of my throat. I screwed my eyes ahead and tried not to think about who Satan did or did not fuck on the pillows I was supposed to sleep on. Most kids thought the idea of their parents having sex was gross, but both parents being deceased put a true somber spin on it.

We kept walking, the silence between us somehow both easier and harder to accept. The farther we went from those pillows, the easier my breathing grew, but the bleakness leaking from Rysten was stifling when I had fewer emotions surrounding me to counteract it.

One thing I never told anyone was how much other's emotions always bled into me, making me love them or hate them before a word left their mouth. In Moira's case it was easy— she was easy—both her and Bandit in terms of being around them. They both were what I liked to call emotionally safe. I knew what to expect from them and it rarely overran my own sense of self. But with the Horsemen, I was only really coming to realize how deep each of their own emotional pools reached. I'd always considered Rysten the easy one because we could sit and watch Netflix while drinking tea on my old faded couch. He indulged me in dates and food while letting me have the emotional distance I physically couldn't keep with the others.

Rysten was supposed to be easy, and maybe that was on me for not seeing past the shields and the masks and the many layers of him. Maybe he held off this part of himself because I wasn't ready for it, or maybe he simply needed time before showing me.

Because in that moment, Rysten wasn't easy. He was anything but. And being so close— yet, so far away —was killing me. But I respected myself too much to give even an inch until we spoke.

"I'm sorry I let her kiss me," he said, and it was hardly a breath.

"Then why did you?" I replied, both aware of what Allistair told me about Iona and their past and wanting to let Rysten explain it for himself.

"I was in shock. And I know that sounds like a terrible excuse, but I hadn't seen Iona in over three thousand years because I thought she was dead. Then she was standing before me, looking like not a day's gone by. I—" He broke off, his hand curling into a fist that he put to his mouth. "I didn't know what to do or say or how I was supposed to respond—and because of that, I disrespected you by letting her kiss me like we were something that we weren't."

I let out a heavy sigh, searching for the words that would help us both.

"Before I comment about that kiss, I need you to

know something." I paused, wanting to look at the ceiling, the walls, the floor—really anything except him. But in the same way he owed me an explanation, I owed him my attention. "Whatever you did before me, that's okay. You are thousands of years old, and I'm only twenty-three. I have a past at twenty-three and while the beast is a jealous entity by nature, it would be naïve and unfair for me to expect that nothing ever happened with anyone." He blinked in surprise, the glazed sheen I saw there slowly leaving. "I don't care what kind of relationship you and Iona had. You're with me now, and what you do now is what matters to me. Not who or what you were then. Alright?"

His lips parted, and he stared at me, the flicker of hope in him growing.

"I never loved her," he blurted out. The beast preened at that. Inside me a warm fuzzy feeling spread before cooling rapidly. There was the L-word again. It seemed to be popping up all over the place now that we were in Hell, and I wasn't sure I was ready to face the confession I suspected was coming next. "Not like I lo—" I lifted a single finger to his lips, keeping those words safe between them.

"It's okay. I'm not just saying that." I paused at the flash of hurt that went through him. No one told me how much more difficult my simpler gifts would be with four partners. The Horsemen experienced emotions on a spectrum that human boys I'd been with didn't seem capable of. I found it incredibly attractive, but it also scared me.

I had everything to lose in this moment, including those words—which is why I couldn't have them. Not yet.

"You stopped me," he murmured against my finger.

I nodded. "For now." Licking my lips, I pressed them together and then continued. "I don't want to remember here and now, with her between us, as the moment you first told me that. I want it to be without pressure or the trials to come looming over us. I want to look back in another thousand years and have it been a moment to remember. Can you give that to me?" I asked him, a subtle purr entering my voice. Inwardly I lifted an eyebrow at the beast and she shrugged flippantly. When had she ever given a shit what I thought?

"I can," he said in slight growl.

The truth of his words resonated in me, and I didn't need Moira's gift to know that he meant it.

"Good. I'm not your owner or your keeper. We're in a partnership, and just like you trust me—I trust you—and that includes making it clear to other females who you're with." My tone wasn't demanding, but there was no room for negotiations or protest. "If you're going to be with me, then you're with me and that's it. If you wouldn't like seeing another male do it to me, don't let someone else do it with you. Understand?"

He nodded slowly, not out of hesitation, but the growing desire inside. Where the empty hole of pain and misery consumed him, that bitterness fueled an underlying need for me. A need to feel something as bright as that blossoming hope and burning fire.

He'd given me a piece of his darkness in his brand and I found it comforting. Maybe he could find peace in my fire.

Rysten lifted his hand to my face, slowly pushing my hair back so he could curl his fingers around my jaw possessively. "You're the only one I want, Ruby. You're the only one I've ever wanted and seeing you here, something just feels so...right. Like it was meant to be. I don't believe in fate or destiny, because I knew your old man. At the end of the day, he was just a man. But you"—he swallowed hard but didn't look away—"you're different, Ruby. Special. And I don't mean because of the brands you wear or the power you hold. You're like fire, and you're going to light up this entire world." A blush crept up my cheeks in the low light of the cave, but with any luck I didn't look like a blueberry. "I'll protect the brand I put on your skin with every breath I have, from now until the very end."

Beneath the warm skin of his palm the brand pulsed with a dark magic that filled me with a very different kind of burning. Desire thickened the air with a headiness that had me swaying for reasons other than exhaustion.

I pulled away abruptly and took a few steps deeper into the cave, flashing him a coy smile over my shoulder. "Are you joining me or standing there waiting for an invitation?"

A smile with just a hint of darkness crept up on his lips, making my heart clench in my chest. I turned back and continued deeper into the cave without waiting. He would follow. Just as he followed me into Pandora's box, and through New Orleans, and even straight to the throne.

A trickling sound pulled my attention to the four-foot gap between one rock and the next, a faint blue light shimmered within. I stepped through the gap and stood two feet from the edge of the first body of water. It was no bigger than a hot tub and heavy steam floated like fog above its surface. Multiple pools in various sizes surrounded the first, staggering in levels and over-flowing from one to the next. Overhead a rocky shelf acted as a waterfall that rained down a heavier stream of glowing liquid into the highest pool.

I grasped the edge of my shirt, feeling eyes on my back. With a quick yank outward, the buttons popped and the flannel fell open. I let it slip off my shoulders, falling to my feet in a pile of dirty fabric and torn threads. Fingers ghosted my back, silently asking permission. I swept my hair over one shoulder and glanced back at Rysten, lifting a single eyebrow. Daring him.

He undid my bra in a single motion and it fell to the ground as a slight groan escaped his lips. He wrapped his arms around me from behind, coarse hands trailing up and down my naked sides, squeezing the flesh at my hips as he pulled me flush against him.

I ground my ass back into his erection, feeling the thickness as he ground into me in return.

"Too many clothes," he whispered around my neck. Lips trailed down the column of my throat, triggering an adrenaline rush like a hit of ecstasy straight to my bloodstream.

"Take my jeans off me," I said softly.

His cock twitched before he pulled away, following my command without even a flicker of hesitation. Sometimes I wanted someone else to take the reins—to let go and feel the release of power— and sometimes I wanted to dominate—to give the orders and feel the power I held over them. Regardless, I was always in control. With my four mates that was possible. They were comfortable with sharing and with each of them I took on a different role that suited our relationship.

With Rysten, our lives were complicated and messy, but our sex didn't have to be. Neither of us were shy without clothes on, and in my transition, I'd learned every inch of him. I looked forward to exploring it again and again.

I turned around to make it easier for him to undress me and was greeted by the sight of Rysten on his knees. He undid the laces on both of my boots, taking the time to take off my shoes, then my socks, before gliding his hands over my pants. I loved the way he made every act something both sensual and caring.

I reached for his hair, running both my hands through his honey-blonde strands without reservation. He groaned again, resting both his own hands at my hips while I pulled hard enough on his hair to force his head back.

"How does it feel when I touch you?" I whispered. I was well aware that the touch of a fully transitioned succubus was like an aphrodisiac, and while the Horsemen had greater self-control than most...I was their equal and they weren't unaffected.

"Like Heaven," he bit out as I dug my nails into his scalp. "Like Hell," he amended, drawing a chuckle from me. I eased my grip, letting his head fall forward. He looked up at me with a devilish glint in his eyes that set my blood to a boil.

"Undo my jeans," I whispered. Biting into the plump flesh of my bottom lip as his fingers skimmed the sensitive skin around the edge of the fabric, popping the button so that it echoed in the cave. Our breathing was hard and heavy, and he hadn't even really touched me yet.

"Lower the zipper," I ground out as his breath fanned over my skin, driving me crazy. He took an agonizingly long time to follow my command, the tips of his fingers running over my thin panties while he did so.

"Now hook your thumbs in the sides of my jeans"—I sucked in a tight breath at the way his nails skimmed straight down my skin—"like that," I groaned.

He looked up at me with an amused smile that said far more than words. While he followed every instruction without refute, it was very much his choice—just the same as I followed Allistair and Julian in the bedroom. The soft scrape of his nails kept me grounded in the moment, here with him and only him.

"And now?" he asked, knowing damn well what his slight touches did to me.

"Take them off."

Rysten had a way of making tenderness sexy. He didn't dive in for the kill or hurriedly rip my clothes off me. He savored me. Slowly, achingly slow, he peeled my jeans and underwear down my legs. Lifting one foot at a time, he placed a gentle kiss on each of my toes, pulling the rough material off me entirely until I stood there naked while he was clothed.

I dropped my hands from his hair to either side of his face, guiding it upward as I leaned down and placed a brazen kiss on his lips, purposely cutting my tongue on his fang.

Rysten took a stuttered breath as the taste of my blood coated both our lips.

When I pulled away, his eyes dilated locking onto the smear of blue. I'd noticed his fascination with my blood over the months, though he never said a word. Now was as great a time as ever to see if my shade had a secret fetish he'd kept from me. Given his reaction and the rumors about blood and sex, I was more than a little curious to see how far I could push before he tried to bite me.

Rysten watched as I walked around the side of the water and slipped one of my feet in, letting out a content sigh. I sat down on the edge of the pool, letting the rocky surface bite into the flesh of my ass as I placed both legs in.

"Do you like this?" I asked him, our eyes locking from across the water. "Or this?" I asked with a husky tenor as I opened my legs wide for him to see just how wet I was. Rysten swallowed, rocking forward as his eyes traveled the length of my body. I dipped my hand in the water and left a trickle of liquid as I ran it up my thigh, two of my fingers dipping down to rub myself. His eyes flashed, the veins darkening to black like they did when strong emotions were at play. "That's what you like, isn't it?" I willed the words from his mouth.

"Yes," he answered and no more. I pinched my clit between two fingers and pulled, drawing a low moan from him.

"Undress for me," I commanded. My fingers stayed, stroking the wetness between my legs while he whipped his shirt off and undid his own shoes. I was writhing against my hand by the time he pulled his jeans and boxers off, standing naked and glorious before me.

He didn't take a single step towards me. He was waiting for me to tell him to.

I smiled knowingly and pointed towards him with

the same hand I had just been using to pleasure myself. Crooking two fingers, I breathed, "Come." He slipped into the water before me with far more grace than I possessed. His feet touched the bottom, the water resting just above his waist, completely transparent.

Only when he stood before me, between my legs but still no contact, did I find the physical distance unbearable. "Touch me."

It was all he needed to hear.

Rysten reached forward, cupping my face in both his hands and then he kissed me. Licking and sucking and biting my lips, he slipped his tongue in my mouth and tasted me. I moaned into him, my hips jumping forward, closer to the edge of the pool so the I could wrap my legs around his waist.

"How'd you know?" he said against my lips.

"Know what?" I asked, the question punctuated with a moan as his fangs scraped over my bottom lip.

"Blood. How did you know I'd be into the blood?" He left my mouth, trailing his lips over my jaws and down my neck leaving tiny nibbling bites, although nothing like the bites I felt like he wanted to give.

"First time," I breathed as his hands wrapped around my hips, lifting me clean off the edge to place me as close as I could possibly get to him, the tip of his cock brushing over the wet opening between my thighs. Close, but not close enough.

"Explain," he demanded, biting a little harder at

my collarbone. I gasped and he pulled back, his eyes wide. "I didn't mean to—"

"Shhh," I whispered, putting a finger to his lips. "The first time we kissed you cut my lip and licked the blood away. It didn't take a genius to figure out you might have a thing for it." I gave him a smile and tilted my head.

"I don't like hurting you, though." A very pained look came over him and I wrapped my arms around his neck, trying to pull him closer again. He didn't budge.

"You're not hurting me," I sighed. "And even if you were, I wouldn't mind it. I like pain, Rysten. I *like* biting and scratching—but I *love* having it done to me."

His frown fell away, but he was still hesitant when he leaned back in. I ran my fingers through his hair, letting my nails bite into the skin at the base of his neck.

"I'm not my brother," he growled.

"I don't want your brother right now. I want you," I growled back. "I want you to show me how good this can feel without the transition coloring what's between us," I whispered, slightly less aggressive.

He placed his lips to my throat in a gentle kiss. "You promise to tell me if it hurts?"

Out of all my lovers, Rysten had the most will power when it came to me, but like he said himself, at the end of the day he was just a man—powerful though he may be. A man I could bring to his knees and savor all the same.

"I promise," I whispered back, loving the pressure of his wet fingers gripping my ass as he moved us through the water. My back hit an uneven edge and one of his hands came around to rub up and down my slit. I arched my back off the rocky edge, throwing my head back in abandon as two fingers entered me and started moving in and out. His thumb pressed against my clit making me squirm, and his other hand roughly gripped my backside.

"I've wanted to do this ever since that night I accidentally tasted you," he whispered against me. A hazy blanket of lust came over me as his teeth tested that tender bit of flesh at the crook of my throat. I pressed closer and his teeth came down hard, breaking the skin as he bit me. The pain, if I could even call it that, was fleeting as my orgasm ripped through me. His fingers twisted inside my seeping flesh and curled to hit my G-spot, while his lips—warm on my neck—drank all that I gave.

Just as I drank all that he gave. Kama gathered on his pores and stirred in the air around us like fallen snow. I breathed it in, reveling in the power this gave me. He gave me.

"I want to be inside you," he groaned. Not quite a question, but still seeking permission.

"Sit on the edge of the pool. I want to ride you."

He wasted no time, lifting me onto the rock and then pulling himself out. Water dripped from his body and onto the warm floor as he took a seat on the ledge, reaching for me as I reached for him. With my legs straddled on either side his hips, I reached between us and guided myself down onto him. My mouth fell open as pure pleasure invaded my senses.

"Oh, fuck yes," I moaned, lifting up and then dipping down. His hands gripped my thighs, slick and soaking from the pool as we both climbed higher and higher.

He leaned forward, pressing his mouth to my nipple and sucking while I chased my release. He rolled the puckered flesh between his teeth, and I knew he was going to bite me a moment before he did. I arched my back, pushing my breast more fully into his mouth. His fangs latched into me—sending me right over the edge.

My mouth fell open in a silent scream as my second orgasm ripped through me, harder and far more brutal than the first. My thighs quaked as I rocked against him, my inner walls clinging to every inch of hardness as his body fed mine. Kama rained down in a torrent as his own release followed on the heels of mine. Thrusting upwards he pumped into me, gripping my hips so that I couldn't move. My knees burned and water pricked the corners of my eyes from the intensity as the last of my shudders died out and we went limp in each other's arms.

CHAPTER ELEVEN

"Everybody decent back here?" Moira hollered from behind the chunk of rock that kept the pools hidden from anyone walking by.

"Ummmm," I drawled, looking over at our piles of discarded clothing. The last thing I wanted was to put on all those dirty, sweaty layers. We didn't have soap, but I felt as close to clean as I was going to get until we reached Inferna. "Is there any chance you have some clean clothes with you?"

Moira let out a harrumph and I could imagine how she was rolling her eyes. "As it so happens, I do." She tossed a stack of clothing through the gap that landed in a heap about six inches from us. "Because you are so unbelievably predictable. I hope you at least made him crawl before you got the D—"

"Okay, thanks, we'll be out in a few," I replied, falsely chipper.

"I've been told to tell you that you have five minutes before Julian comes back here. So, when I say get dressed, I mean—"

"We're coming, greenie," Rysten called back lazily.

A stream of expletives was the only reply she gave as she walked away.

I shook my head at him, lips pursed as I climbed out of the water and reached for the only towel she brought. "Dibs?" I asked, sheepishly holding up the corner of it.

He grinned. "Go ahead. I can use it when you're done."

"Well, in that case, don't mind if I do." I quickly dried off and wrung my hair out three times before handing the towel over.

I dressed in the undergarments Moira brought me, groaning at the insanely tiny jean shorts. Her version of revenge for leaving her so I could have it out with Rysten. I shook my head but donned the booty shorts. We were low on clothes down here, so unless Allistair wanted to magically conjure me a pair of jeans, beggars couldn't be choosers.

Rysten leaned against the cave wall, arms crossed over his chest and a pensive expression on his face as he watched me.

"What?" I asked as I tugged down my favorite Portland State shirt with the green Viking on it. His eyes flicked down my body but then seemed to think better of it.

145

"Nothing," he replied with a wink. I eyed him skeptically but took his hand as we walked back to the front of the cave.

"Finally!" Moira exclaimed, throwing her hands up in the air. "I was beginning to worry you guys were back to doing the horizontal tango again and I'd have to come get you." She threw an arm over her face dramatically, acting completely oblivious to the shade of robin's egg blue my face was probably turning.

"Moira," I hissed. "Are you really giving me shit after that time I caught you spread-eagle on the dining room table while your girlfriend—" I broke off mid-sentence as a blonde-haired, blue-eyed fiend stepped out from behind the Horsemen. The beast hissed and I plastered a brittle smile on my face. "Iona."

It was the only greeting she was getting from me, if not for the kissing thing, then for the sudden cuts running through my chest from emotions that weren't mine. I squeezed Rysten's hand trying to comfort him as best I could. The darkness dissipated to a low fog that I could mostly ignore as he squeezed my hand back.

"Ruby," she replied. Her own expression was arranged in a pleasant smile, though not genuine, and her eyes were hard as cut sapphires. She'd cut me open and bleed me dry with them if she could. I didn't need to be an empath to know that.

"Is there something I can do for you?" I asked, not

trying to be rude, but not exactly kissing ass either. The tension was palpable.

"Actually, there is." Her eyes flashed for a second, flicking to Rysten then back. "There is a feast being held tonight in your honor. I came to ask if you would all attend. It would mean a great deal to the people down here, particularly those of us who are looking forward to returning home once you complete your task." Her words were saying everything right, but her eyes, the set of her lips, the eerie darkness in her heart, and the white brand snaking up the bare flesh of her neck—all said otherwise.

"We're busy," Rysten said in a cold voice beside me.

"We'd love to," I replied at the same time, internally cringing. I didn't want to. I'd actually prefer sleeping on my father's musty sex pillows over putting Rysten in the line of fire and spending any kind of time around her. I deferred from extinguishing the flames for this, though. I changed our entire course of action and put everyone at risk knowing this she-bitch was working for someone that wanted us dead. I needed to find out what she knew for this sacrifice to be worth it.

"Which is it?" Iona asked, looking between the two of us.

"We'll attend," I said firmly, giving Rysten's hand a squeeze.

"Excellent. I've taken the liberty of having an extra boat brought so that all of you and your familiars can attend. We wouldn't want you to roast down here before you could do what you need to." I nodded slowly while lifting an eyebrow in Moira's direction.

Was it just me or was she talking kind of strange? Moira nodded once, scowling at Iona. I still hadn't pieced together what kind of demon she was and that alone was unsettling.

I nodded without saying a thing and she turned for the boats.

I couldn't help feeling like I wouldn't be returning here tonight. Maybe it was paranoia or maybe it was intuition, but something in the back of my mind told me we were being led like lambs to a slaughter. I looked around at our group, from Death to the enigma, and found that they'd chosen a piss poor sacrifice.

I chuckled under my breath and Iona turned at the boats to give me a look before climbing in. I chose to get in a separate one with Rysten, along with Moira and Jax, who was being oddly silent given that we deviated from the original plan. I kept that to myself as Epona followed behind me carrying a very dramatic Bandit. He flopped down on her saddle, lounging back as if this was all very trying for him. I rolled my eyes as he threw a furry arm across his face, then peeked over the edge to see if I was looking. He rolled over and began pulling on her russet colored mane. "That's not going to make her go faster, bud." I shook my head at him, and he chortled ruefully in protest as the boat was pushed off the rocky shore. Bandit switched to gripping the edge of her saddle like a boogie board and started making clicking noises, similar to how Laran did when trying to get her to speed up. Epona and I both looked at him with varying levels of *are you shitting me?*

Jax took the duty of steering us through the Garden while Rysten dropped my hand and wrapped an arm around my shoulders, pulling me close. He placed a tender kiss on my forehead and the tension in my shoulders melted.

"I hope you know what you're doing, love," he whispered.

"Trust me," I whispered back.

"Always."

A steady beat filled the cavern, a deep bass thumping to a lyrical tune. Music called to us, different from the overly machine-edited music on Earth. There was something more primal to this. Almost animalistic in a way. As it drew our attention, flickers of yellow and orange danced against shadows as we approached a cave on the other side of the river. It was so large that I wasn't sure if cave was the right word. The entrance was a hundred feet wide, and tall enough for even Rhiannon to wander inside without a problem. On the rocky beach, a smoldering bonfire roared while masked demons danced erotically and intimately with each other. Where I came from this sort of thing had been looked down upon, considered taboo even. Not in Hell, it seemed.

Our boat came to a halt so abrupt it pulled me from

my stupor, but Rysten kept a firm grip on my waist to keep me from tumbling over. Bandit, the devil-damned raccoon, threw his hands in the air and fell to the side. Moira's wing shot out, catching him just before he could hit the water and the little bugger had the actual nerve to hiss and pout at her for stopping his fun. I wasn't taking any chances after the ordeal with the Kraken, even if the water was crystal clear.

She lifted her cradled wing and deposited him into the bottom of the boat. Bandit jumped to his feet and let out a mewling cry as he palmed at my bare leg to be helped up.

"He's worse than a child," Moira groaned.

"At least he doesn't talk back," I muttered, scooping him up.

"No, instead he grows to be thirty-feet tall and picks you up like he's goddamned King Kong," Moira griped.

"She's got a point," Rysten said, eyeing Bandit distrustfully. I stepped out of his warmth to climb onto the shore, taking a deep breath before I turned to face the demons gathered.

"This isn't so bad, yet," I said. We moved closer to the writhing group of dancers. They were covered in paint and adorned with flowers, while wearing their exquisite and terrifying masks. I could admire the beauty in it, if the magic pulsing through the air hadn't been so constricting. Thick and heady; the closer I came to them, the more it invaded me.

"*Yet.* That's the key word there," Rysten murmured, staying close to me. I didn't fault him with the way I could feel eyes on us, and Iona sidled up beside me.

"They're celebrating the rise of their new queen," she said. I nodded, my eyes darting around for the catch but seeing only smiling faces.

Were they all in on this? Was it just Iona? What about the kids that ran through the groups of people throwing flowers in the air and chanting in a language I didn't understand?

I swallowed hard.

"All of this is for me?" I asked, more than a little skeptical.

"It is," she smiled, waving to the children that approached us.

They wore slipper-like shoes and bright swaths of clothing. Their faces and arms were painted, but also smudged with dirt. A little girl with green skin held up a flower lei. It was made of lilies.

"For me?" I asked. She nodded. I took the lei and slipped it over my head, a distant feeling of ease slowly setting in.

"Lady Iona said you're going to stop the fire. Are you going to stop it?" Her curly green hair framed her paint-smudged face. The imprint of flower petals plastered against her glistening, sweaty skin. Large green eyes the color of spring grass looked up at me with hope, and fear—and more than anything—desperation.

I took both of her trembling hands in mine and sank to my knees, wincing from the bite of the gravel.

"What's your name?" I asked her.

"Elissa," she said in her high-pitched voice.

"That's a beautiful name," I said, a faint upturn to my lips, though I couldn't bring myself to really smile.

"My daddy picked it, but he's gone now."

It took every fiber of my being not to turn away under the weight of the young girl's gaze. There was an accusation in her green eyes that left me with guilt, whether or not it was rightfully mine.

"I'm sorry about your dad. I'm going to do everything I can to stop the flames."

My words rang hollow and the girl backed away. I let her hands drop between us, not understanding what she muttered. It sounded foreign. Melodic. I glanced up at Rysten, but he looked away. A deep frown marred his face and his eyebrows were drawn together in concern. Whatever worries I had about this being a terrible idea, that didn't soothe them.

Slowly, I rose to my feet.

"There's a lot like her, aren't there?" I asked quietly.

Iona nodded. "Unfortunately, yes. Very few are immune to the flames, as I'm sure you know." She cast me a sideways glance that almost seemed like...pity.

"You know," I started, not entirely sure where I was going to go with this but following my gut, "I never knew that I was Lucifer's kid and had this grand destiny laid out for me. When the Horsemen found me, I didn't even think I was a full demon." I smiled at the memory, remembering the way I'd ordered them out of my house. Back then I thought I could close my eyes to it. That if I ignored it long enough, this thing called fate would pick someone else.

Iona glanced sideways like she didn't believe it. "How did you *not know* you were a full demon?" Her voice was incredulous, but I nodded anyway, pretending not to notice it.

"I'm twenty-three and I only just finished my transition four days ago." Her eyes widened almost comically, the reality that was my life seeming to set in. "Before that I just had minor powers. Persuasion. Immunity to fire. Succubus *charm*." I very pointedly left off soul-shredding because she really didn't need to know that. It was a power I was going to save in my back pocket. A just-in-case for when everything else failed.

"The flames?" she asked, her eyes slowly trailing down me like she was only just seeing me for the first time.

"Came to me after the Horsemen showed up, shortly before my transition." I snorted, thinking back at it. "I accidentally started a fire in my living room the morning after they manifested. The Horsemen wanted to whisk me away then..." and just like that, the humor dissipated.

"But they didn't."

I nodded. "But they didn't." She silently looked ahead still, listening to me but not outwardly giving me her attention. Her expression was neutral, indifferent, but as she watched these people something inside her softened. Something that couldn't be seen with eyes, only felt with emotions. "I wasn't ready," I said, admitting the very thing aloud that she would probably hate me for. Part of me felt compelled to speak; to tell her this even though I knew it would likely not win me any favors. "I had no idea how to control the flames. My life was falling apart around me and I hadn't even transitioned yet. At the time I was very...mortal. It was a weakness that I knew would cost me my life if I set foot in Hell before I was ready for it."

"So, you put your life before everyone else's because you weren't *ready?*"

"Iona," Rysten snapped, choosing to step forward. I placed a hand on his arm and gave him the look. The one that told him to stay out of it.

"No, she's right." He opened his mouth to dispute that and come to my aid, but I didn't want or need to be saved. Not from this. "I did put everyone in danger because I wasn't ready. I did, and I can own that." I turned to her and found the blue of her eyes so similar to the color of my flame it was piercing. "But I also had no idea what would happen to Hell. I don't know how much you know about Earth, but I was raised there with humans and without the knowledge of who or what I am. I had no idea what I was capable of. I didn't know that I should try to prepare myself for my new life so many people, like Elissa, wouldn't suffer."

"And if you had?"

"I can't say whether I would have come sooner," I answered honestly. "I think I would have tried, but if I hadn't learned to control the flames, I likely would have only made things worse."

"How do you figure that?" She raised her eyebrows and still I smiled.

"Ever since I got here, I've been working to put out the flames. I can't do anything about the borders until the Sins confirm, but I've been trying to stop it as best I can." She narrowed her eyes a fraction, but didn't dispute it. "If I hadn't learned to control them before I came, I likely wouldn't be able to put anything out and would have lost control, killing everyone instead."

"That's rather prideful of you to assume."

"It's also true."

She gazed at the people around us, but this time it wasn't like she was really seeing them, she just didn't want to see me. "You are not what I expected you would be," she said eventually. "Your youth and ignorance make you both ideal and not for the position you wish to hold. So far you have fallen from your father, but I am unable to forgive or forget the monster he was. While much of Hell mourned, there were many of us that also celebrated."

"I have no idea what kind of person my father was," I said quietly.

"I know," she answered. "That's why I'm telling you." While the echoes and shouts of excitement played, and the shadows danced with their demon counterparts, Iona, Rysten, and I stood apart from it all.

"While many regarded him as the savior of this world, he was also the destroyer. I know, because I was alive when the first true Queen of Hell ruled." I blinked. *First? There was a first?* I wanted to turn to Rysten but Iona's knowing smile kept me watching her. "Her name was Genesis, and this was known as the Garden of Eden. Few remember because most that were there died in the war between immortals. I was only a child myself when Satan bridged the gap between this world and Heaven. His arrival was the beginning of the true fall for this realm."

"What happened to Genesis?" I blurted out. "How did she die and Lucifer become King?"

"No one knows what truly happened to her. Only that she fell madly in love with your father and he didn't return her affections. Genesis died and the entire world shook from her loss. Storms raged. The seas revolted. Genesis was a being of *life*, a creator, who wanted nothing more than to have children of her own. In her death, that's exactly what happened."

My heart beat like the clapping of hooves as the blood pounded in my ears. I could tell this was it. I was on the precipice of what I needed to know.

"While she had made what you now know as demons long before your father's arrival, her death created two beings from the essence of her. Two young girls that much of the world believed held the true claim to the throne."

"Lilith and Eve," I murmured.

She nodded once. "Lilith and Eve. The Fae were born from Genesis's demise, but they were only babies when your father took power."

Suddenly things were beginning to make sense and I could understand why the people in this world might wish that I didn't exist. Lucifer wasn't from Hell either, but nothing stopped him from coming in and claiming it, meanwhile their true ruler died and left behind children that had been denied a birthright. "But now he's dead..." I said hoarsely, my voice hardly more than a whisper.

"Now he's dead," Iona agreed. "And I can't say that I'm sad, but I do pity you." She fingered the flower lei around her neck and mine suddenly felt like a vice. Not just any flowers. *Lilies...*

Deep in my bones I knew it then. It was something I couldn't explain because I only had pieces. Parts. They ran together in my memories. Every flash of a flowered white tattoo that was branded on someone meant to kill me. The imp. The blood magic. The silent *she* that lurked in the back, just waiting for the day to return to her throne.

Eve had come to Earth and died. She created a race of children to hunt demons. The stories of that were clear.

But her sister...

"Do you believe she deserves to rule?" I asked Iona. Emotions collided within me as I struggled to focus on what to think of this. What to feel. Was I truly Queen? Or was I an imposter?

Either way, the flash of surprise in Iona's face couldn't be masked.

She knew what and who I was referencing, still she said, "I don't know who you mean."

"Lilith," I spat her name, causing several around us to look in our direction. Rysten's hand appeared on my lower back and I knew he had moved closer. "Do you believe she deserves to rule?"

Her eyes were conflicted. "I..." She looked away from me, like my gaze was suddenly too much to handle. Guilt swam within in her, followed by regret. Whatever they had planned to do was already in motion, except it wasn't demon magic I needed to truly watch for. No, it wasn't demons at all—but Fae. "I don't think it matters who or what I want anymore. It's not going to change anything."

The words had barely left her lips when a banshee's scream made the ground shudder. My head split in two as Moira's pain flooded me and whatever kindness I felt for the she-demon beside me dissipated.

CHAPTER TWELVE

Blue flames rushed up my arms as I glared at Iona.

"Was this all just a distraction?" I asked, even though I already knew. How foolish I'd been thinking it was Iona I needed to watch. She'd lured me into a den of demons and I'd sang and skipped alongside her, all the while telling myself my eyes were wide open.

I was a fool, but a fool with power.

"There's that Morningstar temper that your father was known for," she murmured. I shook my head and took off through the crowd. Iona would have to deal. First, I needed to find—

"Ruby!" Rysten yelled, his fingers wrapping around my wrist and pulling me to a halt. I looked back at him and a sense of dread filled my stomach. Was he going to try to stop me? "Laran just disappeared. No one can get ahold of him."

Fuck. I was really beginning to wish that I had just lit her ass on fire and been done with it.

"Find him." We locked eyes and silently I was hoping—praying to the beast, to Lucifer, to the Sins, and the monster I knew—I prayed that someone was listening and we would all make it out of here alive.

Rysten nodded and then disappeared into the shadows.

Alone with only my fire and my wits, I ran, following that wisp of a string that tied Moira and I together as people. That bond that would forever keep her by my side.

"Moira!" I yelled, crashing through the crowd. My feet slipped on something liquid and I fell to my knees before her. The crowd jumped back as I waved my arms wide, shooing them away.

She convulsed sporadically, her head whipping side to side. Her eyes squeezed shut and teeth clenched together, I looked her over but could find nothing wrong.

Across from me, Jax kneeled with his eyes closed and hands resting flat over her.

He would be the picture of serenity if I didn't know that inside him a storm was brewing.

Like me, he was trying to figure out what was wrong. His hands clenched into fists as he pulled away.

"It makes no sense," he mumbled, more to himself than anything.

"What doesn't make sense?" I snapped, clutching

her thrashing head in my hands. I moved to place it on my lap, scared she might crack her own skull if this kept up. "What are you talking about?"

"Her!" he yelled. "She told me she wasn't feeling well, then she collapsed. I assumed it was magic, but..." His words trailed off as the brand on her forehead began to glow. I had no idea what that meant, but I bet we were about to find out. "There's no trace of magic on her. If there were, I could stop it. Whatever she's fighting..." he swallowed and looked up at me. "I have no idea what it is."

"Fuck," I growled, wanting to smash my fists in the ground and set it all alight. The beast was already gnashing her teeth, begging to be let out, but I wanted to handle this—I needed to handle this—to show myself that I could.

With no Horsemen, no Bandit, and no fucking clue what I was facing, I had to come to terms with that fact that I was severely outnumbered, outmaneuvered, and out of my depth.

"Moira," I rocked her head side to side. "I need you to wake up, babe." Desperation wasn't leaking into me anymore. It was pouring out of me profusely. "Wake up, Moira. Come on." The fire from my hands engulfed her and the thrashing stopped. I had no idea what I was doing, only that last time my fire saved her and maybe it could again.

But nothing happened.

She burned. She breathed.

161

And yet, she didn't wake.

I pulled away, letting out a frustrated growl. Jax remained silent, watching as I turned to the masked onlookers. "What did you do?" I asked them.

No one answered.

"What. Did. You. Do?" I repeated again, slower. Deadlier. Terror was eating at me. Terror over Moira's unconscious body. Terror over Laran's disappearance. I came down here to find answers and felt like I was going to find an early grave instead.

"They did nothing, Lucifer's Daughter," came a voice.

It was sweet and innocent and all things good in the world. Deception at its finest. Evil at its worst. Darkness that hides under a mask of light and beauty.

"Lilith," I whispered.

"My, my, what a clever girl."

"What did you do to her?" I asked, hating how weak I sounded. Wishing I was half as strong as the world seemed to believe.

She let out a trilling laugh, reminiscent of wind-chimes. "Much like your mother, not clever enough," she replied sweetly, ignoring my question entirely. My blood boiled.

Moira's head slid from my lap as I laid it on the ground and rose to my feet. Her footsteps were sound-less, but the swaths of fabric from her dress brushed the stone. The pounding of my blood filled my ears as she came into view. The woman of my nightmares.

Was it a strange twist of fate that I was the Devil's daughter and she looked like an angel?

Golden eyes blinked down at me and lips that were the palest shade of pink turned at the corners to form a smile. Her gown was made of the whitest gossamer I'd ever seen. So wholesome. So pure. Her hair blended into the billowy fabric as it swayed around her.

"You even look like her." She nodded with the slightest purse to her lips. Disdain, I realized. "But your eyes, those are all your *father's*," she said with a breathy sigh, moving closer to place two fingers under my chin so she could see them clearly

I shuddered against her cool fingers as her nails grew sharp.

The beast decided right then and there that she'd had enough, shoving forward long enough to light her ass on fire. Lilith's grip didn't falter as the flames licked up her fingers, over her hand, halfway up her arm, and the skin beneath remained unearthly pale and smooth.

I'd expected her to burn and this to all be over. I expected my gifts that made me powerful to not fail me. With a cold realization I came to the crux of this. I expected to always and forever be more powerful. To be invincible.

And in thinking that I forgot the very lessons that kept me alive all the years before I had any power to my name.

She cocked an eyebrow, a smirk forming on her face as I scrambled to hide the stricken expression on my own. The flames didn't burn her, which meant I wasn't just in trouble. This time, I was utterly screwed.

The white of her dress turned as black as the essence of her soul. Stripped of her ethereal beauty and cast in only glittering ashes, Lilith stood before me as the last of the fire winked out, and with it, my only hope.

Sin had stripped me of my telepathy. Lilith had taken the fire. Moira was down and Bandit was nowhere to be found. While the Horsemen weren't accounted for, something told me they wouldn't be showing up to save my ass just in time.

I was on my own and my enemy was literally the Queen of the Unseelie. She was about as ancient as it gets.

"Such fire, young one. Your father had that too." She smiled fondly for a moment, her expression nostalgic as she disappeared into a memory. Whatever she was thinking, her heart beat for it. Before I could draw any conclusions her eyes sharpened again, and that same smile turned brittle. Disparaging. "And now that fire will be mine."

"I hate to break it to you"—I paused, turning my cheek to wrench my face away from her grasp—"but that's not possible."

I'd never seen anything so beautiful or wicked like the look she gave me. I swallowed hard against the dryness in my throat. "There was a time when I thought so too, but then you were born and it changed everything."

"What?" To my credit, my voice never wavered, but inside...the beast was silent. Watching. That worried me.

"Well, Lucifer's Daughter, that story started a very long time ago. Back when I was just a girl and your father was just the King—the one who stole my title." Her teeth were pointed and her nails were claw-tipped, but in that brief flash of a second, I saw a woman with mercury eyes and not gold. That realization came too little too late. Still, I kept her talking.

"You see, your father was not a demon as many believed, but a primordial. Just like Genesis. Just like God. One of the fun little quirks of their species is that they can bind themselves to a planet, and by extension its power. But when that being dies...well, so does the planet. Unless, there's another primordial to bond to it." That sense of dread was now magnified. It settled in my stomach and clawed its way up my throat, taking hold of my heart like a parasite—one intent on never letting go.

"Hell started to implode, just as it is doing now—except last time Lucifer bonded to it. He saved the planet and the people made him King. *Not you.*" Those last words were whispered like a goodbye.

If she was suggesting what I thought she might be...the muscles of my empty stomach spasmed as I fought the urge to gag up bile.

"You are clever," she said and clapped happily, but it was all a farce. Did her followers see it too? "Yes. The original Six that Genesis made struck a deal with your dear daddy, and it was only after I got rid of my sister, Eve, that he even found me competent enough to become the Sin of Pride, reducing me to one of his whores instead of giving me my rightful place as Queen." Her hand clenched into a fist and I wondered if she saw the way her pride truly did eat at her. If I had to guess, my father was probably not a good man, but I couldn't see him being worse than this. Worse than her. "I spent centuries trying to convince him to get rid of the other Six, but your daddy—he just had too much *love*, as he would say. I waited, biding my time until he eventually knocked one of them up. In hindsight, I should have known it would be Lola. He always did want what he couldn't have."

There were so many things about this story that struck me as wrong, but I didn't interrupt because I needed every second to try and find a way out of this situation. Chances were if she was immune to the flames, she was immune to other things too, and even if I could get her down, there were still *hundreds* of demons I'd have to fight off as well. I needed to think.

*Think...think...*a slight numbing settled over my skin. A fuzziness entered my brain as I tried to puzzle my way out of this one.

"Are you feeling alright, dear?" she asked, pulling me from my stupor. My pores clogged with sweat as the heat truly pressed down on me. "I must say, I was worried it wouldn't work. But your father fell for the same trick."

I tried to open my mouth but couldn't form the words. My tongue lolled and my head felt too heavy. I squinted as the lights behind her flashed. My feet stumbled even though I was standing up... then my knees hit the cave floor and my heart began hammering into overdrive.

"Lilies grown in the soil of crushed pure black lotus on the Brimstone City will take on the same qualities, except it's far more potent. One touch to the skin or inhaling its scent is enough to kill the average demon within minutes, which is why no one *dares* grow them. As it is, this will likely only incapacitate you for half an hour at most." She paused to laugh... and laugh and laugh. There was a true madness to it and my stomach turned sour. I thought of the children who'd brought them to us. Their hands were bare.

"The children..." In my heart I knew my search would come up empty if I scanned the crowd for that small child called Elissa. My revulsion for this woman that wanted to crown herself a queen only deepened.

"Were orphans. Lower demons with no parents to care for them and no purpose of their own. I gave them a purpose. They were carriers of my crown." Even as she said it, several faces in the crowd turned away. Iona was among them, her eyes glued to the ground. She'd so shamelessly scorned me for a father I never knew, and yet...

I gagged, but no bile would come up. Lilith scrunched her nose with disgust, rolling her golden eyes as she flicked a lock of white hair away from her face.

"You're a monster," I spat as best I could.

"I am," Lilith admitted. "But aren't we all?" She motioned to the demons beyond.

I shook my head and the very ground itself seemed to move. I gritted my teeth, panting hard through the wave of nausea that flooded me. The world had slowed to a crawl.

"Not like...you," I rasped, struggling to make my lips work. Spit flew as I spluttered and shook.

"It's almost time," she said and smiled. "And here you thought I was talking because I wanted to entertain your childish notions. Pathetic girl." She squatted down and put her face eye level to mine. "Unlike Eve and I, you were born with the beast. Your father knew that, so he bound your powers and the monster in a bid to hide you from me so that I would focus on him. It worked for a time, until I realized something. Why wait to control you when I could have the beast all the same?" In my steadily worsening state I saw the monster beneath her skin. The true Lilith—and it was a terrible sight to behold. "Well, I tried and I failed— killing both him and the beast in the process—but you, Ruby, are my second chance. I learned from him where

I went wrong and brought you out of hiding at the same time." She breathed in deeply, inhaling my scent before releasing it like a sigh of relief. "Now, I will have the power of the primordial and reclaim my throne, and you, dear girl, are the one who will help me."

She pressed a chaste kiss to my lips that made me squirm. Her tongue slid over my teeth and she bit down sharply on my bottom lip, pulling back to smear my blood all over her bottom lip like it was the greatest of delicacies. I'd done something not so different with Rysten only hours ago, but the perverted way she went about it made my stomach turn again.

"Mmmm, you even taste like him too," she mused.

Crazy. I didn't know if Lilith was always nuts or — if like Eve—time had turned her, but I needed to find a way out of here right now. A gurgled cry of outrage slid from my lips as she stood to walk away.

In that moment it was do or die, and just like with Danny and the imp, I turned to my last gift.

Blinking once, I opened my eyes and sought out for her soul. It may work. It may not. I was out of options and the Horsemen clearly weren't coming.

I focused on that swirling pit of black in her chest and reached for it—

Only to be blocked.

Impossible.

At least I thought it was. It seemed the more I learned, the more I realized how little I knew. Or how deep the bonds of betrayal could go. Out of the corner of my eye a second figure strode forth, and whatever hope I had of escaping fizzled out completely.

"Siiiin," I moaned. Allistair had warned me. He said that Sin looked out for no one but Sin, and I'd foolishly believed her instead of him. I'd stupidly listened to the emotions I felt instead of the words I heard.

And now it was going to cost me *everything*.

She walked by without sparing me a glance and dropped to one knee. Her head bowed as she uttered, "Mother."

Lilith smiled and it all became so clear. "My dearest one," she purred. Her claw-tipped hands stroked Sin's hair with undeniable fondness. "I knew when you were born that you would be the one to liberate me, and now, I will liberate you. Sinumpa, Heir of the Unseelie, Daughter of Cain, Child of Mine —you are released from your blood oath of service."

Lilith sliced a cut from the corner of Sin's eye to her cheek, leaving a scarlet tear. Blood welled on the tip of her claw as she cut her palm. The wound on Sin's cheek glowed red and then hardened. A scar.

"You are free, Sinumpa, by the rules of our oath. However, this day saddens me so, and you will wear that upon your face henceforth, daughter." My lips trembled out of control from trying to speak but having no control over my body.

"Thank you, mother," Sin murmured. She leaned forward to kiss Lilith's feet and nausea rolled. This is her master. The woman behind the mask. The evil that hid in plain sight. The harbinger of my own destruction.

The beast growled, thrashing about in my mind. Any control that I held was long gone, but whatever affected my body held us both prisoners, here in my mind. My consciousness was waning, even as the crowd of demons began parting to reveal...*them*. My Horsemen.

They were here, but there would be no saving me.

They couldn't even save themselves.

RYSTEN

All our lives we'd been told that our purpose was to serve the next Queen of Hell. To serve. To kneel. To fight for. To defend. To lay down our lives, and before we'd even met her, we were prepared for this day. For the day that we might not survive.

We were prepared to do anything that ensured her survival, even at the cost of our own lives.

But no one prepared us for the soul crushing desperation that would sit on our backs if failure became imminent. No one told us that the sole reason for our existence could be snuffed out with the snap of one's fingers.

No one realized that we would come to love this woman so much it hurt. So deep that it burned.

They didn't tell us those things. Protect. Serve. Defend. That was our duty, and we were happy to do it at the expense of all...until now.

I wished we'd never come back to Hell.

I wished we had let it burn and kept her far away.

I wished we had more time.

I wished for a lot of things that would never come to pass, and I knew that now. I had been smart enough to cherish those moments with her like they would never happen again. Because a small part of me had known that the duty tasked upon us would be our downfall.

And now we knelt on the cold stone floor with poison-laced flowers around our necks, meant to kill even the strongest of demons. Even a primordial.

If Ruby was down, the truth of it was that we never had a chance.

"My boys," Lilith cooed. We weren't her anything and the vile old woman knew it. While she may have helped make us, she was no mother of ours.

Her claws patted my cheek gently, curling around my chin. She wrenched my face upward, but I kept my eyes on Ruby. On the light. No matter what happened now she needed to survive.

"You'll look at me when I speak to you, Pestilence." The prick of her nails was nothing compared to the overwhelming panic of what was to come.

We were the ones that found Lucifer's body last time she'd tried this. Or what was left of it.

I spat and a glob of iridescent blue smacked against her skin. I didn't need to look to know her features contorted with rage; the slap of her hand that sent me reeling was enough.

"The truth is, Lilith, that you're not a queen and stealing the power of the primordial won't make you one." Her foot swung out and Ruby's scream pierced the air as my head slammed into the stone floors again and again. Bone crunched, but I still only felt an inkling of what she was doing thanks to her damned poisons.

"Stop! Get your hands off him!" Ruby screamed, but the words were only barely intelligible.

Lilith stilled, pulling away from me.

"What did you say to me?" she replied in a singsong voice that rang true to madness. She was taking it as a challenge and Ruby didn't know better than to challenge the Unseelie Queen.

"Get your devil-damned hands off my Horseman," Ruby growled. Her hands curled into fists and her nails scraped at the rock beneath her, turning bloody and blue as she let out the most unholy of shrieks. It would have given Moira a run for her money.

"Well, well. You're just full of surprises, aren't you, Little Morningstar?" Lilith grinned. That only incited Ruby further. Her back bowed off the concrete as flames completely consumed her, growing brighter and brighter. I wouldn't look away, even as she grew too bright to truly see.

Her form blurred as the flames wound around her like a living, breathing entity. She didn't scream this time.

She bended and bowed and contorted, but through it all she fought, and the flames raged. She forced her arms to lift her and her knees to hold. She rose with a vengeance and she walked with a purpose. "Did you really think that I would lie down and watch you do this?" she growled.

And then...she exploded.

Fire unlike anything I'd ever seen poured from her, burning out and into the cavern. It raced over the stone shores and the glowing water, snaking up the spires of every tower, crawling over every crook of the cavern walls until it was all that existed—and still she burned.

She burned more than Lucifer ever had, even in his deepest rages.

And she burned for me.

It continued for a suspended frame of time where I wasn't sure if seconds or minutes or even hours had passed. Black and blue and every color in between consumed my vision in the most glorious of blazes, but despite her raw power... despite that immense strength that was buried within her...

Despite it all, she couldn't go on forever—and Lilith still stood.

"You are strong, child," she called out, licking her lips. "I'll give you that." The fire grew thin, showing just how much Ruby had laid waste to. Lilith took an appreciative glance as stalactites fell from the ceiling into the clear waters below. The towers were blackened and crumbling. Every piece of cloth, fabric, or otherwise burned to a crisp and yet...the people were unharmed.

There was only one thing that makes a demon immune to the flames.

"Brimstone," Laran murmured beside me. He must have come to the same conclusion.

"Why won't you die?" Ruby growled in a voice that was half her and half the beast. Her eyes had gone dark, but not truly black. She was fighting for control in a battle she would not win.

"I've spent *centuries* planning, child. Did you really think I wouldn't take into account your primordial power?" Lilith laughed a slight cackle. "No, girl, I thought of everything. Including the possibility that you might be blessed with your mother's gifts."

Lilith snapped her fingers and a silver dagger appeared in her palm. Ruby's legs shook as she took another step forward. Her outpouring of power had left her weak as Lilith circled the four of us.

"What are you doing?" the beast snapped. Ruby's body jerked back and forth as they vied for power. Lilith watched with a slight smile on her lips as she came to a stop before Laran.

She reached down and grabbed a fistful of hair, wrapping it tight around her palm as she wrenched him upwards and moved to stand behind him, the silver edge of her dagger at his throat. We both knew that dagger was imbued with blood magic. "Don't let her break you. You must survive, baby girl. *For me,*" Laran called out to her.

"Teaching a lesson," Lilith said chipperly. "I only need two of them."

Ruby's eyes ran black and the beast took two trembling steps. She knew what was coming. We all did.

And it was too late.

A flick of her wrist was all it took. Laran let out a strangled noise and Ruby's legs collapsed entirely as his blood flowed straight from the vein onto the glittering ashes at her feet.

"Laran," she choked. "Laran, please don't go—" Shudders racked her shoulders as she caved in on herself. "Please don't." She pleaded with the dying demon as she crawled to him. "Laran, please...please!" she begged as tears rolled down her cheeks. She repeated his name over and over again until the gurgling stopped and the light faded from his eyes. "LARAN!" she roared in a voice that could have woken the dead.

Lilith walked to Allistair, dagger in hand, and any fight Ruby had in her was gone by the time Lilith said, "Now, then. You're not going to struggle, are you?"

She shook her head as the pieces inside her well and truly came apart. I saw it in her eyes that she knew she would die, and Lilith knew that. She knew that Ruby would give anything for us.

Including the very heart that beat in her chest.

"Take them to the water's edge, but don't let them

touch it," Lilith ordered. Demons burst into action to follow her every command, and trembling fingers grasped me by the sides. I recognized them, even after three thousand years.

"I'm so sorry," Iona whispered. I didn't have the strength left to spit at her. I didn't have the will power to tell her I'd rather die than touch her. There was only one thing I wanted more in this world than to see Iona burn in that moment.

"S-save h-h-her," I whispered through my broken jaw, through the seeping blood and foggy haze. Lilith's flowers were impeding the healing.

"I can't," she murmured back. "This was the price I paid for life."

"Saaaaa—" The rest of the words never came out. I managed to keep my eyes open as Lilith approached Ruby.

My girl. Her eyes were glazed over when Lilith lifted her up like a child. She didn't struggle. She didn't speak. The spark in her eyes...it was gone.

"Ruby," Allistair wheezed beside me. "Keep... fighting... little... succubus," he groaned. She didn't respond. I felt my body being moved, partially lifted and partially dragged. After the beating to the face Lilith had given me, I should feel every shift, but it seemed that her poisonous flowers had numbed the pain, at least physically.

Iona settled me on the rocky edge of the shore, giving me a front row view of Ruby being lowered into the water. She was naked and her brands glowed faintly, the blue vines limp.

"Gather, my loyal followers, for tonight is the beginning. With this sacrifice we will create a new world. One built on the bones of our enemies." Lilith's words rang in the cavern as all stared on in silence.

"Ruby," Julian growled. "You fight her, Ruby! You don't stop—you understand me—" His words were pointless. She wouldn't lift a finger again. Not if it meant the death of one of us.

Lilith began chanting. Softly at first as she lifted the dagger over her head.

There wasn't a flash of fear in Ruby's eyes when Lilith struck her. Straight in the sternum.

A sickening snap filled the air.

Then again.

Then again.

Then again.

Lilith stabbed her until the water turned bloody and both their skin turned blue.

She stabbed her until Ruby no longer jerked with each strike of the knife.

She stabbed her until the outline of the pentagram on her chest had been cut away, and Ruby...she was only holding on by a thread. There was screaming. So much screaming. Not of Ruby herself, but the three of us bound and unable to stop this. The outcry of a pain so deep that the mind could not grasp it.

My life had been so long. So very long. Never had

it felt so long as it did now. I didn't want to exist in a world where she didn't. She was my light. My soul. My whole fucking universe.

And she couldn't die.

Something snapped inside of me as Lilith began carving away at her own chest, never missing a beat in her chant. Dark magic filled the air. So vile and wicked that it threatened to put her light out, but I gave it all to her.

My magic. My strength. My will to live. I was the strongest shade ever created and I used that power to hold her together. To hold her body together. To try to heal whatever damage I could.

Even as shadows encroached on us, I gave. As a dark void rose from Ruby, I gave.

As the waters ran black, I gave.

It was only when Lilith stood before me that I knew the truth. That hopelessness finally consumed me.

She painted my chest in my mate's blood...and there was no more to give.

I had given right until the final shudder of Ruby's heart...when the world went dark. Truly dark.

And in the blackness, a voice spoke to me. A darkness I knew.

A beast of ancient power filled with so much rage that it could not be soothed after the wrong done to it. It had been stripped of the other half of its soul.

We both had.

CHAPTER THIRTEEN

EXISTENCE WAS SUCH AN ODD THING.

One moment you are there and then you are not. Most believe that the worlds of Heaven and Hell are where you went after— the next plane of existence— but the truth is that no one really knows. Not even Death, who both lived and died on that precarious line in-between.

The veil was a place of existence, less like Hell and more like a state of mind. One that you never wake up from. And I didn't want to wake up. Not now. Not ever.

She took him from me, but what she didn't know was that I followed him well before the last breath left my body. I used that tiny sliver of magic that Death bequeathed upon me to go to the veil and hold onto him. Here we existed together. But on the other side, past the veil...I didn't know. I didn't want to know.

"You can't keep me, baby," he murmured in my ear. "You have to go on. You have to survive."

"I'm not letting you go," I said, clinging to him tighter.

"She killed me, Ruby. You can't change that," he said gently, pressing the pads of his fingers into my jaw as he cupped my face. "It's okay. We were all prepared for this." I swallowed hard and dug my nails into the hair at the base of his neck.

"I. Am. Not. Leaving. You," I whispered in a harsh voice. "It's not happening. I refuse. Do you understand me?" My bottom lip quivered as the tears threatened to fall. His eyes softened as he leaned forward and placed a kiss against my forehead. I leaned in, fighting the emotion swelling in my throat when I realized that I couldn't smell his scent; that tinge of firewood and smoke. That I never would again.

"If you stay with me, you're leaving them behind. You know that, right?" he asked me.

"They have each other. I won't leave you here alone."

"You're leaving Moira and Bandit behind. They won't survive without you." His tone was soft, sweet even. I hated it.

"Stop it," I snapped. "Stop trying to get me to leave you. You can't! I won't!" I pulled harder on his hair and it only drew a chuckle from his lips.

"I'm not making you do anything, babe. I couldn't even if I tried," he whispered against my hair. It put me at ease, but only for a moment. "I'm just telling you what you already know, and you don't want to hear it because the truth is you might be able to survive this if you leave me, but every minute you spend here is another one your body dies more." My hands shook as I held him close, afraid that if I gave any slack, for even a second, he might slip away into the great abyss beyond.

"I don't want to do this without you," I blurted out, taking an unsteady breath. "I don't want to fight Lilith. I don't want to fight for Hell. I don't want to do any of it if it means doing it without you. I don't want to be alone." Tears were falling now. Big. Fat. Ugly tears. They ran down my face and onto his chest.

"You'll never be alone, baby. You know that." But he was so wrong. I didn't know that. I didn't know what came next or when. I never knew when the next time may come that someone I loved died.

Love. Not loved. He was still here. Still with me.

"I'm not going anywhere, Laran. Not without you."

"Actually," another voice interjected. My blood ran cold. "You are."

"Sin," I spat. Laran froze as I spun around using both my hands to grip his arm behind me. "You fucked me over, Sin. This is your fault," I hissed. She narrowed her mercury eyes and cocked her head.

"I warned you. Do not blame me because you made a choice and did not like the outcome." There was a hint of caution in her tone, but I didn't care anymore. She thought this was a game and she was the one moving the pieces, but it wasn't a game for me. It was my life, and it was over, and there were no do-overs for any of us.

"You betrayed me, Sin. I don't care how you twist this. You led me here, feeding me just enough to make me think you were on my side. Laran is dead because of you!" I screamed, finally finding the fury inside. "We both are!"

Sin took a deep breath and released it in a heavy sigh. "I'm sorry for what this war has already cost you, Ruby. I truly am. I told you from the beginning to trust no one. Not even me." Her eyes...they were so old and filled with so much pain. Under different circumstances I might have pitied her. I might have understood.

But I was dead. She said it herself.

"You won't be dead for long, Little Morningstar," she said so softly I almost missed it.

"Don't call me that," I growled, and it was one hundred percent me. No inkling of the beast resided inside my soul anymore. Sin nodded.

"Say your goodbye's, Ruby. We have much to do if we're going to save Hell."

"What? No—"

"I call on the blood oath for the favor owed. You will live, Ruby, and we will fight another day."

The skin on my breast stung as the sliver of blood magic activated on her command. A pressure filled me, pushing and pulling. It disoriented my mind and pressed down on my body. If I had bones here, they might have shattered upon the weight of the blood oath as it forced me to obey its call.

"Laran," I gasped, turning into him. I wrapped my arms around his shoulders and refused to let go.

"Shhh," he whispered. "It'll be okay, baby. Go to the Sins. They'll know what to do." Then the thrashing began. I felt my body again. Every muscle spasmed, attempting to split as if the very atoms that were me could not be contained. Still, I clung to him as the magic began to pull me back.

It could take me, but I wasn't letting go. I would keep him. I didn't come this far just to lose him forever.

I couldn't do it. I wouldn't do it.

I was stronger than this. I was stronger than it all.

And somehow, I would save him too.

"I love you," he whispered. It sounded like a goodbye.

"You're not doing that, Laran. You're not leaving me. I'm right—"

A sudden dull ache filled me, like I had been dropped a hundred stories and then dragged through the street. My back was against something solid and sticky. I clenched my fingers but only found the scratch of my nails against stone.

No. No. No. Where was he? I never let go. Where was Laran?

My eyes flew open as I bent up at the waist and an onset of nausea and dizziness filled me.

"Whoa there—"

"Take it easy, Rubes—"

"Where is he?" I whispered. Broken. Splintered. I turned on Moira and her eyes shuttered. "Where is he, Moira?" I growled, louder this time. Stronger. The muscles in my chest were knitting themselves back together the more I spoke. The bones and cartilage were bending and reshaping and reconnecting the longer I was here. But it was him, the loss of him that filled me so deeply, so acutely, that every single ache and pain and slice and break was *nothing*.

"I'm sorry," she said. Her pentagram eyes swirled with emotion when she opened them to look at me. "I'm so sorry, Ruby. Laran...he's...gone."

Gone.

Gone.

Gone.

It rang in my ears like the last nail in a coffin and I screamed. My head whipped back and forth as I searched for his body on the charred shores of the Garden. Lilith was gone, and so were my other Horsemen.

But Laran, he was dead.

I crawled on all fours, wading through the congealing blood. His beautiful tanned skin was no more. His body pale and void of warmth, his eyes stared, wide open and unflinching even in the face of death. A raw sound erupted from my throat as I started pounding on his chest. "I told you not to leave me," I screamed. "I told you not to go!"

"Ruby—"

"Let her be," Jax whispered to her. "She just lost her mate, the others were taken, and Lilith has the beast. Give her a moment to grieve."

What they were saying didn't register. They sounded far away and cloudy. A vague feeling swimming through the haze that was consuming me as I beat his chest and screamed and cried. "Please don't be dead...I'm sorry...please don't. Please don't. I'm so sorry..."

My tears ran down my face and onto his body, mixing with his blood. I begged and pleaded with him, and when that didn't work, I begged and pleaded for someone else. Anyone else. Save him. It was all I wanted.

"If there is anyone out there in this world or the next that can hear me"—I gasped for breath as the hyperventilating began and I choked on my words —"save him," I sobbed. "It's all I ask. Bring him...back to...me." Tears and snot ran down my face as my throat clogged from too much emotion. I don't know what prompted me to say the words, but in that moment, I would pray to God herself if she would save him.

"You summoned me?" a woman said. Her voice sounded strange here. Too light for the gravity of loss I was experiencing. I wheeled around, covering as much of him as I could with my own body.

The person I saw...

"You're—"

"Morvaen. You freed me, Daughter of Hell."

Holy shit. Had I actually called a Seelie *into* Hell? I tried to see through the tears, but my puffy eyelids blurred my vision. The cavern went silent, as if they just realized the being in our midst was not one that had walked in this world for a very long time.

"Why are you here?" my voice cracked and the features of her face softened.

"You summoned me, my lady. The rune upon your arm was activated. What is it you ask?"

My breath hitched in my throat. Was there really a chance...was this the universe's way of telling me it wasn't over? That this wasn't the end...

"Save him," I choked out. "I don't care what you have to do. Just save him."

A murmur rippled through the room as Morvaen got to her knees beside me. Compassion was there in her silver eyes as she reached for the man I protected even in death. I scrambled to the side, watching her every movement as she began to draw.

Symbols. So many symbols she placed on his chest. His face. His arms.

Magic filled the air, but this time it was not dark or violent.

Like a warm breeze at the end of winter, I felt the first ray of hope.

Morvaen reached for me and I didn't hesitate to

stop her as she started placing the same symbols on my skin. She drew orange runes over every inch of my back, a heaviness building in the space around me. The gravity of it weighing me down.

The very instant her hands lifted from my skin I felt the pressure that had shaped around me snap. The air stood still. My throat constricted each time I tried to take a breath, and as the edges of my vision started to go dark, I heard it.

The beating of a heart.

PART II

CHAPTER FOURTEEN

LARAN LET OUT A CHOKING RASP AND THE VICE around my throat released. An influx of oxygen flooded me and I collapsed forward onto him. The coppery tang of blood laced with his scent of firewood and smoke filled me with...peace. I had feared it would never return. That he would never return. That this soul-crushing loss would be so deep that I might never overcome it because a piece of me had gone to the veil and beyond.

But that piece came back when his arms tightened around me.

"I told you I wasn't letting you go," I breathed.

"I never doubted you," he whispered.

All wasn't right in the world. Three of my mates were missing. Lilith was gone, and she took the beast with her.

I came here for my crown and lost my life.

Now…I was coming for it all, and this time…

I looked to my best friend and the enigma that watched over her carefully—to my raccoon and the way he sat at Laran's feet—to the four horses that now watched over us—to the crowd of demons staying as far away as they possibly could—and finally, to the dark-skinned Fae sitting across from me

"Thank you," I told her.

"I owed you a debt, Ruby Morningstar. Now it is paid." Her eyes searched as she took in our surroundings. "But I must ask, where are we?" The brush with death one too many times had left me exhausted to the bone and a weary grimace was all I managed.

"You can't tell?" She eyed me warily and I took that as a no. "We're in Hell."

Her mouth fell open and she said, "You summoned me…to *Hell*?"

"It appears so."

She went quiet, then, "How?"

I groaned, pressing my cheek against the steadily heating skin of Laran's chest. "I'm not entirely sure." Rough hands clung to my side, his fingernails biting into the skin as he held me, almost as if he feared letting me go.

"I see," she said eventually. Her dark lips curved downward before she turned and started to assess the demons cowering in the corner. "Should we be worrying about them?" she asked.

"Probably," I grit my teeth against the soreness in my muscles as I tried to pull myself up. Laran was there helping me even as his own limbs shook with exertion. The clacking of hooves and a wet nose pressed against my face had me pausing to look over at the ridiculously large mare. Her soulful eyes looked deep into mine as she pressed her muzzle against me and then brushed up against Laran.

"Hey girl," he murmured to Epona. His gentle hands brushed over her side as he muttered sweet things under his breath. It filled me with a sort of bittersweetness. I was so grateful that he was here and alive to soothe his familiar, but as I looked over at the other three horses...my heart broke all over again.

Tears threatened to fall from my eyes, but I couldn't wallow in my grief. I took a deep breath and scooped up Bandit, letting his claws prick my bare skin as he climbed up to my shoulder. The light flashes of pain grounded me, reminding me of Julian and what I stood to lose should I fail. Emotion swelled in my throat, making me swallow hard.

A shuffling of feet drew my attention to the crowd as it parted and a hollow-eyed Iona stepped forward. In an instant something shifted inside of me. I growled, waiting for the beast's snide remarks about skinning her alive while fire danced just beneath the skin of my fingers. But there was no beast and there was no fire. Only glittering ashes and memories.

That pissed me off even more. I strode forward as a

snarl ripped from my lips and Iona, she had enough wherewithal to flinch, but made no move to block me as I swung a wild right hook that landed true. Her breath stuttered as her neck whipped around. A crunch echoed across the cavern. She fell to her knees before me and wept.

I grit my teeth against the urge to wrap my hand in her hair and see just how many times I had to smash her face into the stone for her head to crack open. Violence wasn't my first choice. It had never been, until the beast.

And now it seemed that she had changed me inexplicably. The call for restitution rode me hard, even as she let out the most awful sobs, blood and snot and tears smearing her face. "I'm so sorry," she cried. I wanted to kill her, but deep down I knew she wasn't the one at fault. Not truly.

"She stabbed me in the chest six times. She killed me. She killed Laran. Now she has the beast and took my Horsemen for Devil knows what," I spat harshly. "It's a bit late for sorry, Iona."

I turned my back on her. There would be no forgiveness for what she had done. Not now. Not in a hundred years. I may not kill her, but she could live with the guilt.

Feeble fingers grasped for my ankle. I stilled. "Rysten and I were raised together. I love him, not as a mate—as a brother—and he loved me."

"You have a fine way of showing it," I replied scathingly. She winced, but didn't contradict me.

"Your father saw that he cared and threw me into the burning lake of Inferna. I would have died...I did die...but Lilith saved me. She gave me life in return for my soul and that debt was only paid by bringing you here." She shuddered again, her teeth clanking as the adrenaline in her system crashed. "I didn't know he would love you," she whispered. "I-I didn't know s-s-she would take him t-too."

"If you're telling me this because you hope you'll get sympathy from me, you're shit out of luck. You didn't just bring this on yourself. You brought this down on me and mine, and for that..." For the shaking mess that she was, I was the picture of indifference. It was that or fall apart, and I couldn't do that again. Not here. Not in this moment. "I could have understood your hate for me after what my father did to you, but you sold your fucking soul. What did you think would come of it?"

"I didn't know," she sobbed.

I smiled coldly because that was a lie. I no longer had my empath powers, but I didn't need them to know what she felt. "You knew. You just didn't care. You thought you'd have Rysten in the end and I'd be the spawn of Satan Lilith told you I would be." I turned and strode away, not even flinching as her wailing echoed through the cavern. The sound of despair cemented me in that moment. Her pain kept me from coming unhinged. It calmed me. Even though my hands shook with the need to break something. The need to burn something.

I no longer had even a trace of power. I could feel that as steadily as the bond between Laran and I. She'd taken everything, and while I might be immortal...I was useless.

I was weaker than I'd ever been in my life. I'd lost three pieces of my heart. I'd lost a part of my soul in the beast. I'd lost my powers, and the next time I came face-to-face with Lilith I would fucking roar.

But first I needed to find my way out of here.

"We need to leave. It's not safe here," I began, pausing when I registered Jax was still here.

After I'd burned every inch of the cavern... he should be ashes right now. But he wasn't.

"We need to get to Inferna," Laran said.

"Find the Sins," Moira agreed. I continued watching Jax while she spoke, analyzing his every move. "Ruby, why do you look like you're about to stab someone?" Her voice was weary.

"You should have died," I said to Jax. His eyes narrowed on me, but I couldn't tell if it was confusion or something darker.

"What do you mean?" Moira asked, looking between us.

"I mean I let it all out. The beast and I used every trace of fire I had in me to try and take Lilith out, but she and her minions didn't die and the fire kills everything it touches." Moira's eyes widened, and she took a step away from him. "How are all of you alive?"

"Brimstone," he answered as Moira started to circle around him. "The punch they were drinking was laced with brimstone. It's the only substance that is immune to the flames, but it's also a poison." He looked pointedly at Moira. "Unlike the demons down here that I'm sure have been working up a tolerance for centuries, Moira hasn't."

"That doesn't explain anything, enigma," I replied. "She didn't need brimstone. She's immune to my flames and that has nothing to do with you."

"She's a legion," he said, as if that explained it all. "Pain can be delivered unto her, but she will return it sevenfold. Moira woke with a vengeance and when she touched me, the brimstone she consumed passed." I frowned as understanding flashed on Moira's expression.

"What do you mean *it passed*?" I asked.

"The mark of Cain," she said slowly. "I didn't know if it was true. That it could return pain sevenfold. All I had to do was touch him, though..." She gnawed on her lip, looking between us. "I don't know what to say when I barely understand it myself. The brimstone moved from me to him, and then you went supernova."

"It saved me," Jax replied. "If you hadn't woken when you did, I would have died from the flames." He didn't have any tell-tale signs of a liar, but after what I'd just gone through, I wasn't taking any chances.

"When we leave, you're going back in the bottle until we get to Inferna." It wasn't a question or a request, and I could tell he knew it by the set of his jaw.

"I'm not your enemy here." His eyes strayed to Moira with concern.

"You're not my friend, either. And right now I can't afford that." I crossed my arms over my chest and stared blankly at the underground lake that was no longer glowing or clear. Dark blue waters stained the shore where blood covered the rocks.

"And if you're attacked getting to Inferna?" the enigma asked.

My tone was flat when I replied, "Well, you'll be about as much help as you were this time."

"That's completely—"

"It won't be an issue," Laran cut in. He settled one arm around my shoulders and pulled me close. "Lilith took the beast and bonded to Hell in the waters of the Garden. That means the landscape will no longer be shifting and the fires should be out." I blinked, looking up at him.

"Are you saying we can pyroport straight there now?" I asked in a breath.

"I am."

We could get to Inferna in minutes. I could be seeing the Sins in mere minutes. The thought no longer terrified me, but in my current state it was diffi-cult to feel much of anything. Instead of taking out my rage on Iona, I'd given in to the apathy so I could func-tion. The pain was still there, the grief and the anger and the twisted feelings that I didn't even understand were still with me.

Later, I promised myself. *I'd deal with it later.*

I turned away from those thoughts and focused on the people. On the pricks of Bandit's claws as he protectively wrapped around me, purring softly under his breath. Laran's warm arm around me that held fast. On Moira's blue pentagram eyes, watching me with such open sadness that I flinched away. Laran looked at me with that same worry and I just said, "Open the portal. There's nothing left for us here."

He watched me for a heavy moment. I was torn between wishing I knew how he felt and embracing the solitude that may very well be the rest of my existence —if I couldn't get my powers back—however short it may be if Lilith learned I was alive. "As you wish," he nodded, holding out his hand to conjure forth a ring of flame.

It burned bright from the crimson tendrils to the sunburst heart. I looked at the colors and felt heat, but for once the warmth didn't soothe me.

Morvaen crouched on the floor, looking very unsure of all this.

"You can't just portal home, can you?" I couldn't bring myself to feel bad for calling her when she saved

Laran, but I could understand how she was out of her element. I knew that feeling all too well.

"I don't think so," she answered. "It is not my magic that brought me into this world, but yours." Her fingers traced a rune in the air, but no matter how much magic she summoned, a portal would not form. Her hands contorted as she fisted them in frustration, her head hung low. "The door won't open," she whispered. Anxiety colored her tone as her dark grey skin blanched.

I held out my hand and she looked up at me. Her lips parted as she followed the tilt of my head to the flaming ring. For a brief second, indecision warred with the sorrow of being trapped before she reached out and her fingers grasped mine.

"Hell does not like my kind," she said as we faced the portal.

"It seems it doesn't like mine either," I spoke without turning. "Maybe together we can manage to stay alive."

Laran stepped up to my other side and gripped my hand tightly. The four horses walked in first. Then Moira and Jax, and finally it was our turn.

The first time I walked through a portal of flame I thought I was a girl on fire.

While I was no longer that girl and there was no fire in me, I found that I still burned. Even in the depths of grief. The deepest parts of my soul still held embers, but this time when I ignited, it would be pyres of reprisal that I lit.

A reckoning was coming after what Lilith did here tonight, and when I was done Hell would never be the same again.

CHAPTER FIFTEEN

I HAD STEPPED INTO A PORTAL OF FIRE AND I didn't know what I had been expecting, but it wasn't the dull roar of a crowd assaulting my senses. Light poured down on us, blinding me as a gust of warm air wrapped around my body. The glittering ashes of my past drifted in the wind, settling on the baked earth around me. I pressed my toes into it, curling them inward. My hands shook at my sides as I took in what I was looking at.

"Where are we?" Moira yelled.

The reddish-brown earth spanned out before me, shifting to rocks of various heights and then past those, farther up, were stands...seating. I turned in both directions, both awed and terrified at the rows upon rows of demons. They surrounded me so fully and their cheers were deafening.

I thought back to what the Horsemen had told me,

about what exactly the gate to Inferna was. It was only when Bandit let out some horrible screech in warning that I knew where we were.

"The coliseum," I muttered. "We're in the coliseum!"

"Run!" Laran yelled. Morvaen took off at a dead sprint. I only got a glimpse of something large and dark as my feet stumbled and she half-dragged, half-carried me. Bandit held fast to my chest just as I clutched her, trying desperately to pull my knees up, only to feel the burn of skin being shredded by friction against the rocky ground. I let out a grunt and put everything I had into hooking my feet under me and putting on a burst of speed.

I found traction, just as a massive rock loomed before us.

"We need to get on top of it," I panted, gripping the Seelie woman's hand for dear life and praying that Laran could handle whatever that thing was. In a fight between demons and monsters, I was no longer the biggest one of all. I was the weak link, and I hated it.

"We must jump." Morvaen sounded like this was a mere walk in the park to her and it occurred to me she was going slower so that I wouldn't fall behind. I was going to owe her a damn debt before this all was over.

"I'm not...a great...jumper," I panted, completely out of breath. Her plum-colored lips curved upwards in a feral grin.

"No worries, my lady," she called out. Her hand

tightened around mine as she sped up. I was just starting to stall out when she bent her legs and launched into the air, dragging me with her. My arm felt like it was being torn from my body as we went airborne. I dangled helplessly beside her and Bandit let out a cry of dismay as the flat top of the rock was closing in too fast.

Morvaen landed lightly on the balls of her feet as my own body hit the stone in a heap. Bandit, for all his strength, was flung from my chest and into the low layer of dust that filled the coliseum below us.

I couldn't see him, but I could sense that his presence was there. Given that Bandit was better equipped to protect himself than I was, it shouldn't have worried me as much as it did.

I scrabbled to my feet despite the bone-deep exhaustion. Pain prickled over my fresh wounds, but even without my powers they were healing incredibly fast. Small blessings, I supposed. Weak or strong, at least I was hard to kill.

I pulled myself up so that my knee wasn't bent at an odd angle, flinching when it popped loudly. A slight burn spread around it telling me that whatever my crash landing had fucked up would be fixed soon.

"Your mate is strong," Morvaen commented as the dust settled enough to see Laran. Naked and covered from head to toe in both his blood and my own, he stood alone against a hellhound of epic proportions. This thing made the one in New Orleans look downright small as it towered over him, drool dripping from its jowls. Crimson eyes watched him with malicious intent as it stalked around him in circles. The hell-hound made no move to attack, but its raised hackles gave notice that it could at any given moment.

"That thing could swallow him whole," I answered in a voice that sounded far calmer than I felt.

"He is War, is he not?" Morvaen asked. She didn't sound worried, but we were far enough back from the fight now that we were as close to safe as you could get in an arena of hell beasts.

I swallowed hard and nodded. I had to trust him, just as he trusted me. "He is War."

Storm clouds swirled overhead as the skies darkened and the first hint of rain misted. The winds grew rough, sweeping away the dust to reveal Moira and Jax fighting their own battles on the other side of him. Morvaen gasped as the creature they were backing into a corner became visible.

"Is that a—"

"Cerberus," I answered with a grave nod.

Hellhounds were one thing. The damn things were vicious to the bone and only obeyed the call of its master. A Cerberus was in a whole other category of its own. Unlike the savage Hellhounds, taming a Cerberus was near impossible. Legend had it that each head possessed a different ability and a mind of its own. Getting all three minds to agree on a master was not easy. That had led to their near extinction.

Or so I'd thought.

By the looks of it this one was in rough shape. Blood dripped from its side where claw marks had slashed through the skin. Moira stood before it, hands on her hips. I couldn't see her expression from here, but I got the distinct impression she didn't want to kill it. Hellbeast or not, she had a soft spot for dogs...even the ones with three heads.

A rumbled whine drew me back to the hellhound. The beast no longer looked like it wanted to kill Laran, rather like it wanted to...play. The great giant sat back on its haunches and lowered its head. He reached forward and pet its snout. I couldn't hear him from where I stood, but I wouldn't be surprised to find that he was speaking to it much like he had Epona.

"Where are the horses?" I asked with a jolt. They'd gone first. Was there a chance that it ate them? I shuddered in horror right as Morvaen pointed to another peak to the right of us.

"They fled behind there." I let out an exhale and nodded, but that still left one.

Bandit.

I looked behind us but there was no flat ground, only jagged rocks, and none of them held a black and blue raccoon or any sign of blood and fur. My pulse quickened as I turned back towards the rest of the arena. He wasn't known for staying out of trouble. The hellhound's ears perked up suddenly, glancing to a spot on the left side of us.

Oh no...a ball of fur and fury launched itself across the coliseum.

"No!" I shouted as the dog took off like a hound on a hunt. Bandit was fast, though, diving between its legs —narrowly missing the paws that could kill him with a single step as he went straight for Moira. No. Not Moira...the blood drained from my face as he went for the Cerberus.

Three sets of large green eyes swiveled to Bandit as he ran full speed, stopping right before it. Dread filled me as I judged the distance. We were a good twenty feet up and several hundred out. Powers or no powers, I needed to get off this damn rock. Sinking to my butt and never taking my eyes off Bandit, I slid forward. The sharper edges of the rock sliced through my naked skin with ease, but the drop was harder. The impact jolted straight through me as my feet hit the ground. Still I ran.

Hobbled. Broken. Bleeding. I ran.

And then Bandit did the most peculiar thing of all.

He rounded on Moira and Jax, snapping his teeth. Jax took a step forward and blue fire shot out from Bandit's mouth as he started to grow in size. Five feet. Ten feet. Twenty. He kept growing. His body becoming so large it surpassed the Cerberus that was huddled behind him. From this angle I could see his tail, the way it flicked back to wrap around the three-headed beastie.

He was protecting it.

But Moira was not the greatest threat here.

The hellhound watching him was.

A pounding started in my head, combatting the dizziness from blood loss and over exertion as I ran as hard as I could. My fists clenched so tightly the nails dug into my palms. I only barely felt the prick of skin breaking. My single focus was to get to him. To reach him in time. I didn't know what I could do, but I just couldn't be useless again. I couldn't. I wouldn't.

A whisper of something foreign raced through my veins. The pounding continued, growing so loud it was all I could hear. It was all I knew. A flash of pain raced through me, starting at my palms and spreading through my entire being. I grit my teeth, sprinting as fast as a I could. It happened in the blink of an eye. The impossible.

I went from over a hundred feet away to standing inches from a snarling hellhound.

Each of its teeth were as large as my face. I swallowed hard against the urge to run as I took a step back. It let out a loud harrumph, its rancid breath blowing the stringy, blood-caked pieces of my hair away.

It took a step forward and I took a step back. Fur brushed against my naked body and I recognized the scent of Bandit immediately. I didn't know what just happened. I couldn't wrap my mind around it, but somehow—someway—

"Ruby?" Moira asked, her head whipped around to

where I had been just a moment before. "How did you—"

"I don't know, but we've got bigger problems at the moment."

Moira nodded, raising two fingers to her lips. I frowned right as Jax clapped his hands over his ears. Her whistle sliced through the crowd like a knife through butter. The crowd fell silent. The hellhound stopped. Everything in the arena seemingly froze.

A slow clapping began. I looked around, trying to find where it was coming from as the clouds overhead cleared. A single beam of light shined down into the center of the coliseum and that's when I saw her. Dressed in battle leathers, an oversized battle-axe strapped to her back, wearing that strange half-smile I hadn't seen in two years.

"*Dina?*" I asked, squinting in disbelief.

"Hello, Ruby. It's been a blink since I last saw you."

CHAPTER SIXTEEN

Laran groaned, running his hand over the stubble on his face. "You know her?"

I nodded. "That's Dina. She was my mentor. She taught me everything about tattooing..."

"No, babe." He shook his head, looking at her as he said, "That's Hela, the Deadly Sin of Wrath."

I looked back and forth between the two, my mouth hanging open as slow realization set in. My lips pressed together as my feet began to move. I wasn't exactly sure what I was going to do when I came to stand before the woman who'd been my teacher and friend. The woman who'd bought oranges by the dozen because they were the closest thing to human skin a novice could tattoo on. The woman who spent count-less hours shaping me as a person and an artist.

No. I had no idea what I would do, but the rage inside me did.

A crack split the air and I looked from my hand that I hadn't noticed moved, to the darkening blue palm print on her cheek. I couldn't find it in me to be sorry or feel scared.

"That was for lying to me about *everything*," I said.

The coliseum was quiet. A dead sort of silence filling it. I'd already died twice. The veil didn't scare me. A second crack snapped me from my own controlling anger as a second bright blue palm print appeared on her other cheek. Dina—or Hela—didn't look quite so happy now. "That was for leaving without saying goodbye."

Her eyes softened as tears gathered in them. "I deserve that," she whispered as she wrapped her arms around my shoulders and pulled me close. I let her, not because I forgave her, but because I needed to feel something—anything other than this anger and grief and despair so sharp and deep that I feared I'd bleed out from the inside before I could ever recover.

So, I let her hug me and I embraced her fiercely in return—but I didn't cry. The time for tears was over. I'd lost it all, and in the depths of rock bottom I was regaining it piece by piece. I needed to hold together, and if I cried, I would come apart at the seams.

"I've missed you, Blue," Hela murmured softly against my hair.

"Why did you lie to me?" I asked in a scathing tone. She pulled away and took any semblance of peace with her. The blue of her eyes shined so bright, far more vivid than it ever did on Earth.

"I had no choice. None of us did." She smiled even as a single tear slid down her cheek. She brushed it away and turned to wrap an arm around my shoulders. With her other hand she lazily drew a circle with two fingers and a ring of fire appeared. I tensed. "It leads to my home," she said, answering my unspoken question. I eyed her warily and then turned to look for the others. Laran watched Hela with a neutral expression. Moira looked downright pissed and that probably had to do with the same reason I was. Morvaen was slowly making her way to us, eyeing the hellhound that hadn't moved a single inch since Hela had appeared.

"Does your house have clothes and a bath available without anyone trying to kill us?" Moira asked. Hela eyed her with fading amusement as she really took in the state of us. Something like guilt flashed in her eyes, but I couldn't be certain.

"Of course," she said before looking back at me. "The other Sins would like to see you, though. If you're up for it?"

"Do I get an actual choice?" I asked, already knowing what I was going to do but needing to ask it anyways.

"Yes." The tightness around her eyes showed me how much that question pained her, but there was understanding there too. "You have always had a choice. Just as we have always been watching."

I frowned. "What do you mean by that?"

She smiled but it was filled with trepidation. I didn't get the same feeling I did in the Garden; an unknown sense of impending doom I never had any chance to prevent. Instead I felt...anxiousness. "You'll see," she answered, stepping forward into the flames. She left me there to decide for myself, the hellhound following after her. I looked back at Bandit and motioned for him to come to me. Usually it only took once, but he looked uncertain, glancing around us before eventually shrinking down to his usual size. The Cerberus whined as he brushed against her before coming to me.

I arched a brow, glancing between the two of them as Bandit bounded up to me.

"Of course, you choose a damn hellbeast to get cozy with." Bandit waggled his eyebrows, casting a last look of longing over his shoulder. I scooped him up and turned for the portal. If he wanted a girlfriend, he'd have to wait.

Moira came over beside me and squeezed my shoulder. "It's been a long day, Rubes. You just gotta last a little longer," she murmured under her breath for my ears only. I nodded, staring into the bright yellow flames.

"It's not me I'm worried about."

We all followed after her and into the portal as one. When we stepped out there were no crowds or coliseums. The sudden hush of silence apart from bare feet slapping against the sleek surface was uncomfortable. The towering pillars only served as a reminder as to how small I was. Hela stood before us holding out several thin robes. I took one without speaking, not that it stopped her from looping her arm through mine and guiding me down the hall. I kept my head slightly turned making sure no one appeared behind us.

"Time has changed you, Blue." It was a simple statement, but it cracked through my armor, if only for a moment.

"You have no idea," I snapped, trying to shrug her arm off. Hela didn't let go. She was assertive. She always had been. "I've been fighting my ass off for months just to survive while you've been doing what? Hiding here? Playing gladiator in a devil-damned coliseum? What the fuck?"

Her skin grew hot against mine as her eyes flashed with streaks of lightning. The hellhound trailing behind us let out a growl and Bandit returned the sentiment. "There are many things you do not understand, Ruby. I cannot blame you for that when we are the ones who chose to keep you in the dark, but I can ask you to at least hear us out."

"You left," I said harshly. "Walked out. Poof." I snapped my fingers. "I needed you and you disappeared overnight without even a note or a goodbye. Do you know how much that hurt?" I yanked my arm roughly and she finally dropped it. "You don't get to make demands of me."

Hela stalked ahead of me, lithe and graceful even in armor. "You don't want to listen to me?" she called over her shoulder. "Fine." She stopped in front of a pair of doors that were ten feet tall and black as onyx, a silver pentagram adorned the center, divided by the seam. She grasped the handles and flung them open, breaking the star. "Maybe you'll listen to them."

My heart skipped a beat, suspending for the moment it took me to look at the four women standing around the longest dining table I'd ever seen.

"No fucking way," Moira blurted out. "*Sadie?*"

"You two have gotten into far too much trouble ever since you moved out of my house," the green-eyed shade said with a smile. The tips of her fangs toyed with her plump bottom lip. She'd been the house mother at the orphanage where Moira and I had met.

Another woman scoffed. This one I didn't recognize. "They got in too much trouble *in* your house. There's a reason it was me Ruby came to every week." She smiled, and it was a cruel thing. Her beauty was too much to be real. Her white-blonde hair and pale skin made it difficult to tell what she might be.

"That's only because I wasn't there anymore," another woman smarted off. I took her in. Her black hair was striking against her pale skin and ruby red lips. I knew this wraith. Mere. She was one of the orphanage mothers I'd spent the majority of my formative years with until I'd gone to Portland.

"Oh, please," the cruel beauty smirked. "Hela and I

are the only ones she actually missed." Her sharp brown eyes landed on me. "Aren't we, Ruby?"

"Uh..."—I stifled a yawn—"I don't know who you are."

"A nightmare," not-Mere said flippantly.

"I'd rather be a nightmare than a wraith," the beauty snapped. The Horsemen had said that the Sin of Greed was a nightmare. Her true name was Saraphine. "At least I'm not haunted by the souls I send to the veil."

"That you know of," not-Mere muttered under her breath.

The fourth woman, a banshee sitting in the corner, let out a cackle as she leaned back in her chair to kick her feet up. Heavy boots hit the long wooden table with a thunk, mud and grass falling in clumps while she leaned over and grabbed a handful of grapes, plopping them in her mouth. "You're all jealous, yet *I'm* the one that's green. Oh, the irony," she smirked. The blonde nightmare rolled her eyes and slowly her form changed...

"*Martha?*" I asked.

Speechless.

The sharp-eyed owner of my beloved diner back in Portland blinked and flashed me a smile as she crossed her arms over her chest. "You must be having a mighty hard time without bacon or coffee in these parts," she drawled. Her voice changing to that of the woman I'd known for over a decade. My throat constricted.

"I left you everything," I whispered, stumbling back. The form of the old woman disappeared in an instant and it was again the blonde...Saraphine standing before me. This time her eyes weren't quite so striking as a softness formed in them.

"You're a kind girl and you take care of your own," she said. "Let it be known I never doubted you would make it this far. I knew from the very first day you walked into my diner."

"Me neither," Hela agreed, though the expression on her face made it clear she didn't often agree with this woman about much of anything.

"She's always been destined for greatness," not-Mere concurred.

"She was destined for something, I'll agree with you there," the banshee said around a mouthful of grapes. I lifted an eyebrow and she grinned fiercely, her form shifting before my eyes into...Joe...

"You gotta be fucking kidding me," I said, mostly to myself. The middle-aged cop with the receding hairline and beer gut smiled tepidly.

"Did you really think we would let our sister's daughter grow up alone?" he asked, shaking his head the way he used to. In a blink, the banshee reappeared with a rueful grin. "You're smarter than that, Morningstar," she said, mockingly using my last name the way Joe had during our frequent encounters.

I looked around the room at each of the women that had been involved without me knowing it throughout the span of my life. "I don't know what to say to this," I said honestly.

"Thank you, perhaps?" the banshee suggested, making Saraphine—Greed—roll her eyes.

"She's in shock," said not-Sadie.

I turned to Laran, not sure if it was anger or just surprise riding me when I said," Did you know?"

"Who they were?" he asked, looking around them in shock. I nodded. "No," he shook his head. "Never."

"Of course not," the banshee said and yawned. "We had to keep it from the likes of Lilith. You four really had no chance." She examined her nails, looking quite proud of herself and reminding me a little too much of a certain other banshee. I swiveled to glance at Moira who was watching the she-demon at the table with narrowed eyes.

"You lot have been following her this entire time?" Moira asked all the sudden. The Sins looked her way and nodded. Not-Sadie's lips thinned as if she knew where this was going. "Then you either suck at your job more than the four fuckers who brought us here, or you purposely turned the other way all those years because not a single goddamn time that she's needed someone have any of you been there."

Hela looked like she swallowed something sour, but the banshee—not-Joe who's name I didn't know— just dropped her legs to the floor with a heavy thump and rose to her feet, arms crossed over her. "You really think that she kept herself out of trouble with the law all those years? Possession? Assault? Arson, really? No charges ever pressed against her and she never saw a judge? And yet you came and paid a bail. And she always dealt with me. That's not how any of that works. Don't be so obtuse," she chastised Moira, rolling her eyes before my best friend could respond. "Turned the other way? Please. If she'd kept her nose clean it would have made my job all that easier. I could have been sitting on my ass all day eating donuts while I glamored myself doing shit, but no. I was constantly overriding the damn files to get her off with nothing more than a slap on the wrist," she groaned and leaned back against the table. "It was exhausting. I'm fucking glad to be back here."

Well, at the very least that answered who she was. Only sloth would bitch about me causing more work for her when she had the least hands-on role of them all.

"Lazy," not-Mere griped.

"Jealous," the banshee smiled.

"Can we get to the fucking point?" Moira asked bluntly.

"The point," the Sin of Sloth said, "is that we've been in the background all these years. Raising you without you knowing it was us. We watched over you, keeping away the worst of the monsters so that you would live long enough to one day be able to do it yourself."

"But who are you?" I asked, an anger beginning to

form inside the more I thought about it. They seemed taken aback, but how could they not realize that this wasn't just a shock. No...it was a betrayal. I needed to know who they were—who exactly I was dealing with all those years.

"We're the same people we've always been, Blue—"

"Who are you *really*?" I interrupted.

Hela sighed. "You already know I am the Sin of Wrath."

"And you?" I asked the banshee.

"Sloth," she answered. "But you can call me Ahnika."

I looked at the nightmare. "Greed?" I asked.

Sadness emanated from her as she took me in and nodded once. "Call me Saraphine." Her lips were pressed to hide a frown and the pinched corners of her cheeks showed her strain.

"And you?" I asked not-Sadie.

"Lamia," the sweet-faced woman said. "Sin of Revelry." She stroked the dark blue sapphire that hung from her neck with an admiration.

"Not Gluttony?" Moira asked.

"I am a glutton by nature, but my taste is for the finer things in life," Lamia said. "You would like my realm," she added. "I throw the best parties."

"Like Satan you do," not-Mere griped.

"No need to be a jealous ninny, Merula—"

"Envy?" I asked, cutting Lamia off entirely without apology. I didn't have time for their bickering.

"In the flesh," the woman who had raised me in my formative years answered.

I mentally counted down the Sins...

"There's only five of you," I said. Six sins. Everything had been very specific about this before. Not seven. Not five. Six. "Who is missing?"

They all seemed to share a look with each other without moving an inch, and regardless of who these women were to me, I froze. *More fucking secrets?*

I opened my mouth to say as much when a voice spoke and ice spread through my veins.

"I see you all started the party without me."

Standing behind me was one of the last people I ever wanted to see again. In the blink of an eye I reacted, turning on my heel to slam my palm into her temple. She sidestepped easily, blocking my rebound and the following three blows I let loose after that. It was only when the shiny metal crossbow materialized on my arm with the bolt already cocked that her hand came up to grab my wrist, stopping me from letting it fly.

I let out a growl, but it was Laran that said, "What the fuck are you doing here?"

"Great question," she said offhandedly. I moved to punch her with my other hand and she was forced to let go of the crossbow to sidestep the swing. I wasn't a bad fighter by any means but going up against a several thousand-year-old opponent wasn't exactly a recipe for winning if you played fair. I concentrated on her with all I had and snapped my wrist to fire. The rest was left to chance.

The bolt flew true, striking her chest cavity with enough force to break the bone. Sin took a step back and glowered. "Feel better yet?"

"Hmm," I drawled sarcastically. "Three of my mates are missing and my soul was ripped in half, so I'm going to go with a solid no." She sighed, wrenching the bolt from her chest. The site of her blood cooled my own some.

"At least they're not dead," she scoffed.

"No thanks to you!" I roared.

My fingers twitched and I felt it again, the makings of something stirring within me. Like an ember of power that if only I could grasp it, it might grow to an all-out flame. I reached for it, but the ember evaded me.

"Guys?" She cleared her throat, looking over my shoulder. "Can I get a little help here?"

"You're lucky she doesn't have more Hela in her," Merula replied. Sin gave her a flat look and snapped her fingers. The bloody clothes were instantly replaced with clean ones.

"What is she doing here?" I demanded angrily. A growing unease was beginning to fill me.

There were five...now there are six.

"Ruby," Hela sighed. "Meet your mother's replacement. Sinumpa—the Deadly Sin of Lust."

CHAPTER SEVENTEEN

I OPENED MY MOUTH AND CLOSED IT THREE TIMES, trying to find the right words to say. That's the thing, though—there weren't any.

"Replacement?" I said softly, but my voice sounded hollow. Cold. "You mean to tell me that you replaced her with the bitch who got me and Laran killed?"

Again, the Sins looked between each other, but Sinumpa—she just watched me. Her eyes were slightly narrowed as they skated over me from the top of my head to my bare, dirty feet. "*They* didn't replace anything," she said.

"Oh?" I lifted both eyebrows. "They didn't?" I scoffed callously. Bandit wound himself around me tightly. "Please tell me who exactly made you the Sin of Lust, then?"

Sinumpa let out a sigh and her shoulders dropped a fraction. "Your mother."

"Bullshit."

"Is it?" she asked, daring me to contradict her. "You were just a little babe when I found you both in Atlanta. Your mother knew the score. She still begged for me to spare you. Not her. *You*." I swallowed hard because I hadn't wanted to hear about my mother days ago and I didn't want to hear it now. "She passed on her title to me so that I had the power to keep you hidden until it was time for you to be found. Did you know that?" She unbuttoned the top four buttons on her blouse and pushed the material aside. "Did you know that she branded me before she ordered me to kill her and mutilate her body so that my mother would believe she had been thoroughly interrogated and died during torture while refusing to give up where she hid you?" There on her skin was a deep magenta brand made up of swirling lines that overlapped each other. "Did you know that, Ruby? Did you—"

"I get the point," I spat, biting the inside of my cheek. Bandit braced himself on my shoulder, baring his teeth at the Fae woman.

"No," Sin continued. "I don't think you do. The only way you can become the Sin of anything is if the last Sin passes on her brand and title to you. Lola gave me hers when I found you in Atlanta. *I* was the one that hid you before the rest of Lilith's children came looking. *I* was the one that hunted down every monster that got too close so that the other five could watch over you without blowing their glamor. *I* was the one that kept you alive for twenty-three years, so don't tell me you *get the point.*" At the end of her little speech I wasn't left with an immense gratitude I assumed she expected I should be feeling.

My entire life had been a lie, but that wasn't enough. Raising me to never know the truth was not sufficient. They had to lie to me about who they were as well. It made the time on Earth and the experiences I cherished feel cheap.

Deceived was not a strong enough word.

More like the ultimate betrayal.

"Was any of it real?" I asked. This time my tone was not cold. Nor was it burning. It was empty. Like the hole in my chest where my mates had been carved out from. "Or was it all just preparation to keep the heir alive, only for me to fail because no one told me a fucking thing?"

"We didn't want to keep you in the dark," Saraphine said. I didn't want to call her Martha. She wasn't. She never had been in the first place. Saraphine was a stranger—just like the face that looked back at me—and I preferred it that way. "But we all had our roles to play. Roles that were agreed upon before Lola died. Not even Lucifer knew that we had left and gone to you."

"Why though? Why bother being there at all when you could have just brought me back to Hell, or sent the Horsemen sooner, or any number of things that wouldn't have ended the way today did." I lowered my head.

"You didn't fail," Hela said. "Today went exactly the way we'd expected it to go—with the exception of War almost being killed." My neck cracked with how fast my head lifted to look her in the eye.

"You knew that was going to happen to me?"

"We planned for a great many things," the banshee —Ahnika—said. She lifted the grapes high over her head, dropping them into her mouth one by one. "If you'd all take a seat, we might even be able to start at the beginning," she continued lazily. She quirked an eyebrow as another grape fell, her teeth clanked together as she bit it in half mid-fall, the other slice toppling to the ground. She didn't seem to notice.

I took a deep breath, glancing at Moira and how she had her arms crossed over her chest. Beside her, Jax looked torn between remaining there and splitting. He'd done his job after all. He'd gotten me to Inferna alive. Past him, Morvaen idled by the door, watching everything around her with narrowed eyes. She didn't trust this place, and she was right for that. I still hadn't figured out what we were going to do with her, but at the moment getting some answers and getting my Horsemen back were the top priority.

Laran came up beside me and squeezed my side gently, placing a scratchy kiss on my temple. It steadied me for what was to come, and I went to sit at the opposite end of the table from Ahnika.

I crossed my legs as I leaned into the soft cushioning. My right arm rested on the arm of the chair, curling upwards so that I could brace my chin on my closed fist. The crossbow remained cocked, jutting just far enough out that if I were to fire, the bolt should miss me and still fly true. I didn't expect to need it. Hell, I didn't think it would do much more than anger whoever I hit. I was without power, though, and this metal contraption gave me a piece of that back. I clung to it even as my fingers grew so cold, they felt numb. "You wanted to talk, so talk. From the beginning."

Ahnika's eyebrows bunched together for a moment before her feet dropped away and she leaned forward on her elbows, steepling her fingers. I had her attention now. "Alright, Baby Morningstar. From the beginning."

She nodded once, and the other Sins took their seats. A calm settled over me as I tilted my head. Inside there was a Ruby that hurt. A Ruby that bled. I couldn't afford to be her right now. I couldn't afford to lose my head. There was no beast to balance me anymore, and for that I had to balance myself. Right now, that meant putting aside all my feelings, because feelings wouldn't save anyone.

But the truth might.

And so, I listened.

CHAPTER EIGHTEEN

"IN THE BEGINNING WHEN EDEN WAS NEW, A primordial of great power came into being. Her name was Genesis," Ahnika began.

"I've already heard this story," I sighed.

"You've heard Lilith's version of this story, but she was barely a babe when Eden came to an end and Hell was born," Hela answered. I closed my mouth and inclined my head for them to continue.

"Genesis was the primordial of creation. She created us first, Lola included, as the original six. We each held an aspect of her, and that feature became what we were known for as she created others. She divided our world into provinces and gave us each a piece, tasking us to watch it while she watched over us all, and for a time it was good." Ahnika leaned forward and dropped the empty grapevine on the plate in front of her.

"And then Lucifer came," Merula said. She pushed her silky black hair over one shoulder, her cherry red lips twisting in a grimace. "In a blaze of fire, the primordial of the flames tore a rift in the boundaries between the worlds. Genesis was smitten the very moment she'd seen him because Lucifer was the first being she hadn't created. The attraction only grew the longer he remained, until it reached the point of obsession." She curled her fingers, showing the blood red shade of her nails. "After his falling out with God, Lucifer would not find himself tied to one woman—"

"Why?" Moira asked. Merula sent her a chiding glare, but the question was a valid one.

"Because he had already done so for God," Ahnika answered. "He gave her everything. His heart. His soul. They'd been created as equals—him the primordial of fire and her the primordial of light. A perfect harmonious pair..."

"She wanted more," Hela said, taking over. "God wasn't fulfilled by Lucifer's love alone and decided that she would no longer be bound to one. She would be worshipped by many. A being above him," she said. "A God."

"Lucifer would not be tied down again after that," Merula said. "This drove Genesis mad, and in her madness, she revolted in one final act of creation. She'd wanted real children so desperately she split herself in two—creating the Fae—while dooming her world." She shook her head of dark hair with disapproval.

"The world started to break apart at the seams because Genesis had bonded to it," Merula explained. "Primordials do not *have* to bond with a world, but if they do it vastly increases their power. And that planet, that realm they've bonded to, becomes dependent on the primordial to sustain life. If that primordial dies, the only true way to stop it from imploding was for another primordial to now do the same. Lucifer was our only option, contrary to what Lilith might have told you. Without him, Hell as we came to know it never would have existed because Eden—the world—would have died. Us along with it."

"That's not to say that your father was a saint," Lamia chimed in. "He quite enjoyed the indulgences that being bonded to Hell earned him and he grew to be known as King. Lilith was only a baby when he bonded to the planet and your father took it upon himself to raise her and Eve. She grew up a selfish little twat thinking that she deserved to rule simply because she and Eve were born out of Genesis's death. Much like her creator, she focused on the wrong things. Obsessing over her lack of primordial power instead of the very people that Lucifer gave her by making her one of us. She abused it. Dabbling in dark magic at terrible costs, all the while he refused to see her as anything but the sweet little girl that looked just like Genesis." She rolled her eyes to the crystalline chandeliers above us. Her lips pursed as she looked directly at me. "Then Ragnarök came. A banshee of such great power that he didn't just herald the death of those around him, but the end of the world. He foretold of a future where Hell would burn like it never had before. The borders between this world and any other's Lucifer bridged would be set aflame. Billions of humans, demons, and even angels would die."

"Heaven would burn too?" I asked.

"Yes," Hela answered. "Your father was the purest form of fire forged into the body of a man. He would pyroport between not just distances in Hell, but worlds themselves. It was how he came here, and how inevitably everything he touched would die—if not for you."

"But I did die," I interrupted.

"You did," she nodded. "But you came back. Ragnarök foretold of a daughter that would be born unto fire. That she would wield this great power and ultimately be the key to stopping the apocalypse. This girl would be brought back to her people by four horsemen and put an end to the burning."

"But I don't understand—" I began.

"You will," Merula stopped me. "By the time Ragnarök revealed his prophecy, Lilith was already as mad as the woman she called mother, but ten times more ruthless. Genesis was a selfish deity, not unlike us. We were created in her image after all. But the child she created was a true monster." She shook her head. "I was with her when the prophecy was spoken. I saw that gleam in her eye. I know jealousy when I see it and the moment Ragnarök foretold of you, Lilith began making plans."

"And my father never saw this?" I asked, skeptical. They all shook their heads, solemn but angry. They had every reason to be.

"She was once a master of deception," Sinumpa began, taking over the story. "But over time she began believing the lies she told. She became delusional, falling into her own web. Ragnarök's prophecy made her desperate, because she knew that one day Lucifer would fall, and when he did there would be someone that could take his throne—the throne she viewed as rightfully hers from the beginning." She lifted both eyebrows as she stared down the table at me. Her nails tapped the long wooden table with enough strength to rip a heart from a man's chest. "She got the idea in her mind that if your father could sire a primordial, then she could give birth to one, if she had the right child with the right bloodline." I swallowed the bile in my throat. Revulsion eating at my insides. Sinumpa smiled coldly. "I see my title and lineage didn't escape you in the cavern. Sinumpa, Child of Lilith, Daughter of Cain." She spat her mother's name like it was venom. "Right around the time Lilith got the idea that she needed a male Seelie, one of Eve's spawn came tearing through Hell with the mark of Cain on his head. She trapped him and then she raped him. Again. And again —until she became pregnant with me."

A child born of blood and pain. A girl raised by a

monster dressed as an angel. I pitied her, even if only for a moment.

"My fath—Lucifer allowed this?" Her lips tightened at my change mid-sentence.

"Lucifer didn't know about it. Nor did he find out about the hundreds of other males she held at different points across the years. And while I'm quite unique, I'm not a primordial—unlike you." There wasn't a hint of jealousy in her tone, only bone-deep weariness. The kind of tired that wasn't brought on by a bad day or week. It settled in you day after day. Growing. Eating away at who and what you are until only a numb sense of emptiness remains. "Each one raped until they were able to sire a female child."

"Why female?" Moira asked.

"Males are inferior in the Brimstone City. Used as slaves and breeding studs by the women of Pride. She considered them too primal. Prone to giving into base urges instead of capable thought," Sinumpa answered without having to even think about it.

"Harsh," Moira mumbled. Sinumpa only shrugged.

"She was building an army out of children that would live for eternity. Some having children of their own that would also be enslaved from birth. It was only this very night that I earned my freedom."

"How was she able to hide this if she was the one pregnant?" I asked. Demon women carried their children to term for two years before giving birth. Were the Fae the same?

"She didn't," Ahnika answered. "Hide her pregnancy, that is. Your father didn't take issue with her having children. They were never...romantic. He raised her, after all. He never thought it strange that she would want children given Genesis was her mother. It wasn't until the Horsemen came about that he started to realize what she really was." All of the Sins nodded and once again the conversation passed onto another.

"Like me, Lilith shares an affinity for Greed," Saraphine said.

"She really shares an affinity with each of us, if we're being honest," Ahnika sniped. Greed nodded her head, clearly not disagreeing.

"She does, but her Greed became prevalent the day Lucifer came to her with a proposition." She didn't smile as her gaze slid to Laran. He froze under those sharp brown eyes that in this light held the reddish tint of a nightmare. "He believed in the prophecy that Ragnarök spoke, that you would be returned by four horsemen. But they were not demons that existed yet. So, he made them. Made you, that is." I reached out to grasp Laran's hand, clinging to his warmth. "He wanted you to be the perfect guards for his little girl when she came into existence, so he bargained with the monster he raised. Four women volunteered to be the mothers of the Four Horsemen, knowing they would not survive the process. Four sterile women, I should add. Lilith impregnated them with her own blood magic and Lucifer's power. Just enough fire that they would be immune, just enough strength that they could contain you. No more."

"What did he give her in return?" I asked, dreading the truth.

I waited as Laran took a deep breath and then answered me.

"Our childhood," he said. "She already had free reign in her domain and he couldn't give anything that actually belonged to any of the Sins, so he bargained with us."

"This was before she killed one of the she-demons carrying a child," Sinumpa inserted.

"What?" Moira and I said simultaneously.

"I was closing in on a millennium at the time, so the details from my adolescence are a bit fuzzy," she said, turning to Hela beside her. That she considered a thousand years adolescence said a great deal about the woman I was coming to see more clearly.

"She poisoned one of the she-demons and Lucifer found out. He was enraged by it, given that he was supposed to hand over the babes once they were born. Forced to strike a new deal now that so much was at stake, he swore on a blood oath that as long as she did not physically harm the Horsemen, or allow them to be harmed, then as long as he lived no one could kill her without meeting the same fate—including himself." Her lips pinched, telling me what exactly she thought of that blood oath.

"It was a desperate move that he never should have made," Ahnika stated.

"But he did," Hela sighed "And when the three she-demons gave birth, one was carrying twins. Even at the time he felt that this was his best move for you and for Hell. The odds of one mother dying and then one having twins was too much to be a coincidence. In his mind, the Four Horsemen meant that Ragnarök's prophecy was inevitable."

"It was a self-fulfilling prophecy that might never have come to pass were the Horsemen not created," Ahnika snapped.

"A prophecy that has come to pass, nonetheless" Merula sternly.

"A prophecy that kept us from taking out the bitch before she massed enough power and support to actually become a problem," Ahnika replied.

"Can we cut the arguing and get back to the story?" I cut in, leaning forward onto the table. I grabbed an apple off the platter in front of me and took a bite.

"For many years we continued with this uneven truce. As promised, the Horsemen were raised by her and passed into the transition, at which point they were free to do as they pleased. Years passed. Millennia went by. Then Lola became pregnant. It changed everything." Hela looked at the wooden table in front of her and the expression on her face made me think she was seeing something the rest of us couldn't. "You changed everything. Before you, primordials were never *born*. They came into existence when they were needed. Your arrival meant change was coming, and with it the new age." I held up my free hand to stop her and Hela paused, inclining her head forward for me to speak.

"I hear what you're saying, but I'm not a primordial. I'm only half. My other half is succubus." I was fairly certain of that given that I drank kama like an addict in need of a fix.

"That's only partially accurate," Hela said hesitantly. "You require the sustenance a succubus might, but your power is primordial. We sensed it when you were born. It was the reason Lucifer bound your beast. He'd hoped that would keep the power confined until the Horsemen came for you."

"I've had low-ranging abilities my entire life," I said. Moira scoffed and I ignored it.

"You did," Merula agreed. "But that is because your power is not the flames as we thought it would be."

"What are you talking about?"

"Oh, Little Morningstar, you have much to learn about your kind," Ahnika said with a cackle. "There is no such thing as a half-primordial being. Just as the abilities that you've exhibited were no accident. Genesis held the power of creation in her fingers. Your father held fire. God held light. Others have come, both on Earth and in other worlds, before and after Genesis's death. Yet you sit before us, completely ignorant to the fact that you are the most powerful primordial ever known to date. I would wonder if you were faking the humble behavior had I not interrogated you before. You're not exactly what I would call a great liar." Several of the Sins snickered, no doubt recalling memories of me with fondness that I now thought of with a sense of betrayal.

"What are you talking about, Ahnika?" I asked.

"Until your father died no one could lay a hand on Lilith. She was unstoppable by the time he crossed the veil. She took your beast thinking that it would give her the power of the primordial—your power—but your power doesn't lie solely with the beast."

"You're speaking in riddles I don't understand. Of course, my power lies solely with the beast."

"No, Ruby," Hela said. "It doesn't."

"Lilith is currently operating on the assumption that you are dead, but if she had killed you, the beast would have died as well. It's a symbiotic relationship," Sinumpa said. I couldn't call her Lust. That was Lola's Sin and that just felt too odd. I couldn't call her Sin because we weren't friends. We were simply allies until the greater purpose had been achieved. "She thought you were a half-primordial—something that doesn't exist—and because she hails from Genesis, she thought she knew all there was to know about your kind. She didn't realize that you, dear girl, are not a primordial of flame like your father. You're a primordial of *magic*. You absorb the powers you come into contact with, making them your own." Her mercury eyes glowed eerily, reminding me of the day she stole my telepathy...that I sort of stole from her. She'd said something similar at the time, before making me unable to talk to my Horsemen or anyone else about this. She smiled, like she knew that's where my mind had gone.

"You did this with your father's power as a baby," Merula said.

"And your mother's powers," Saraphine said.

"And when you killed that boy in my house at sixteen," Lamia added. I spluttered for a moment.

"You knew about Danny?" I asked.

"Child," she smiled. "You think that you could kill someone and I wouldn't notice? Who did you think cleaned it up with the authorities?" I felt Moira's hand snake under the table to wrap around my knee, squeezing gently. I didn't like to think about Danny. What I did that night. The way Moira and I became blood sisters.

"After I entered a blood oath with you, you showed signs of my magic," Sinumpa chimed in, nicely leaving out that she also blocked me from showing anything once she figured it out.

I stared around the table from one person to another and I realized this was it. They really, truly believed that I could stop Lilith because I was some ultra-powerful primordial.

The thought was...I couldn't contain the snigger that started under my breath and built to a full-on cackle. I laughed so hard that tears formed in my eyes and slid down my cheeks. Until there was a cramp in my side and even when it hurt, I still laughed...and when it finally died out into the heavy silence, I spoke.

"You guys put your hopes and dreams in the wrong girl." Another chuckle slid from my lips that bordered on insanity. "Lilith killed me. She stole the beast and my power. I have nothing."

And I truly believed that.

Hela said, "You're wrong, Blue. You have your blood."

"What?" I shook my head a little, not sure they were really listening if we were back to this. I came here hoping for answers so I could fix what happened. Not be told I'm the messiah they've been waiting for. Weren't they listening?

"Your power is in your blood, Little Morningstar," Ahnika said. "It is the reason we tested you the way we did. You had to go to Lilith. Sinumpa had to be freed of her oath. All of this had to happen. It was the *only* way."

The back of my legs hit the chair as I stood in an instant, thankful they couldn't see my shaking limbs below the table. "The only way for who?" I demanded.

"For any of us," she whispered.

"Why?" I pushed. Her answers weren't good enough. The pounding in my skull from dehydration and blood loss aiding the righteous anger.

"Because you now possess the power you need to

win this once and for all," Sinumpa said. I opened my mouth when Moira spoke.

"Blood magic," she whispered. Her blue pentagram eyes turned up to me, swirling as the always did. "In killing you, Lilith used *her* magic on you."

I froze. My breath hitched in my chest as all of what they'd told me came together and I finally understood.

Lilith was powerful enough that even the Sins couldn't take her on. If I had her power and the Sins at my disposal...

"That's not all you have," Sinumpa said suddenly. She motioned to my hand. No, she motioned to the... ring. My 'get out of jail free card' as Allistair called it. I don't think he meant it this way. "I locked a tiny sliver of your magic inside of it. Everything that was your mother's and father's is there, when you're ready to take it."

Take it. I played those words over in my mind.

Lilith had taken everything from me. She'd taken everything from every person around her. My Horsemen. The Sins. My father. Her own children.

She bit the Devil. It's time she learned this Devil bites back.

CHAPTER NINETEEN

Drip.

Drip.

Drip.

I pulled my knees in close and tucked them under my chin. Bloods and scabs and dirt and leaves swirled around the cobbled shower floor. The rounded pebbles were uncomfortable against my skin as I leaned back into the wall behind me, vaguely listening to falling water. The cold droplets splattered against my body. Images of Laran's severed neck flashed through my mind. I tilted my head forward onto my knees, trying to calm the storm inside.

They were gone. Not dead, but gone.

Stolen.

Yes. That's what they were. Stolen, along with my beast.

I hadn't even known that was possible until this

night. Then again, I didn't know what I really was either—or what I was really capable of. They said I still have magic, that my blood itself is magic, that Lilith will never be able to take my true power.

I was thankful for it. Now more than ever. Losing everything had been a wake-up call. Never in my life had I been so cocky, so overconfident that I thought my powers would save me. I wanted to say that if I'd been smart enough this never would have come to pass, but I didn't really believe that. The Sins had set me up, and at the end of the day I didn't have a choice. They set the stage, and like the puppet I was—I danced.

Last time I took my powers for granted. I took my safety for granted. I took it all, hoping like a child that it would all be alright.

That hope almost broke me.

My hand closed around the iron handle. It screeched in protest as I turned it. The water slowed.

Drip.

Drip.

Drip.

I wasn't going to hide in here and hope. I wasn't going to sit on the floor and cry or scream or pray. They all had the same result.

Nothing. They would do nothing.

They would save no one.

I sucked in a breath as my arms fell to my sides. I pushed my splayed palms into the ground. I let my hands feel every uncomfortable inch of it as I pushed myself off the bathroom floor and rose on my own two legs. They weren't shaking anymore.

And if I had my way they would never shake again.

I went to stand before the mirror.

Drip.

Drip.

Drip.

Water splattered the floor behind me as my wet hair plastered itself to my face. I stood cold and naked in front of the mirror as I took in every scar she left, every brand she stole, every bare flawless inch...and I hated it.

I hated the scars, not because they were ugly, but because it was every cut and stab of the knife that took my beast. Every bare inch of skin where the Horsemen's brands should have been were an empty chasm in my heart as I realized that even with my magic, I could no longer feel them.

They were gone.

But not dead.

I had to remind myself of that. That there was still a chance to save them. That I could still take back everything I'd lost and more, because if I didn't remind myself, if I didn't focus on that...I may have had the power of a primordial, but I still had the heart of a woman. A woman who was rapidly losing the battle inside herself. Before, the beast had threatened to burn the world. I was scared to admit that without her I very well might, and not a soul could stop me. I was terrified that the Sins could see the truth in my eyes, that I'd lost more than my mates tonight. Lilith had stolen the beast, half of my soul, and it was changing me. I wanted to save Hell...but if I lost them all, I may very well be what destroys it.

Drip.

Drip.

Drip.

My lips pinched together in a severe scowl as I traced my fingers over the hardened scar tissue on my chest. It formed a pentagram of its own, the skin slightly raised and uneven in its healing. The blue vines that had once danced all over my body now curled tight around that wound. I swallowed hard, my eyes drifting upwards in the mirror to where Laran stood. He leaned against the stone wall, shirtless and stoic. The runes Morvaen had given him to save his life had faded from his skin over the last hours. The ones on my back still remained—bright and glowing—an iridescent orange that had not faded.

If I wore them for an eternity I would still get on my knees and thank her. Those marks on my skin were such a small price to pay for what she returned to me. I would never forget it.

Drip.

Drip.

Drip.

We didn't say anything to each other. Both of us had been lost in our own minds when Hela had shown us to our room with the promise to return in the morning. We had to prepare, she'd said. For Lilith, is what she didn't say. Even with all the power in the world, I'd had my ass handed to me once. I couldn't let it happen again. I would not get a third chance.

Again, my eyes drifted back to my body. So bare by comparison to what it had been before. They had made me a work of art, but Lilith had laid my canvas bare.

I didn't like it. The lack of brands made me feel more naked than the lack of clothes ever could. It wasn't so long ago that just the idea of brands scared me. What they meant. The commitment involved. That certainly wasn't the case anymore.

Drip.

Drip.

I shuddered.

Laran pushed off the wall. Something in his gaze changing, morphing in time, and not so very different than the darkness I felt settling around my own heart. There was a fire there tonight, one that I knew would consume me if I let it. I wondered if he saw the same thing in my eyes. If he saw the same shadows that danced.

Warm hands settled on my shoulders as he swept my hair to one side. His fingers traced over the very runes of power that saved his life and mine. I trembled.

He didn't stop.

He traced every line and when there were no more, he continued tracing. His fingers greedy as he caressed my skin, pressing to every nick, feeling every cut. His nails bit into my hips with a sudden fierceness, and through it all his eyes blazed with a dark fire. I wasn't the only one who had lost things tonight.

"I'm so sorry," he whispered hoarsely. I refused to close my eyes and shy away from the intimacy I saw.

"This was not your fault," I said back, my voice just as rough.

"I never should have agreed to let Lola take you to Earth," he said suddenly, surprising me. "I never should have let you leave my sight. I should have fought hard, done more—"

"There was nothing you could have done," I said softly. "The Sins decided my fate before you all were born. They picked and chose what to tell you. They hid things from the Devil himself. There was nothing you or anyone could have done to prevent what happened tonight."

Except perhaps me. Maybe.

My thoughts were only that, just thoughts, and yet they seemed so very loud in the confines of the bathroom. Laran's gaze grew steadily darker.

"You're doing it again," he whispered. I could see my own eyebrows draw together in the mirror, just slightly. A pucker forming in confusion. "You're projecting your thoughts."

The breath hissed between my teeth.

That only meant one thing.

My silence had been broken.

Something hardened inside of me that reflected in his eyes. I didn't ask what it was, because I knew. He was finally hearing all of the things none of them had been privy to. The dirty little secrets I held against my own will. The bargains I struck. The choices I made. The inevitable vice of crushing failure that weighed on me, and the bitter taste of loss that ate at my heart. He was hearing the things I wasn't saying, and I made no move to hide them from him.

Splayed out like the pages of a book, I let him listen and I let myself feel.

My breath hitched as he leaned forward and pressed a soft kiss to my naked shoulder.

"I hear you," the voice of his thoughts whispered through my mind. *"I hear you, and I want you to know something."* His lips skated across my skin as he ran them over my collarbone and up the crook of my neck. His breath fanned the hollow shell of my ear as he stared at me in the mirror. I put my hands on the counter in front of me as he said, *"I love you, Ruby. I love every broken and damaged piece of you. I love the ugly parts. I love the beautiful ones. I love your strength, and above all, baby, I love your fire."* His teeth bit down on the lobe of my ear, drawing a low gasp from me. My fingers curled, wrapping around the edge of the counter.

"You're going to set this world on fire, Ruby, and we're going to burn for you." The front of his body pressed firmly against my back as one of his hands

came forward and parted the delicate flesh between my legs. My eyes stayed on his as he started circling my clit with two fingers. A low groan slid between his lips and my pupils dilated. *"Tell me what you want."* His silent words wormed their way into my mind, far more intimate than anything before. I pushed my hips back into his erection as one of his fingers slid inside me.

Everything. I wanted everything. I didn't want to be numb or unfeeling because I'd lost. I wanted to feel it all and remember what it was like to live. I wanted to hold onto that, to this, because when you're dying in a lake of your own blood and fighting for every breath, this is what you fight for.

I wanted this, because next time I faced her it was all or nothing.

Either we were all walking away together, or no one was.

His fingers slipped out of me and slid forward to press on the bundle of nerves. My own wetness made it easy for his fingers to glide, pulling my body tighter and tighter. I grit my teeth, arching my back. I wanted him, and I wanted him now.

Laran didn't waste time toying with me. There were no power games between us. There was no restraint. Only pure, unbridled passion as he thrust inside me and I moaned. My head tilted back into his shoulder and Laran stilled.

"Look at me," he said. *"I want to see your eyes."* He rocked back before slamming into me again. My head

lolled forward as he gripped my hip with one hand and rubbed my clit with the other. Flesh met flesh as his hips slapped against me. Losing himself to this thing between us. This beautiful and savage thing called love.

My legs quickened, going straight as a rod. I watched the black of his eyes as sweat beaded on his temple. Right as I approached that mind-numbing bliss, his fingers slipped away and with it, my release. I bit back the growl of frustration as his hand slid along the length of my body, settling over my heart.

What was he doing?

As soon as I thought it, I felt it. *"You asked for everything. I am giving all that I am. Whatever you need, I will be with you to the end because you are mine..."* The embers of power in my chest caught fire as the sizzling heat beneath his palm poured into me. I breathed in the faint wash of his kama as the pulsating length beneath my legs slid in and out of me, driving me higher and higher.

A scream built in my throat, not of pain, not of power, but of an emotion far greater.

All-consuming, the blazing inferno ripped through me, and still I gave him my eyes, watching him as he watched me. *"...and I am yours,"* his mind whispered.

I shattered into a million pieces as he let out a groan and several shallow thrusts. His cock twitched inside me as my inner walls clamped around him, pulling more and more. Fire glowed beneath my skin as my veins lit up in a blaze of red and blue.

We continued like that, giving and taking from each other all night until it didn't feel as if we were two people at all, but one.

It wasn't until the next morning that I saw the scorch marks on the stone counter.

Two blackened handprints, glittering like stardust.

JULIAN

Our bodies were puppets. Prisoners in our minds.

Lilith stole us to use as instruments against the very she-demon I loved.

She took us from her. She took her from me.

I saw her soul wavering in the space in-between. Well, half of her soul. The other half now resided within us. The beast.

Lilith had ripped her in half and still they both clung to life. Clung to each other.

The beast was enraged. She was vengeful and murderous and dark and twisted. It was a wonder to me how Ruby held up against the immense power of the beast when I could barely hold a fraction.

Time stood still in this suspended state of being alive but not living.

I had no idea how long had passed, only that I had

to hold on—for her—because if we gave in, the beast would well and truly destroy us all.

Even me. I'd never thought about dying because I didn't think it possible.

If we failed them, though, I had a feeling I might just find out.

I didn't fear the veil. I feared losing her. If we lost, the beast was kind to end my misery.

I would help her tear this world apart myself, piece by piece.

And so, I held on.

We all did.

CHAPTER TWENTY

"SUMMON THE CROSSBOW."

I growled under my breath. My fingers curled into fists, biting into the skin. "I already told you I don't know how," I snapped. The white-haired Fae only tsked, her fingers weaving violet runes mid-air. Whatever she was casting I wanted no part in it.

"You did it once, Lucifer's Daughter." Sinumpa smiled and it was a treacherous thing. "Yesterday you had the audacity to pull it on me because you thought I meant you harm. Have you forgotten so soon what I did to you?" she taunted me. Toyed with me.

I wanted to shoot her in the devil-damned face just so she'd stop smiling like a jack-o-lantern on Halloween. The problem was that I truly did not know how I summoned the crossbow. One minute I had nothing and the next it was there, already strapped to me. Cocked and loaded.

With a flick of her fingers the rune spiraled high above me. It pulled together and then broke apart with a bang, a light sheen of purple descending around me .

"What is this?" I demanded. From the sidelines Bandit let out a rumble and it took both Moira and Laran to calm him down enough so that he didn't launch straight into this fight with me. The Sins each sat on their thrones looking down at us with varying levels of calculated interest.

"A trap," Sinumpa said. Her voice pure with malicious intent as her mercury eyes darkened. My blood quickened as I looked around wildly. Trying to find a way out.

The magical barrier touched the ground and began shrinking inward. A real and true panic started to hit me. I couldn't be confined. Not again. Not ever again.

"Summon the crossbow, Ruby. It's the only thing that can break it," the Fae woman called. I took slow, measured breaths.

"You can do this, Ruby. I believe in you," Laran's voice whispered into my mind. I found solace in that. Not peace, but drive. A burning motivation to get myself out of this. One way or another.

Think, Ruby. Come on.

I grit my teeth focusing on the crossbow with all my might, but the impending shield was getting closer. Shrinking faster. I was out of time and the damned crossbow wasn't coming. Which meant I needed to find another way out of this.

I rubbed my hands together, feeling a true calm wash over me.

It was moments like this the beast usually took over. She got me through the hard things with a detachment I'd never felt until now. A forced stillness that spread inside me, twisting and warping my mind. The eerie silence filled me.

I lifted my hand and pointed.

Burn. The word echoed in my mind.

Fire ignited, a mass of swirling red and blue. My father's flame and Laran's. It built at the tip of my finger, compressing in on itself, like a star preparing to explode. Sinumpa tilted her head curiously as the fire snapped free.

It hurdled towards her barrier at a breakneck speed, tearing a hole through it, sailing straight for its true target.

The breath hissed between her teeth as she realized my intent. Shouts rang out as something dark and ugly swirled inside me. This wasn't the beast.

Oh, no. This was me.

Every ounce of rage I held came forward. She dropped to the ground, narrowly missing the swirling ball of flames. I snapped my fingers and it swung around, returning to me. The room fell silent as I walked forward, my boots thudding softly against the polished stone floors.

Sinumpa tilted her head, looking up from the ground. I held the swirling orb of chaos in one hand

and nothing but a closed fist in my right as I leaned down beside her.

"I will never forget what you did to me. I don't even know if I'm capable of forgiving it, though it would certainly be easier on me if I did," I said softly. "You didn't just help her take my life away. You brought me back to use as a tool in a war I shouldn't have to finish." Something like regret flashed in the depths of her silver eyes. I ignored it. "I will never be the same girl I was in Portland because of what you've done. I had to change in order to survive this, and I will. I wasn't the one to start this war, but I will finish it. And when all is said and done, and your mother is nothing more than ash on the ground—I will still remember what you did, and you had better hope"—I paused closing my hand around the orb. The power extinguished in a flash of light—"no, you'd better pray that when I get them back, they can piece me together again. That they can quench this rage, because anything that I perceive as a threat to them is where I'll be setting my sights next, *little Fae*," I whispered so softly. You could have heard a pen drop half a mile away with how quiet the palace had gone. It was as if time itself stood still and took note of what I was and who I was becoming. "You took everything from me and if I have to build my own throne on the bones of my enemies, then so be it. Remember this next time you think of taunting me. "

I stood and walked away.

Laran and Moira stood with me, letting Bandit loose. His feet echoed on the cold stone floors as he launched himself up and into my arms. I caught him squarely against my chest and paused.

When I looked up to the Sins, these women that I'd known all my life, I think they saw it. That whatever their hopes had been, whatever they had been striving for—no matter how things had to happen—the way they chose to go about it was wrong.

"You asked me to train and I will," I told them. "But not with her." My fingers tightened in Bandit's fur as he curled around me.

I thought I could do this. That I could train with her as they'd asked.

I would not be a puppet any longer.

In their betrayal I'd become someone else entirely.

Heaven help the next person that crosses me after what they've done, because nothing in Hell will. I was done playing their games, and as I walked out of the throne room, I think they realized it too.

This time we were going to play my way.

CHAPTER TWENTY-ONE

WIND WHISPERED OVER MY FACE. A GENTLE caress as I leaned against the balcony. Several hours later and my temper had only marginally cooled. With a night's rest and enough food, the magic was coming back at an alarming pace. Fire roared to life like it had in the old days, except this time I knew how to control it. All of my other gifts the beast had taught me how to control were there too, just waiting to be used.

My chest constricted. A pang of emptiness hit me.

I missed her. I missed our conversations. I missed the presence that sat by me in the fire, guiding me through my nightmares and urging me to take my destiny by the horns. I'd never truly wished her gone, but it was only in losing her that I realized how much I'd come to rely on her. We were two halves of the same whole. Or we used to be.

She had been my darkness and I had been her light.

Something told me we both had fallen in this. That I wasn't the only one suffering.

My hands tightened on the railing as my skin began to glow again. The sky overhead darkened, and lightning flashed. I swallowed hard, pushing down those emotions. I couldn't afford to lose it here.

I heard the door in my room being opened. A faint whispered conversation. A rustling of feet. The curtains to the balcony drifted lazily to the side and I felt her. The burning fire of Wrath as she plopped down beside me and pushed her legs between the rails.

"Mighty fine weather you've conjured here," she said, squinting at the brewing clouds. I let out a steady breath, trying to will them away. War's power over the elements was strange still, and not something I had expected to need to learn so quickly after he branded me.

Maybe Hell itself was responsible for this as well.

"I didn't ask for this," I said quietly, waving my hand at the clouds. Hela smiled kindly, lifting her own hand. The clouds broke apart and sunlight seeped in. It bathed the sprawling city before us. Lighting up every alley, every home, every demon that dared walk in the streets when a somberness had stolen us all. Lilith hadn't come yet, but it was only a matter of time and we all felt it.

"None of us did," Hela said. Her fiery hair swayed

in the breeze as her lightning eyes flashed, not with fury but something else. I didn't want to feel it, but I did. I suppose I had Lola to thank for this. "Our paths were set from the moment Genesis brought us into creation."

"You chose how to handle me. You chose to keep me in the dark, Hela. That is not something Genesis, or Lilith, or anyone else chose."

She nodded. "We did choose that. Do you want to know why?" she asked me.

No, I thought. Her lips curved up. She must have heard it.

"Well, I'm going to tell you anyways," she said, patting the ground beside her. I pressed my lips together but took a seat all the same. Pushing my legs through the railing reminded me of better times. Of the late nights we shared in her flat, sitting on a balcony grate that was far more uncomfortable than this. We used to talk for hours, watching the sun die in the sky and the moon be born. I bit my cheek because that wasn't who I was anymore, and neither was she. Those memories wouldn't do me any good in the coming battle. "I can sense your internal struggle, you know. While I was not an empath like your mother, your telepathy is so strong that you project your thoughts. I know you don't want to hear it, but Sinumpa was right to mute it. If Lilith had realized what it is you truly do, she would have drained your body dry, and that very well may have taken your magic, even if Sinumpa could save you. As much as you hate us for what we have done, remember that we did not ask to be the rulers of Hell. We, like you, never chose this." She waved to the people below us. "We were created and given a purpose. Similar to you in many ways, except we wanted more for you.

"The six of us made a pact when you were born. Your mother included, being the Sin of Lust at the time. We decided that while you were destined to save Hell, you were also only a child. A baby. We could not change your destiny, but we could alter the path towards it, so to speak." She nodded to herself, her eyes staring down unseeing. "In Hell, you would never have had anything resembling a normal childhood, even for a demon. So, we chose a different path for you. One that gave you time to learn and to grow and to experience all that life had to offer. We gave you as long as we could on Earth, because time was all that we ever truly could buy you. It was our gift to you, though you may not see it that way."

I sighed, leaning forward to rest my head on the rails. I didn't want to feel sorry for her; for any of them. I didn't want to feel anything for the Sins, but I did.

"Will I die?" I asked.

It was one thing the prophecy didn't really cover. There were a lot of vague notions about me saving Hell. About the flames. About the Horsemen.

None of it ever said what happened at the very end.

265

"I don't know," Hela answered. I appreciated her honesty, but damn—it stung. "For a primordial to bond to a planet, a great sacrifice must be made. Sinumpa said that Lilith stabbed herself as many times as she did you, effectively bringing herself to the edge of death before bonding to the Horsemen so that they could act as an anchor for the beast."

"Haven't I sacrificed enough?" I asked, more to myself than her. That didn't stop her from answering.

"You have sacrificed more than anyone should have to. Should you truly defeat her and survive the encounter, you will be worthy of so much more than the broken world you've inherited."

"And the trials?" I asked. A light mist blew through the valley, spraying us on the elevated balcony.

"You've already passed them," she said with a twinkle in her eye. "We were going to tell you today, but then, well..." she trailed off, but the implication was clear. Then I stormed out of my first "training" session with Sinumpa.

"I meant what I said. I'm not training with her." My hands fell away from the rails, crossing over my chest.

"I'm well aware," Hela said. "But you still have much to learn and very little time. While the flames can handle many things, Lilith will have had her army consuming brimstone long enough now that they will be all but useless. Laran's gifts now run in your veins, but I should know well enough that the power of the elements won't be enough to bring Lilith down. The crossbow given to you is a Seelie weapon. Their magic is one of the only things left in this world that can still harm her."

"I don't want to rely solely on a weapon when she's already proven to think ahead," I said. The Sins were convinced the power Donnach had put in the little gauntlet crossbow was enough to kill her, but after what went down in the Garden...I wasn't so sure.

She will plan for this. She had to. And I had to be ready for that.

"It's better than relying on the flames as you do now," Hela said reproachfully.

"That won't be the only thing I plan to use when the time comes," I snapped. I didn't want to disclose everything to her. At this point I didn't really know who I could trust, past those that were bonded to me.

"What do you mean?" Hela asked, sounding more curious than angered by my tone. Odd for the Sin of Wrath, but then again, our years spent together may have at least earned me some patience.

"I mean"—I paused, exhaling a breath—"there are other ways. Things that haven't been considered. Lilith came out of nowhere last time. She already proved to be powerful and now I'll have my own gifts to contend with as well. I have very limited time until she hears I'm still alive, and that's assuming she hasn't already. How long do you think it will take her to arrive?"

Hela grimaced, her head leaning side to side as she

internally weighed the numbers. "Weeks at most. A few days, more likely."

"Exactly," I murmured. "That's not enough time to train me on anything really. After months I've only just mastered the flames. It really makes no sense to put it all on me because ultimately, if I were facing her alone, I would fail. Lilith has been planning for thousands of years just how she might destroy me. I would be a fool to think I could train hard and that any one thing could save me and end this."

The wheels had been turning since last night. The makings of a plan.

"What are you talking about?" Hela asked me.

I looked out over the city again. To the children that clasped their parents' hands. To the people that stuck to the shadows. To the shiny lake of flame. All the way to the volcano that sat at the mouth of the valley, acting as an entrance. I could hear the roar of the coliseum if I tried hard enough.

"Lilith has been planning this for an eternity. I plan to throw something else at her. Something she doesn't see coming," I paused, looking over at Hela. I wouldn't tell her everything. Hell, I wasn't telling *anyone* everything. Not even Laran. In my spiraling anger, I found the part of myself that survived so long, not on power, but something far simpler. "I was raised in the human world thinking that I was a demon with very little power, but surviving, nonetheless. I may never be that person again. But being her for twenty-three years taught me enough to know there's a better way and I plan to find it."

Hela went silent, her eyebrows slowly inching up her forehead. A laugh rang out and lightning arced across the sky.

"Ah, Blue," she smiled. "You and Sinumpa are far more alike than you realize."

I didn't say anything as I looked over Inferna. I had no idea what she was talking about, but in that moment, I didn't really want to know.

ALLISTAIR

The bitch's cackle made me flinch internally, though my muscles no longer moved at my command. I was chained to the feet of her throne. It was a chair built from the bones of her own children.

Failures, she called them. Disappointments put to better use.

She was fucking crazy.

"Did you hear that, my sweet Famine?" she chimed. I wished I could stiffen. I knew what was coming.

"Yes, my love," I answered, though not of my own accord. The beast thrashed, wanting to rip and slice and tear and *kill*. I had no doubts if she ever got free that she would end her for what she had subjected us to.

It would not be slow if the beast had her way.

It would be savage. Bloody. Ruthless. Brutal.

She would fucking destroy her.

As it was, she was caged. We all were. I prayed to Ruby for the thousandth time. I prayed that she hurried. I prayed that she was safe. I prayed that no matter what happened she got through this.

"Oh, how I just *love* you like this," Lilith purred. I wish I could gouge my own eyeballs out when she let the thin fabric of her white dress slip from her shoulders and fall to the floor.

I tried to stop myself. To resist. But I wasn't in control anymore. I was a prisoner in my own mind as she had me sit upon her throne.

I was unable to stop her from grasping my length and squeezing. Her hand jerked up and down and my revulsion reached an all-time high. This was not the first time she'd done this. It wouldn't be the last.

My dick hardened against my will and she gripped the base, straddling me on her throne of pain and lies.

"Tell me you love me," she breathed, placing herself directly over me. She slid herself down my cock, her wet cunt dripping with poison.

I'd never hated what I was until this moment.

I'd never wished to die.

I loved Ruby. I loved her so very much, but I didn't know how much more I could take of this.

My lips parted and said the words she wanted to hear. "I love you, Lilith."

She moaned, her breasts bouncing up and down as she clenched around me.

I hated myself when my hips jerked, and I emptied inside of her.

She cried out, climaxing around me and a small part of me died as she leaned forward, breathing in my scent. Her kama stank, invading my pores as she licked up the column of my throat and hummed merrily.

"Go back to your place, Famine. I want to play with Pestilence." Internally I flinched as she pulled away and lifted her naked body from mine. The mess of her release and mine pooled into my lap.

"Yes, my love." My legs stood, the liquid falling and smacking against the concrete surface, echoing in the silence of her throne room.

I couldn't control a damn thing as I took my place beside Julian, watching Rysten as he was forced to sit upon the same chair.

I had no choice but to see and feel my brother's despair as she climbed on top of him, her cunt still wet from Julian's release...from mine...

If I ever got free...

I would rip her limb from limb and feed the pieces to Bandit. I would carve the Devil's mark in her chest and pull out her still beating heart just to crush it with my bare hands.

I would let the beast flay the skin from her body, layer by layer until the damaged husk of that monster matched the person she was inside.

As it was, I waited.

I waited for Ruby.

I waited for freedom.

I waited for this to end.

The beast roared in fury.

But I could do nothing.

So, I held on to that small sliver of hope, and I waited.

MOIRA

He closed the door softly behind him, turning into what he thought was an empty hallway. I crossed my arms over my chest and tilted my head.

"Going somewhere, genie?"

"Moira." It was all he said; my name coming out in an exasperated sigh.

"My question still stands, Jax. You're wearing a jacket which means you're headed outside, and the backpack leads me to think you might be leaving entirely. So..." I drawled out. "Are you?"

His purple eyes settled on me as I lifted my eyebrows.

"Don't give me that look," he groaned.

"What look?" I said sweetly, batting my eyelashes. He rolled his eyes to the clouds.

"*That* look..." he muttered. "Like you're disappointed in me or something."

"On the contrary"—I wagged my finger back and forth—"I expected you to leave much sooner than this." He narrowed his eyes slightly.

"You're not mad?" he asked, genuinely confused.

"Mad?" I asked. "We fucked. It's not a proposal, big boy. I had an itch and you scratched it. Don't make this awkward." He scratched the back of his head, looking perplexed. Like he wasn't quite sure what to do with me.

"Alright, so, why are you here?" he asked, crossing his arms over his chest. I tilted my head to the side, listening to my surroundings. The howling wind and occasional errant breeze caught my attention, but it was otherwise quiet. Excellent.

"I needed to ask you a couple of questions before you left," I said. "Like, where are you going?"

His eyes widened for a moment at my straight-forwardness and then he coughed. "Typically, girls don't ask that if—"

"I'm not looking for a hookup," I rolled me eyes. His cheeks darkened from a blush. "Don't get me wrong; you were good and all. I'm just not looking for any sort of relationship—not even a casual one. The world is ending and I've got enough people to keep an eye on as it is." He nodded as if he understood, but there was something in his eyes that I pretended not to see.

"I see," he muttered. "If you must know, I'm meeting up with someone."

"Sin?" I asked. He blinked twice.

"Possibly."

"She was the Sin that called in a favor to escort us to Inferna, right?" I brushed a hand over my sleek green braid, flicking the tail over my shoulder.

"She was."

"And your debt is paid now, yes?"

"It is."

"Good," I smiled, clapping my hands together once. "You see—the thing is—I hear things. Lots of things. And a little birdie told me the most *interesting* thing about Sinumpa, but it seems that every time I manage to track her down, she simply disappears. Why is that?"

"I'm not sure," Jax said, blowing out a rough breath. "You'd need to ask her."

"I plan to," I nodded.

Well," he started as he went to sidestep me, "if that's all—" The words caught in his throat.

Jax started coughing. "Not...possible..." His eyes bulged in alarm, shocked by what was happening. I sighed, taking my time to stroll to a stop in front of him. I leaned down, putting us at eye level.

"Enigmas are only immune to magic from those *beneath* them in power, Jax. I'm a legion; the familiar to the strongest primordial to ever come into being. You heard it yourself. So, let's make this easy." I blinked, and the pressure fizzled out as he found himself able to breath. "I want to know where Sin is and where you are going."

"Can't...tell...you..." he managed to choke out between coughs and heavy panting.

"There, there," I patted him on the back. "You know how rough I can be in bed, enigma. And I know you like it. Do you *really* want to push this—"

"Blood...oath..."

I sighed and clenched a fist, choking him again. It didn't escape my notice that he was hard, and I couldn't help but find it rather amusing.

"You were looking for me," a voice whispered through the shadows. I smiled, letting Jax have another couple of seconds to sweat it before loosening my grip. He collapsed onto his knees, leaning into my right thigh.

"You're...going...to be..."—he coughed hard and cleared his throat—"the death of me." I winked at him and patted his dreads for a moment before turning to spare Sinumpa a glance.

"You're leaving with the enigma," I said. "Where are you going?"

Her silver eyes glowed like the light of a dying star. She was the most beautiful being—male or female—I'd ever seen, and she was appraising me with interest.

"I get the impression you already know," she answered.

"Earth," I whispered.

Sin nodded.

"The borders are closed." I swallowed hard and looked down the corridor at nothing in particular. "How is it possible that you can portal between worlds?"

"How did you know where I would go?" she asked, ignoring my question entirely.

"You're splitting town and nowhere in Hell is safe. That doesn't leave many places..." I trailed off, but it was only a partial truth.

"Tell me." Sin strolled forward, her leather boots silent on the stone floors—even to my ears. "Do the dead talk, green one?"

I looked to the ceiling, the corner of my lips turned up. Yes. Yes, they did. Incessantly, really. But just as I could shush the living, so too could I silence the dead if I so chose. Usually I just let them chatter away. Never knew what stories you might hear.

"Sometimes," I admitted. "But this did not come from the dead."

"Then who?" she asked. There was a sharp edge to her tone and I didn't like it.

"I'll make you a deal, Sin," I said boldly. "I want to know why you're leaving Ruby to face your mother alone. If you can tell me that—and tell me the truth— I'll tell you how I found out."

Sinumpa grinned as she stepped right up to me with a swagger, starlight shining in her eyes. She extended a hand, and I swear my heart damn near jumped out of my chest.

I didn't hesitate for even a second. Our hands joined, and I saw it. In my mind, I saw the truth...

If Sin stayed, we would all die. Lilith had bound her so tightly in blood oaths that her presence would end us all. The Sins. Bandit. Me.

The *only* one who could end this was Ruby.

Sin was leaving because there was no other way for Hell's humanity to recover should she stay. It was a risk —the largest one of all—because it left the weight of the world on one woman's shoulders. But it was also a gift.

The only gift she could give for what she had already done.

CHAPTER TWENTY-TWO

My footsteps were silent as I padded from one room to another. I'd left my boots next to the door so that I could be as quiet as possible and not disturb the sleeping raccoon. He was sprawled on Laran's chest, drooling everywhere. Laran had conked out as well, but I wasn't as worried about waking that one. He was sleeping like the dead since we'd returned here. Said it was something about the land returning him to full strength. I didn't dwell on it, or his reasons. He needed his energy for what was to come, and I needed to be ready.

Stepping past Moira's door, I ignored the inkling of guilt that niggled at me for not talking to her about this first. The less each person knew, the better.

In a world where even your thoughts weren't private, I needed to be wary of how much I let anyone know. Then again, that's why I was here.

My closed fist came up to knock on the door, hovering mid-air when it swung open before me. I blinked as Morvaen leaned out and looked from side to side before motioning for me to come in. I swallowed once and nodded, lowering my arm as I stepped over the threshold.

"You knew I was coming?" I asked, slowly striding forward into the suite. Two armchairs were arranged to face each other with a small table between them.

"I suspected," the Seelie woman said. She took a seat in one of the chairs, waiting for me to sit in the other.

"Why is that?" I continued, plopping down across from her. The leather pants I'd been given stretched to the max as I crossed my legs. While tough and durable, they weren't exactly the most comfortable. The movies never mentioned that. Then again, they didn't mention a lot of things.

"You're fighting an enemy that has already beaten you once. An enemy that demons no longer remember how to beat because they've been in her clutches for far too long. A smart individual would speak to one of the two creatures in this palace that have an understanding of the Fae." She leaned forward, lifting the teapot from the table and pouring two cups. I leaned forward and accepted mine gratefully while she continued. "You cannot be in a room with one of us without trying to kill her. So, it is no surprise that you came to me as the lesser evil."

I took a sip of the steaming herbal brew. "You know what I am, yes?"

"A primordial of magic."

I nodded. "And you know how I gain new magic?"

"By coming into direct contact with it," she answered. "Much like you have with mine," she added. I pressed my lips together in a tight smile.

"I haven't seen traces of your magic yet, but after everything I've been told, I do believe it is there." I took another sip, settling deeper into the armchair. A contentedness filled me.

"I do as well," Morvaen said. "Is this why you have come to me?"

"Yes." The word bubbled up and spilled out of me before I could think. I swallowed another sip of tea and frowned. "I came because I want to understand the difference between blood magic and rune magic."

"It's really quite simple. When Genesis split herself in two, half of her essence created Lilith and half created Eve. Lilith received the magic of the body and all that is tangible. It relies on blood sacrifices in return for power," Morvaen said.

"And Eve?" I prompted.

"The magic of the mind. Rune magic is far more nuanced in that it works with what cannot be seen. Its power comes from inside us." She motioned to a spot on her chest, over her heart. "The soul."

"Donnach made me a crossbow with Seelie magic," I said. The words came to my tongue without thought or effort. "The Sins are convinced the crossbow is the way to kill Lilith, but the truth is I'm not very good with it even though it is spelled to hit whatever I'm aiming for. Nor do we have the time to fix that," I continued. "And I believe relying on something so simple is foolish, really. I need to find a way to beat Lilith so that she doesn't see it coming." I frowned again, looking at my cup.

Morvaen nodded, setting her tea in front of her. "You'll have to forgive me for spelling the tea with truth. We Fae cannot lie, but your kind can. In this world I need to know who you truly are, Ruby Morningstar, if I am to give you what you seek."

"And what is that?" I asked her, deliberately taking another sip of tea. I had nothing to hide from this woman. All the better that she sees it.

"The power of the Seelie. The reason Lilith feared our kind enough to send her own sister onto another plane of existence knowing that it would ultimately kill her." I nodded, tipping the cup and drinking the last of my tea. The rim hid my smile as I let out a breath.

"Right," I drawled. "I want to know it all. I want to understand, but most of all—I want to save this world from her. I need my Horsemen and the beast back. The people need peace. The land needs time to heal. I don't want a war, Morvaen. I want an execution."

She nodded, and in her silver eyes I saw understanding. She leaned back, crossing her hands on her lap as she watched me. Long hair so black it looked like liquid tar hung over one shoulder, showcasing her runes along the other. "You're a curious woman. Do you know how many times in the thousand years I've lived that I have given another my rune of protection—the same one I placed on you—so that it may call on me for a favor owed?" I shook my head. "Twice. Once for a lover that betrayed me. The second time was for a girl I thought to be my enemy. You could have ordered me to do anything with that rune once called upon, and all you asked for was to save your mate."

"I will never be able to show you my gratitude for what you did," I found myself saying. She blinked and I could tell that surprised her. "I am only holding onto my humanity by the barest of threads. I want to save this world, but I don't want to live without them. The rage will consume me until I will either destroy them all or wish I were dead myself. Maybe both. You saved a piece of me from dying that day, and for that, words will never be enough to show how I feel."

This rage was a terrible thing. It made me strong enough to live through what I had, but not so strong that I might overcome it if things don't go my way when this is all over.

Was this the price of such power?

Or was I simply not strong enough to begin with?

"Spelled tea or not, your honesty comes out easily for a demon," Morvaen said simply. "You are humble for a primordial being, but more than that, you have lost all there is to lose and still you cling to humanity. You are worthy of the knowledge you seek." She stood from her arm chair, offering me a hand. I took it, setting my empty cup aside. "Many of the Seelie lost their magic in those early days on Earth. They feared losing their story with each passing generation, and so my father devised a spell unlike anything we had seen before."

Her fingers began to twirl and orange strokes of power came to life. I watched, transfixed as always. "What does it do?" I asked.

"It is the holder of all knowledge," she said. "Every Seelie child performs this spell at least once in their life upon reaching the age of maturity. Once it is cast, that Fae is bestowed with the knowledge of Seth and every Seelie that has performed it after him." One by one the runes began to float in a loose circle, and the more she added, the more they started to lock together like pieces of a puzzle.

"Did you say Seth? As in Eve's son?" I asked.

"Aye," she nodded. "He was my father. Cain, his brother, came to Hell for glory. Abel died as a sacrifice. My father wanted the Seelie to live on. He settled in New Orleans and after many generations of children, I came to be. Some of us are born with more magic than others. Not all Seelie can withstand time and settle into immortality. He created this spell because of it." I stared at her, near speechless.

"Why would you do something like this for me?" I asked her as the runes started to move faster. They locked together forming a mandala of light.

"You are the future of this world. A future I would like to be a part of," she answered. Her fingers stilled and the intricate circle of light stopped. "Which is why I offer this not as a gift, but as a bargain. I will give you the knowledge of all that we were and are so that you have the power to put the Blood Queen down, but in return—when all is said and done—my people get to return home."

I stilled. That wasn't what I had been expecting. Answers? Maybe. A trade? I had considered brokering one, but I hadn't expected this.

"Will this truly give me what I seek?" I asked her.

"You will know our history. You will understand our power. You will know what my magic is—the magic that now runs in your veins—and you will know how to use it. I have never offered this to another soul, but then again, there has never been one with the power to complete the ritual and survive. Only the power of the Seelie will do." As she spoke, goosebumps formed over my arms. There was something in the air that whispered of ancient power and forbidden secrets.

I'd come here to bargain for something else entirely, but what she offered...it could change everything.

"And what if I asked for something more?"

"I have nothing more to give," she answered steadily.

"Could you bring your people here?" I asked. Soldiers. That's what I'd come to ask for. Seelie soldiers that could fight blood with magic. The hunters of all demon kind.

Morvaen shook her head. "As you already saw, I am unable to open a portal directly to Earth, not even to bring someone in. That power lies with a being who is bonded to this planet and the only way to surpass it would be both blood and rune magic. Neither of which you are proficient in." I cursed because she was right. I hadn't the faintest clue how to use the blood magic. It was the reason I wanted the Seelie on my side to begin with. "And even if I could open such a portal," Morvaen added, "I am not at liberty to offer my people for your war. Seth's Wisdom is the most I can give."

I took a deep breath, looking between the glowing mandala, the Fae, and the greater world beyond. I had no idea what this would do to me, or who I might become. I could never go back, though. Only forward. If this knowledge gave me the power to defeat Lilith, then so be it.

I held my hand out to her, well aware this may come back to bite me in the ass, but I was out of options.

Morvaen took my hand in both of hers, turning it palm upward. She scrawled a symbol into the flesh before pressing her own palm against mine. A searing ripped through my skin, fading to a stinging ache before I could even react. Morvaen smiled and I had the distinct feeling it was genuine, despite the way it looked like a sharp grimace.

"Let's get started."

CHAPTER TWENTY-THREE

It felt like my flesh was being peeled from my body, but I drew every damn line of that spell.

Seth's Wisdom, they called it.

It was a rune that exacted so much from you that only those with a purpose greater than themselves could survive the crushing weight of the knowledge it held. Morvaen could have warned me, but she didn't. I'd be more pissed about it if it would have made a difference. I was getting everything it had to offer, no matter the costs. So even when my bones seemed to break, and my blood began to boil, and the pressure in my mind became so strong I thought my skull had been split in two—I kept drawing.

The very moment my fingers completed the final flourish, a darkness consumed me. Pain racked my body to the point that all I could do was separate myself from it and focus on reaching for the only light. The spinning rune. Seth's Wisdom.

Their faces flashed before me.

Bandit.

Moira.

Laran.

Allistair.

Rysten.

Julian.

Me.

I was doing this for us.

I would not fail.

A doorway appeared and I didn't hesitate.

I didn't falter.

My fingers wrapped around the handle and I felt it.

Knowledge.

Power.

Everything.

LARAN

Three days.

She'd been comatose for three days. All the while Lilith drew closer.

I tried entering her mind, but my telepathy was not strong enough.

I sent Moira, but she could not breach whatever place held her.

Bandit curled himself around her feet as we waited.

I'd fallen asleep when she was on the balcony. I'd woken to her in bed beside me. No one knew what had happened. No one knew how to fix her.

I held her hand in mine. The pale skin stretched taut over blue veins. Moira paced at the foot of the bed, snarling at anyone who dared enter.

She couldn't last much longer like this, and the war would not wait for her.

I needed her to come back to me.

I needed to know she was alright.

I just needed...her.

"*Soon,*" a voice whispered. I blinked and looked to Moira. She had stopped and was looking at Ruby like she'd seen a ghost.

"Did you hear that?" she asked.

"I did."

"*Soon,*" the voice repeated.

Nothing about her changed. The blue strands of hair stayed limp on her pillow. Her breathing never faltered. Her pulse never jumped.

But Ruby would be waking up.

Soon.

I just hoped it wasn't too late.

CHAPTER TWENTY-FOUR

My eyes opened after an eternity of pain.

I'd lived every nightmare.

I'd suffered every torture.

I'd felt every single death that the Seelie had endured.

I saw their plight.

I saw their struggle.

I saw their persecution.

And in the end...I understood them.

Seth's Wisdom had aged me centuries. At the end of it—when I had lived their lives and known their sorrows—when the bitterness and resentment of all that had been done to them subsided, I got what I came for.

Every single rune that had been created since the dawn of time now sat on my fingertips.

Every single event that led us here sat in my mind.

A choking noise pulled my attention. I blinked, turning my head. The soft fabric of a pillowcase brushed against my cheek. A cold wind blasted the baby blue curtains in the air like streamers, chilling me to the bone as I took in Laran's face.

"Wh-what's wrong?" My voice was scratchy. My throat dry. I felt like I'd swallowed sand and then tried to speak, and the craggy sound that came out was pitiful. *How long had I been asleep?*

"Three days. Almost four," Laran murmured. Black eyes so dark they reminded me of ashes from my flames looked at me with sadness. "What happened? Where have you been?"

There was no easy answer.

The body and mind were two different things. While I had taken a journey that felt closer to a millennium in my mind, my body had been lying in bed. I'd lived a thousand lives and died a thousand deaths in the span of days. I'd hunted demons and had been the hunted. I'd seen rape and torture and cruelty that could turn an iron stomach. All at the hands of Lilith.

I now knew Morvaen and every other Seelie that had crossed through Seth's Wisdom and come out alive. I knew them as well as I knew myself.

Where had I been? The question turned over in my mind.

"Everywhere," I answered. Knowing that wouldn't appease or makes sense, I sat up. Stretching my arms high over my head, I reveled in the series of pops as my stiff body came to life again. "I'm not able to disclose what you want to hear. I'm sorry," I added. "It's not my secret to share. I went looking for a way to beat Lilith."

He opened his mouth—paused—then asked, "Did you find it?"

Did I find it?

"I found..." I hesitated, a breath exhaling from my chest. My fingers fisted in the black satin sheets. The ornate tapestries that hung on the wall drew my attention as I struggled for the right words to say. "Answers."

"You're not going to tell me, are you?" He didn't sound upset, but I still felt the need to explain.

"No," I sighed. "Lilith has my power. She can get into anyone's mind. Now more than ever I need to hold the truth close." I unclenched my fingers from the slick fabric and slid my legs over the edge of the bed. The dark stone floor felt warm beneath my feet as I stood, still leaning back onto the bed while I faced him.

"I know. It's better this way," he said. His mouth moved to form a smile, but it fell short. The corners of his eyes were strained. I blinked, taking in the dark circles from lack of sleep and the sallowness of his skin. My heart clenched.

"Is everything alright?" The uneasy look in his eye said no, it wasn't alright. In fact, something was very wrong.

"You were...*asleep*...for a few days," he started slowly. My pulse quickened. It hammered unnaturally as he looked toward the ceiling and his hands clenched tight around nothing. "During that time, we got word Lilith is on her way."

Pounding turned into an all-out gallop, but I didn't move an inch.

I simply asked, "How long?"

He lowered his head, and in the early afternoon light I could see several days of growth on his beard. I didn't say anything as he looked me up and down. A pleading entered his eyes, and I knew what was coming.

"How long?" I asked again.

"Not long enough."

"How long?" I repeated, harsher.

"Damnit, Ruby." He clasped my jaw in his hands, holding me like I was the most precious thing in this world. And I knew I was. "I'm scared, alright? I trust you that whatever happened you truly believe you've found the way to end this, but I am scared. You've already given so much..." Desperation leaked out of him. I closed my eyes as he leaned his forehead against mine.

"It's okay to be scared," I whispered. "I'm scared too."

"I don't want to lose you. Not again."

"You won't." I opened my eyes and leaned back, ignoring the gut-wrenching pain as his hands dropped away from me. "Just as I won't leave this world to her. She has the beast, she has my mates, and she holds the people of Hell prisoner to satisfy her every whim. That is unacceptable."

"You've changed, baby," he whispered. I pressed my lips together to keep from flinching.

"My soul was ripped in half and I survived. Everything has a price, Laran. You know this," I said, fighting my own desperation to comfort him as I stood strong.

"I do, which is why I won't ask you to run. We've already lost too much. I just wish we had more time."

"How long?" I asked softly. He must have sensed this was the last time I would ask. My next move was to walk out the door and find out for myself. A darkness passed over the balcony, casting the room in shade.

He swallowed hard. "It's already begun."

CHAPTER TWENTY-FIVE

I RAN TO THE BALCONY, IGNORING THE LOOSE swaths of fabric as they twisted around my limbs, trapping me in their confines as I looked up. A mass loomed over us, a hundred times greater in size than the enormous palace I stood in, blocking the sun and blanketing Inferna in a bleak shadow.

"What is that?" I breathed.

"The Brimstone City," he answered gravely. "It was once known as the province of Pride. Lilith's domain."

"It's *floating*. Why is it floating?" I asked, unable to stop the panic from coloring my tone.

"Lilith wanted a city that no one could enter without her knowing; a city that transcended the barriers of magic. She sacrificed one hundred of her children to create the spell that keeps the city airborne."

Horror washed through me. I clenched my teeth together as the world turned dark, seemingly bleached of color as the sun disappeared entirely. It was only the torches lit below us that kept the city visible in any way. In the span of minutes, Inferna had gone from a sprawling wonder to looking like a hellscape straight out of the Bible.

"People are warring in the streets." I wouldn't have believed it would happen that way if I hadn't seen it myself. The way two friends turned on each other mid-stride and began trading blows with torches. Parents turned on children. Brother on sister. Wife on husband. Inferna descended into chaos as the floating city sat directly overhead, crushing the atmosphere with its very presence.

"That's the power of Famine at work," Laran said behind me. "He toys with their emotions. Makes them feel what he wants them to feel."

"He can't be doing this by choice." There was no way. Allistair was many things...but not this.

"She took your bonds with them," Laran muttered. "There's no telling what she's truly done in the days they've been gone."

"No," I contradicted him. Frowning, I tapped my chin. "She took the magic of those bonds that held us together. She didn't take the feelings behind them. They chose to be my mates, which lends the question— how much awareness of this do they truly have?" I murmured.

"Her magic helped create us," he said. "It's hard to say." The wind howled through the valley and the biblical references weren't lost on me. I was about to walk through the valley of the shadow of death, but I wasn't praying to any god. I was prepared to finally be one.

"We'll get them back, Laran. I promise."

"Don't make promises here, Ruby." He let out a rough exhale, the knuckles of his fists turning white. "Just...be safe. Be careful. Don't overplay your hand. I have fought so many battles and won many a war. The loser doesn't always lose because they were not good enough, or strong enough. It's because they made a mistake." He shook his head slightly as he remembered things that I'd never lived through, but some of the Seelie had. "A single mistake could cost your life and I don't want to lose you. The first time you faced her, we both died. You barely survived, and haven't trained with the Sins but once. I don't know how you're going to pull this one off, baby, but..."

I stared at him—knowing the mighty Horseman I saw but only now truly seeing the man. Even demons, powerful as they might be, had weaknesses. I was his.

"Trust me," I whispered, taking his hands in mine. "Trust that I know what I am doing. Trust that I am strong enough. Trust that..." I grasped at the fire in his eyes. "Trust that I will not fail—that I can put this world back together again."

He brushed the hair away from my eyes, placing a kiss on my forehead. I leaned in, but I did not yield.

I wouldn't. Not now. Not ever. Not for anyone.

"I love you," he whispered.

"I know you do," I said with a sad smile. This was the only goodbye I would get with him, with any of them, if I fucked this up. "But I need more than your love this time. I need your complete trust to not try to stop me. No matter what."

He leaned away as I took his hands in mine. "Ruby, you are the only woman—demon or otherwise—that I will bow to ever again. I trust you and that you know what you're doing...even if I don't understand. I will stand by you until the day I die. I've done it once already and I will do it again. If that day is today, so be it."

We kissed and it was everything. It was fire and passion and desperation—that connection that all people sought. Human. Demon. Fae. Mortals and immortals alike spent entire lives looking for this thing between us. Some called it soulmates, but I refused to believe there was only one person in the world you're meant to be with. It's an awfully big universe, after all.

I found my match in four exceedingly possessive, sometimes devious, and always devoted mates. They couldn't be more different from each other if they were born centuries and worlds apart. They weren't perfect, but they were mine. I'd experienced the love that some people never found in all their searching, and I'd felt it four times greater.

With it had come this loss so crushing that I was left with nothing but scraps of a soul and wisps of power when they had been ripped from me. I'd loved so fiercely that when I lost them all, it was the most devastating experience in the universe. To have a love so consuming that it burned, and you burned with it. Bright. Fierce. True.

That was what we had. That was what *we all* had.

A love that changed the worlds.

A love that could and would overcome anything.

I sucked in a breath as a harsh wind whipped at my skin, rattling my bones. My teeth grit as I stormed back into the bedroom and readied myself—not for battle—but for war. We dressed silently, clothing ourselves in the fighting leathers of Hell before we stormed the palace halls. Our footsteps echoed in the empty silence as we made our way down to the throne room. My footing slipped on the bottom step of the quartz stairs and Laran steadied me with a single hand—not missing a beat.

I mumbled my thanks as we approached the onyx doors with a silver pentagram engraved on them. The wood panels hung ajar, the metal hinges melted or broken.

Backs to us—I saw them.

My Horsemen.

Pestilence stood to the right wearing armor made of

gold. His blonde hair appeared honeyed, his cheek bones strong and sharp. My Rysten had always seemed so carefree, but this man in metal was merely a phantom apparition of his previous radiance. I turned to Death, standing regal and glistening in the starkest of whites. He'd always been a stoic sort that straddled the edge of cruelty. Now, not even a hint of warmth resided inside him. Even with his back to me, I could sense the swirling abyss eating him alive. The darkness that swallowed all light.

I couldn't say that the last one I saw was the one that hit me the hardest, but it was a blow to my gut, nonetheless. Allistair did not carry the light that Rysten did. Nor did he harbor the demons of Death. Allistair was a man who wore a mask. A fiend that walked into your life and stole your heart before you even knew he was reaching for it. To see him dressed in onyx, painted a dark knight...I saw the duties that confined him. The rules that bound him. The lecherous chains of submission that buried the man I knew so deep underneath...I had no doubt he wasn't truly in control as he brought about anarchy.

They stood, soldiers of pain.

Bringers of destruction.

The apocalypse.

And I wondered...I wondered if it wasn't the flames I was meant to stop. If it wasn't the barriers between the worlds—I wondered for the first time...if it was *them*. If they, the Horsemen who brought me here under the guise of a savior, were the very apocalypse that I was destined to be the savior of—or to fall myself and bring both the worlds with me.

A cackle pulled at my attention.

And I knew who stood there—the woman in white that stole them.

A crown of lilies adorned her head, their color tainted in comparison. Her dress, if it could truly be called that, was two panels of fabric hung over both shoulders and bound around the waist by a golden chain.

"I heard your rumors. That the girl lived..." her voice carried as she stared down the Sins—all of them but one. Sinumpa was absent, but she'd already betrayed me one too many times for me to think she'd stick around. I don't know what my mother was thinking, but she chose a coward. Both her and Jax were gone, but not the others. The Sins and Moira were armed and ready to defend without even knowing if I would make it in time. Bandit stood tall on her shoulder, teeth bared and eyes blazing. Pride swelled within me. "How pathetic."

"Pathetic?" Hela asked, her voice carried as well, fueled by an errant wind. Her flaming hair lifted as lightning's wrath filled her gaze. "You killed the very man you claimed to love after killing the mother of his child. You've sought vengeance for a throne that was never yours. You've tried to steal the power of the primordial, and committed war crimes against our people and yours—all in the name of a throne that doesn't belong to you." Power radiated in every word as that rage she was known for came to life. She stood like a beacon light against the darkness. "Your end is now, Lilith. Lucifer is gone, and we will not allow this madness to reign in our domain any longer."

"My, my," Lilith mocked. "You have grown rather big for your britches, Hela. Tell me, is there any bite behind that bark." She flicked her fingers and the flames leapt at *her* command. My flames. That rage I'd kept so close to my heart came bubbling up as they incinerated Hela's clothing. It seemed she had been smart enough to consume brimstone before this fight.

"Is that the best you've got?" Hela taunted, throwing her hand in the air. Thunder roared as a bolt of lightning came down on her. The hairs on my arms rose when she pointed to Lilith and the electricity at her fingertips struck her with enough force it rattled the building. I held my breath as she stilled, neither falling nor retaliating.

"You should know by now that these childish abilities you have won't work on me," Lilith spat. The sweetness of her tone had dried up. "You were merely a *flaw* created by Genesis. I am of her blood. Her very *soul*," she said, her tone dripping with disdain.

Hela's fingers balled into fists, and while she'd never show it, there was very real fear there. It was palpable.

Lilith lifted her hands as if in a gesture to say, *my*

turn. Demons did not play fair, though. The moment she moved, both Moira and Ahnika stepped forward and let out a scream.

As a child, she was strong enough to shatter an eardrum. As a transitioned banshee-legion, Moira held the power to bring down buildings. That was by herself.

When the Sin of Sloth let loose her own scream, they had the strength to cause an earthquake.

The ground began to rumble as the earth protested against the mighty power being thrown at it. Lilith clapped her hands over her ears as all three Horsemen before us fell to their knees under the strain.

Lamia stepped forward and the veins around her eyes turned black as she extended her hands toward the fallen woman and whispered a word I didn't have a prayer of hearing, if not for her thoughts.

"Bleed."

At her command, Lilith's skin split. The arteries of her neck exploded, raining blood upon the dark navy floors. Her legs collapsed, her white dress stained red as her blood seeped into the fabric. Lying in a pool of her own blood, the earth split and opened its gaping mouth.

Her body tumbled into the chasm.

Lost to the darkness within.

The screams died away, drowned by a sea of silence and apprehension.

No one rejoiced or applauded. I did not dare to even speak as the gaping mouth closed shut.

Because deep down—knowing what I did now—I knew that even I could survive that.

Which meant Lilith could as well.

The moments spanned in time, but the Horsemen never rose. Behind me, Laran had grabbed a handful of my shirt to steady me as something thick and pungent began to clog the air.

Dark magic. Blood magic. Only it wasn't Sinumpa or me using it.

The ground shook as a great power built beneath it. Chunks of stone the size of baseballs rattled. Poison burned at my nostrils.

No one had even a moment to dive for cover. One second the ground quaked as a whining sound resonated deep inside. The next, it didn't just split. Oh, no. The stone itself fractured and caved in.

A figure cloaked in red and black rose, floating upwards as if suspended in water. The lilies in her hair were crushed into nothing more than bloody petals and broken stems.

"Did you really think that would work?" she asked them. I heard it in her voice in that moment. She meant death; if left to her own devices, she would destroy the very world she wished to rule if it meant obliterating the Sins.

Her hands raised and a phantom darkness wrapped around her. It took only a second to realize what was happening. I'd never been on the outside when I used that particular ability.

I never saw the way one's own soul poised to strike.

She intended to rip every soul in that room from its body.

But she hadn't planned on one thing.

Me.

My fingers twirled as the depraved soul of a mad woman sought its victims. If you blinked, you would miss it. The glow of a rune so bright and blue it hurt to look at. My rune. My power. My protection.

A barrier snapped into place around her, trapping that hideous soul within. I squinted, searching the blackness for even a spec of blue, but there was none.

Lilith looked every which way, spinning around.

The Sins faces were set in shock. Moira's in a smirk, despite the odds as she knew them.

But Lilith's—her lips were set in a grim smile.

"Well, well, well," she purred. "The bitch wasn't lying after all. Little Morningstar came to play."

There was a time when her taunting set fear in my heart, but when I smiled over the head of my enslaved mates, it was all teeth and no fear.

She thought she was the biggest, baddest bitch on the playground.

But I was the Devil now, and you don't steal from the Devil without paying your pound of flesh.

CHAPTER TWENTY-SIX

Rage was a dangerous thing.

It was all consuming as fire itself. It was as vast and expansive as the sea. It settled deep within, festering and rotting if you let it. But more than anything, the reason rage was so powerful was because you couldn't simply choose to lift it.

It came and went as it willed. Sitting on your chest like a demon in the night until it decided to leave you and afflict another.

I could not change it. I could not calm it. I could simply live with it, and in that I found power among the powerless.

Most people stricken lost themselves in the grips of passion, but I honed mine into a strength of its own.

My rage guided me. It fueled me so that I had no reservation when the end came.

She'd stripped me of everything, and for that she was going to lose it all.

"I must say, you look better than when I left you," she noted. Her eyes carefully straying towards my chest. My brand. "Tell me," she murmured. "How'd you do it?"

I smiled even though I wanted to rip her limb from limb. Her clawed hands formed fists. It bothered her that I'd survived. She was unsure of herself now. Unsure of her power. Unsure of mine. I reveled in it.

"Well," I started. My boots thudded against the floor as I slowly started for her. "It was really a number of things. As it was, my body was slowly trying to stitch itself back together, but with so little blood I would have died and stayed dead, were it not for Sinumpa."

Her eyes flashed with a fury, and if for some reason I did not succeed, I had no doubt that she would hunt down her daughter to the ends of this world or the next. I pitied her, Sinumpa, in that moment. She was a cursed child who grew into an imprisoned woman.

"Sinumpa?" she said, attempting and failing to hide her surprise. I flashed a Cheshire grin that only served to piss her off more.

"Oh, yes," I nodded. "You see, while you've been planning my destruction, she was planning yours. Her actions are what set all of this into motion, after all." I waved a hand at the palace around us. "She found me when I was a baby, made a deal with my mother, then convinced you she became the Sin of Lust because she "took" it. You were so desperate to believe that someone truly wanted to see you on the throne that you didn't see her for the double agent she has always been. Not that I blame you there," I added. "I'm an empath and I didn't see her for what she was until that moment in the Garden. She led me to be slaughtered only to bring me back with a blood oath."

Rage. It was a dangerous thing. Lilith loved to toy, but if there was one thing I realized in all those Seelie memories I'd lived through, it's that she was a slave to her own emotions and too prideful to see. It was going to make for the sweetest of endings.

"So, you lived." Her eyes slid to Laran. "And you somehow managed to save the spare. You're insistent. I'll give you that." Between us, the three Horsemen rose and closed ranks around her.

"They can't save you," I said. Her expression froze.

"You may have lived but you have no power. The beast lies within *them*," she growled.

"The beast wasn't the holder of my true power," I replied steadily. Her pupils thinned to slits, making the gold of her eyes that much brighter.

"You're lying!"

"No," I smirked. "But you wish I was."

My taunting pushed her over the edge. Flames raced to greet me and I greeted them as my own. They licked at my skin and burned away my clothes until I stood nude for all to see.

"Impossible," she whispered as I cut the flames out

with a snap of my fingers. She stared at the brand on my chest. Over the hardened scar tissue, blue vines curled protectively in the form of a pentagram.

"Clearly not if I'm standing before you," I said, reveling in the way her pale cheeks darkened to a pink. "You see, for all the great time you've spent plotting my death and your eventual rise—you never took the time to properly realize what I am." I gazed at the apathetic faces of Pestilence, Death, and Famine. On the outside, they appeared so empty, but inside they were drowning in such darkness. Such pain.

"What...you...*are*?" She let out a cackle that would give Moira a run for her money. "You're *nothing*. No one. You think because you survived me once that you will again?" she smirked, but I sensed her growing unease just as she could feel my calm.

The blackened soul in her chest roused a second time, aiming for me. I thought it so very telling that while she might look like a saint, inside she was a monster of the worst kind. An animal bound to its instincts. A madman with no control.

Lilith moved to strike, and this time I didn't block her. I met her head on.

Our phantom forms met in a collision of great power, but try as both might, there was no harming one another. She could not hurt me, just as I could not hurt her. It was an impasse.

"You see, Lilith—the thing is—you stole my magic without understanding what it could really do. I don't

314

blame you. I myself didn't truly understand until now." I shrugged with a faked nonchalance. Our souls continued to twist and twine, but there was not a thing she could do. "In stealing it, though, you put us on a level playing field. You can't hurt me, because all you have to throw at me—is me. You understand?" She gnashed her teeth as her soul continually attacked but made no ground. "We are so evenly matched that I knew I couldn't defeat you like this. It would never work, and given enough time, you'd probably outsmart me because you're far older and more experienced. I never had a hope if that's how I planned to beat you."

She switched tactics, using her nails to slit her own wrists. Fresh blood slicked her fingers as she began to chant.

Still I smiled. Desperation was eating at her.

"That worked on me once," I nodded, gesturing to the magic gathering around us. Without an outlet, it would inevitably fizzle out. "The only problem is that you've already used that trick. You stole the beast and ripped my soul in half. It was the most painful experience in all of my life. It will probably be the worst thing I endure until the end of times." As I predicted, the magic flared and like a firework on display, it burned out.

"How are you doing that?" she snapped. The angelic mask she so loved to wear fell away as the cold-hearted murderer beneath finally looked out and realized that something was very wrong.

Or very right, depending on your perspective.

"I've already told you"—I paused to wag my finger —"I'm not a demon. Just as you are still only a blood Fae."

"That's preposterous—"

"Is it?" I purred. She was seeing red, but her bag of tricks was running empty. "I think you're only just realizing that I'm telling you the truth. I am the same as I've always been. A primordial of magic." I waited, letting that sink in, continuing only when she opened her mouth to speak. "And by using your blood magic to kill me, I also hold that power now too. Which would make us truly equal, if not for one *little* thing." Her features had gone stark white. Her pulse was through the roof and anxiety was clawing its way up her throat. She was well and truly scared.

She was right to be.

"You killed my mate, and to bring him back I accidentally called on a favor from the Seelie. Do you know what happened then? Do you know what she did?" Her lips moved, but no sound came out. Her mind was working a million miles an hour to keep up. "She tied my body to his using rune magic. Directly on my skin." I turned a fraction for her to see the runes and she began shaking. "Yes, you're a clever girl, aren't you?" I mocked coldly. "Figured out that I now have the one and only thing that can beat you?"

"You won't do it," she said, barely attempting to taunt me, though it fell short on her breathless lips.

"Oh?" I asked. "And why is that?"

"Because I tied the Horsemen's lives to mine. If anything kills me, they'll die too." She was so smug that it infuriated me.

"You think that only just occurred to me?" I asked her. She blinked, not saying a word. "I'm not the fool you take me for. You're selfish. Rotten. As much as you think yourself above all others, you build in safety precautions, just in case," I said. "But this time they won't save you."

The Sins took in a collective gasp. No one had seen it coming. That was the beauty of it. The unpredictability.

"You wouldn't do anything that would kill your mates."

"Who said anything about killing them?" Both my eyebrows rose as she tried to control her expression and manage the emotions riding her. She was as much a slave to herself as Josh had been, and in the end, what goes around comes around.

"You look confused, so I'm going to spell it out for you," I told her. "Rune magic is so very special. It's both the one magic that can stop you and the one magic you don't possess. I can deflect you. I can cage you. I can do a great number of things around you—even to you—but you won't pick up the magic that way." I lifted my hand and began to draw. A blue luminescence followed my finger. It was the essence of my soul, and I painted the symbol of an upside-down lotus with it. "When they grant a rune of protection for a favor owed, it is the receiver's magic that is used when it is time to call upon it. I learned this in New Orleans after the tangle I had with La Dan Bia. I saved a Seelie woman's life and she granted me a favor. When I called upon it, it was my magic that pulled her into Hell. Hers wasn't strong enough to get in or out." Next, I drew a skull shrouded in shadow. She still hadn't figured it out yet. "I made a deal with that same woman. She gave me Seth's Wisdom. Do you know what that is?" The last symbol was a modified biohazard sign. She recognized them, but she still hadn't figured out what I was doing with them. No one did.

"It allows me to relive every Seelie ancestor's life that has ever cast it. In the span of four days I lived through thousands of years, and for what you have done to the Seelie alone you deserve to pay, but I don't have the patience to extend this out much longer," I said. Then I began drawing one last symbol. This one was important because it wasn't Seth's Wisdom that gave me this idea.

It was Sinumpa.

At a certain point I had to wonder if she knew what this would bring about—if she knew that is was this rune that changed everything.

I poured everything I had into that rune. Every hope. Every fear. Every bit of me that I could. I gave it my all, and when my fingers lifted, the three Horsemen dropped.

It all happened so quickly after that.

"What have you done?" Lilith screeched. It pained me to do it to them, but that pain would be temporary. I appeased myself with that knowledge as a slow realization dawned on her.

"The very first life I lived was Eve's, your sister." I paused. The power to silence three of the Horsemen was immense and keeping it up this long wasn't easy, but I needed to get this out. Not just for me. But for Eve too. "I saw what you told her. I lived the horror through her eyes when you said you were going to take the beast from Lucifer, and I lived every gory detail thereafter. I know exactly how you planned to use the Sins, but they were too strong, and you were too weak. You improvised with Lucifer originally, and because of it you learned you couldn't hold the power of the primordial yourself. You needed someone to hold it for you. To bear the brunt of the darkness." The rune of silence became downright crushing, but I was reaching the end of this sorry tale. "Eve was a kind girl, a bit of a pushover with you, but even she wasn't willing to let Lucifer die for your delusions. She threatened to tell him, and you had her framed for opening the portal *you* used to talk to God. She was cast out of Hell and went mad, but not before she gave her memories to Seth—and his children gave them to me."

This was it. The end. The moment that I didn't just kill her.

Oh, no. I did something worse.

"I've silenced the Horsemen, which I'm sure by now you've realized also cuts off your connection to the beast. Which means you can no longer protect yourself with my magic. I'd ask if you had any last words, but I don't care even if you did."

I let go. She screamed. Oh, she screamed.

I listened to every single note as I tore her soul straight from her chest and consumed it whole.

And after thousands of years, Lilith's reign in Hell finally ended.

CHAPTER TWENTY-SEVEN

SHE SPENT SO LONG TERRORIZING THE WORLD THAT when it ended there was only silence. It dripped from the ceiling and spanned the length between her body and me.

Lilith was not dead. She was gone.

Her soul didn't go beyond the veil because there was not a soul to be had. She was destroyed indefinitely, but her body remained, because her body is what kept them alive.

Without a soul, the body itself would wither and die rapidly.

It would, if not for one thing.

The beast.

Her soul was never taken into Lilith. She couldn't have held the beast if she tried. Now she was an empty vessel still tied to the Horsemen. I didn't have to lift a finger to prompt it—I simply had to lift the silence.

And as the runes I'd drawn began fading into the distance, the heavy smothering of that power dwindled too. I eased my grips on the last of it, sucking in a heavy breath as my knees shook and collapsed. The shuddering crack that ran through me echoed in the empty hall.

Then she spoke.

"Ruby?" a neutral voice said. It no longer sounded anything like the voice of the monster it belonged to before.

"Hello, Beast," I replied softly with a true smile. Free of the rage and pain and destruction. "This must be very strange for you."

"She took me," the beast said. There was confusion in her voice. "I lost my light. I lost *you.*"

My throat closed up and I began to crawl. No one moved an inch as I pushed against the straining exhaustion in me and dragged myself to her.

Curled inward, she tilted her chin to look up at me. It was Lilith's face—undeniably—but it was not her eyes that stared out. It was not her soul that now dwelled there.

It was not her body anymore.

It was the beast's.

"I'm so sorry I wasn't strong enough the first time," I told her. Those pale lips pinched together. Displeasure. I knew her emotions as well as my own.

"Do not apologize for wrongs that you did not commit," she told me. That brought a faint grin to my lips. "You have freed *us* of her black magic. You did what no other before you could. Do not apologize, for you are a true Queen worthy of me."

I nodded slowly, a single piece of me healing with her words. I wrapped my arms tight around the shoulders of my other half, and the tears began to flow. She did not cry. She was not capable of such emotion, and I understood that. Slim pale arms wrapped around me in return, though, clutching me to her just as I held her to me.

There were other arms then. Other hands. Other bodies.

I smelled seduction and sin as whiskery lips placed a short kiss to my lips, promising of so much more. Allistair tasted of scotch and honey and my own salty tears. I cried even harder as a fair head leaned down over my shoulder, Rysten's sunshine hair tickling my face as it stuck to my wet skin. Laran's warm hands grasped my waist, holding me as close as he could while huddled on the floor with me at an awkward angle—and then there was Julian. My white knight. He kneeled behind the beast and reached past her to grab my chin, tilting my head. We worked in perfect sync as I parted my lips, kissing him with abandon. A wild war cry sounded as Bandit ran at full speed, leaping to land right in the thick of things with a clash of fur and nails. The beast let out a huff but didn't make a move to stop him from clawing his way between us and settling on our chests with a purr of contentment.

A mighty groan from far above us had me pausing. I looked from each of the Horsemen, to the beast, to the ceiling—where a series of booms blasted from the rafters like thunder.

"What is going on?" I asked, my weak legs protesting as I attempted to stand. Julian reached down and plucked me from the ground, clasping one arm around my back and one under my knees.

"It's the Brimstone City," Moira said. The ceiling cracked and pieces began dropping. "It's falling."

"Devil-damned bitch," I cursed. I couldn't have one fucking moment of peace, could I? "She put in a fail-safe, didn't she?"

It was the beast that nodded once and said, "If you killed her body, you would have killed the Horsemen. She didn't think she would die, but she planned for it. The Brimstone City is indeed falling."

"Can you stop it?" I asked her.

"Can you?" she replied.

Shit. No. No, I couldn't. My powers had been completely exhausted. I was unable to stand on my own two feet. There was no way I'd be able to hold a falling city.

"What options do we have?" I asked, looking between the Sins. Their faces were grave.

"There is no time to evacuate all of Inferna," Lamia said. "It is simply too large." Abandoning the hundreds of thousands of people that lived here wasn't an option to me. There had to be another way.

"Could you blast the city apart?" I asked Moira. Her eyes widened.

"Are you crazy?" she demanded.

"Sometimes," I answered. "Can you?"

"No!" She looked at the ceiling as if judging the possibilities. "If I managed to somehow break it apart, we all would be crushed beneath the rubble, as would the rest of Inferna."

My head landed against Julian's chest as I scrambled and searched my brain for something—anything inside all of Seth's Wisdom. But the problem was that this was blood magic; a blood spell. Something I didn't know how to use yet.

"There's got to be something we can—"

A crackle of light. A flair of color. An ember guided by a phantom hand.

An ancient rune to open a portal between worlds appeared in violet.

Sinumpa.

She hadn't abandoned us after all. My heart pounded and my palms grew slick. The incandescent rune exploded in a bang, tearing a hole between the realms. I put a hand over my eyes to shield them against the blinding light.

A pair of boots clicked. I parted my fingers, glimpsing between them.

Backlit by the shimmering glow, Sinumpa came striding in. She took one look and flashed a Cheshire grin. "It seems I've arrived just in time."

"You came back..." Moira murmured. Stunned. "Can you stop the Brimstone City from falling?"

"No," Sinumpa said. She hooked her thumb over her shoulder, pointing to the portal behind her. "But they can."

Behind her, people started pouring out of the portal one by one.

Morvaen came first, followed by Donnach and many more. I didn't know what to say as the Seelie came into Hell, leaving the safety of Earth to come to a land that was going to be crushed in a matter of minutes. Dozens. Hundreds. They came, and when the portal finally closed...they kneeled as one. Every single man, woman, and child that crossed through dropped on all fours in front of me.

I squeezed Julian's bicep, our silent communication for him to let me down. I approached Morvaen on shaking feet. I got on my knees and touched her shoulder, concern leaking through my voice. "What have you done?"

"You and I made a deal...Ruby," she said, testing my name on her tongue. "I gave you Seth's Wisdom and you promised to let us come home."

"But the Brimstone City is falling," I told her. "You've doomed your people."

"We have not." It was not her who answered, but Donnach. He got to his feet and the hundreds of Seelie followed in his stead. "You and my sister were not the only ones with an agreement." He glanced at Sinumpa who stood to the side watching the ceiling crumble away.

"You made a deal with Morvaen to gain the ancient knowledge of the Seelie," the white-haired Fae said. "I struck a deal with Donnach. In return for my ceding the province of Lust, he would stop the falling city. We have to live here, after all."

"You...I...how...what the fuck, Sin?" I stammered, looking for words. "You didn't have any guarantees I would beat Lilith, but you bet on it all the same?"

I wasn't sure if I should be flattered. She'd already proven to be a gambler of fate. Who's to say she wasn't on her way to being as crazy as Lilith had gone.

I'd never seen her look so young or carefree; a lightness dancing in her eyes for the first time. Looking at her, you'd never guess a city was falling above us. "I knew you had it in you, but I couldn't tell you anything. So long as Lilith was alive, I was bound by so many blood oaths that would have not only taken my life, but the lives of all my siblings. I couldn't do that to them anymore than you could kill your Horsemen. We all made sacrifices, girl, and once we fix this you are going to do what you've said you would all along."

My lips parted as I breathed, "And what is that?"

Sinumpa stared. Measuring. Weighing my worth. Judging the girl I once was and the woman I had become.

"Make the world a better place, and if you have to, burn out the rot with your own hands."

I stared back and then I nodded. For all she had done, I didn't know if I could forgive her—it was still fresh and raw and much too soon. But that didn't mean that I didn't understand her. Why she had done it. Why she was willing to sacrifice so much for me to become the woman she knew I could be. I was a child born to not just flame, but magic. Shaped and molded by the Six Sins, honed to be a queen; in creating me, they lost the girl I was. She had kept much hidden from me, I sensed her regret in that—if only for a second.

Sinumpa was a proud woman that would not apologize.

I was aged by the things I had survived through, and I would not forgive. Not *yet*.

But we reached an understanding.

And for that, Hell would go on.

She lifted her hands and began to draw. They all did. Every single Seelie. They drew in shades of violet and crimson and navy and every color that existed. They wielded their magic with such unity that demons could never manage.

And as they put the floating city back in the sky, I realized that they had something all of demon kind could learn from.

A unity born not only of loyalty and purpose, but of strength.

The strength to survive.

JULIAN

She'd changed. I could see it in her eyes. As she paced before the bed, I noticed a grace in her movements that hadn't been there before. There was a worry that troubled her despite winning the war. A weariness that only age and time could give you.

My woman was not the twenty-three years her body was anymore.

She had become something far older in a span of days—doing the unthinkable to save us.

I didn't have words to convey how freedom tasted after being reduced to a prisoner in my own mind. I was simply content to watch her and to know that no matter what happened from here, no matter how much damage had been done...we would find our way through it.

Together.

"Killing her was too kind for what she did to you," she spat. It wasn't just fire in her anymore. If you watched closely you could see the shadow too. The darkness that had settled next to the flame. That wasn't going away anytime soon.

"You made her pay..." Allistair murmured softly.

"It wasn't enough," she whispered. "It wasn't—"

"Stop," the beast ordered. Ruby looked over to where she sat upon a chaise in the Queen's Suite. The dresses Lilith loved had been replaced by leather trousers and long shirts. She wore fur-lined boots to go with the discarded jacket on the floor. The white hair of the woman I'd hated had been shaved from her head, leaving her bald.

The beast was more content for it.

She didn't like being without Ruby, but if she had to reside in this body for now, she planned to make it her own.

Ruby stared at her and something silent passed between the two. The beast's flat expression softened for a moment. "You saved us," she said to Ruby. "You ended what so many before you could not. Do not dwell on what you could have done. Focus on what you will do now."

"I will never forgive myself for the things she did to them," Ruby said softly. Tears stained her cheeks as she cried utterly silent. These were not the racking sobs of loss, but the cold feeling of shame and regret.

"You did not do those things to them," the beast growled.

"But they happened," Ruby snapped. "They happened and I wish they hadn't. I wish I could have done something sooner. I wish..."

I rose from the corner of the bed and pulled her to me. "Listen to me." I leaned forward and brushed a lock of her hair away from her face as she leaned into me, resting her cheek on my chest. "The beast is right. What was done, was done. You cannot change it. You could not prevent it. You gave everything you could, Ruby..." I swallowed, searching for the words to help her. To help us. "And in the end, you saved us all. You made sure that she can never hurt anyone again. That gives us closure." It was the truth, every word. "You did that."

She looked up at me, her cheeks colored a light blue from the flush of tears.

"Will it ever stop?" she asked me. "The rage. The despair. This feeling of powerlessness. Will they ever go away?"

I opened my mouth, but I didn't know what to say. I didn't know what to tell her. She couldn't just get over it. That wasn't an option. She'd lived through too much. Seen too much for that to ever be possible.

So, I gave her the only thing I could, even knowing it might hurt her.

"No, my girl, I don't think they will." The look in her eyes...it was crushing. Truly soul-crushing. "But with time, it will lessen. They say that time heals all wounds and that's not quite true. It softens the intensity of them. Until it's only a memory of the pain, but as you've learned, memories can still be quite painful." She nodded and I knew she was thinking of the Seelie then. Of the thousands of lives she'd lived. "It will get better, though. For all of us."

Both Rysten and Allistair nodded. Laran was battling a different sort of turmoil. Much like Ruby, he blamed himself because he was spared from Lilith's touch. He was not the type to grieve as Ruby did, but he had his own way. We all did.

"Do you promise?" she asked, her voice thin from exhaustion.

"I promise."

And I meant it. It would get better, for all of us.

Her eyelids fluttered as the day started to take its toll. Allistair stepped in front of us and held out his arms. *"May I?"* he asked silently. I picked her up and handed her over to him.

He held her with a reverence, whispering words meant only for her ears as he carried her to bed. As he placed her in the center and moved the blankets to cover her, her hand snapped out, grabbing his wrist faster than the blink of an eye.

"Stay," she pleaded. "I don't want to be alone right now."

We looked at each other and I knew it then. After

this there would be no separating again. Not for safety, or protection, or worry over her life.

Simply because we needed her, and she needed us.

To heal and to live—truly live.

And in my mind I whispered to them all, even the beast. *"You will never be alone again."*

MOIRA

"You're leaving again, aren't you?" I asked into the darkness. Below me, Inferna was celebrating with a party that took over the streets and raged into the early morning hours. But above—on the rooftop where I stood—there was only me, my thoughts, and *her*.

"I've done what I set out to do," Sinumpa replied. "The Brimstone City will not fall again. Hell is free. There is nothing more for me here."

"You know," I said, turning away from the railing, "you kept that whole bit about the city falling to yourself when you left the first time." Her eyes were shadowed, but a weary smile sat on her lips.

"Another oath," she answered vaguely. I nodded.

"And telling Ruby that your siblings were the reason you left?" I asked her, more curious than anything.

A single sigh. It said everything she didn't.

"They were part of it," she settled on. "Not all, but part. Ruby didn't need to know what my being there would have cost her. She's angry—rightfully so—and I don't need her approval to move on."

"Another gift?" I turned my cheek a fraction, grinning at her. A cool breeze whistled around us. This high up it was a world away from the festivities below.

"Maybe," Sin conceded. "She doesn't blame me. Not truly. But having somewhere to aim it now that Lilith is gone...it will help."

I nodded because she wasn't wrong. "Thank you." Her right eyebrow twitched and I elaborated. "Thank you for all that you did. For her...and for me."

Sinumpa stood there and it was like she saw the sun for the first time in a very long time.

"You're welcome...Moira," she spoke softly. Intimately. I liked the sound of my name on her lips.

"Enjoy your freedom, Sinumpa," I told her. It was a goodbye, but not forever. Something told me our paths would cross again. One day.

She turned and then paused. Over her shoulder, she said, "Until we meet again."

No, not forever. Just for now.

I stayed on those rafters until the break of dawn. A thunderous applause broke out over Inferna at the start of a new day, and I knew it was time.

Time to finally answer that voice that had been speaking to me.

Time to answer the Cerberus's call.

CHAPTER TWENTY-EIGHT

THOSE EARLY DAYS OF SETTLING WERE NOT EASY. Many long and hard meetings had to be held about the fate of Hell, the Seelie, the Brimstone City—and where I fit into all of this. Tempers were short and nights were long. I savored every moment of it because you never knew when the end would come. We were immortal, but not infallible. Lilith had proven that.

The Sins themselves were as divided in opinions as the divisive lines that were drawn between their provinces. Sinumpa had stepped down and vanished into the night, leaving Lust without a representative. Donnach filled that space upon my own suggestion and tensions were smoother for it. He appreciated my willingness to give them their own seat of power and it went a long way in easing the Fae's worries. The Seelie were given one of the most ravaged parts of this world, and because of that I was going with them when they journeyed there to help with the restoration. I wanted to truly see my mother's land and make this as painless a transition as I could.

My Horsemen were coming with me, but Moira was not. As much as it hurt us to part from one another, she felt a call to go to the Brimstone City and oversee that rehabilitation as an ambassador on my behalf. Without a true successor to that province, the Sins and I saw it best to hand over the task to the only person who was up for the job. Lilith had kept her children and people as slaves. The physical damage to the city during the falling was sparse compared to the damage to their minds. As a survivor of abuse, like called to like. It didn't hurt that the Library of Pride had the most in-depth knowledge on legions in all of Hell.

It saddened me, but she had a familiar of her own now who would keep her more than safe. I smiled over at the Cerberus who stood smartly beside my best friend. They'd tied a blue bow around its neck to make it look less frightening for the ceremony. Not that it lasted long. Bandit had taken a liking to the three-headed female Moira named Fate.

The dog was scared of its own shadow, but if she thought you were trying to harm Moira...familiars don't fuck around.

Yeah, Moira would be in good hands.

I smoothed my dress nervously, running my hands over the feathery soft fabric. After all I'd been through,

I refused to wear white this day. It was no longer the color of purity in my mind, and there was nothing pure about me anyway. Instead, I'd opted for a deep blue floor-length gown, the same color as the jewel-toned sky and sea.

My feet were bare as I padded down the long aisle. All around me the demons and Fae of Inferna looked on with respect and happiness. I felt their joy, and while it was fucking nerve-racking to take this last step, they gave me my strength. I stared straight ahead. On the left side of the aisle stood Laran, Allistair, Julian, and Rysten. None of them had truly recovered from these last months of being hunted. We were still seeing shadows when there were none, but after all that had happened, it would take time to get better. The pressure of the beast had changed each of them inextricably those last days.

Julian was gentler. Rysten was rugged. Allistair was…struggling. We all were, but he—more so than the others—was struggling with what had happened to them during their time with Lilith. Struggling with having his choices taken from him. Struggling with what he was as a demon and what he thought I needed him to be as a man. He lost himself in me every night, trying to forget what was done, but there was no forgetting…

Immortality was a blessing and a curse. We would never forget what brought us here, but we would cherish every moment we had. Every image. Every touch. Every sound. Every feeling. We cherished them more.

"Ruby?" Moira asked, drawing my attention. I'd stopped in the center of the aisle. Taking a deep breath, I continued to walk the rest of the way, turning my head and my thoughts to the Sins.

While there was still much to be done—and it would not come easy—the one thing they'd all agreed on was my right to become Queen. I'd earned it, or so they said. It was a bittersweet day for me; I would ascend, but the beast would not be with me. Much as we tried to find a way to free her from Lilith's body, we still hadn't discovered a way to free the Horsemen if we did. Neither the beast nor I were willing to risk their lives on anything short of a guarantee, no matter how much it pained both of us to be apart.

She stood at the top of the stairs, watching me. A secret smile twisting her lips that the rest of the world would mistake for a grimace. Not me. For a jealous being by nature, she held no qualms with this arrangement. In her mind we would find a way to reunite us, eventually. It was an oddly optimistic view, truth be told. Not that I told her that.

"Focus, Ruby. This day is important," she chastised in my mind.

I pressed my lips together to hide my own smile as I started up the stairs. At the top of the dais stood the Sins. The women who had raised me.

Hela was the first to step forward. Her flaming red

gown was the same shade as her hair. Lightning struck high above us. The throne room still hadn't been fixed and most of the ceiling was missing. I didn't mind the open air one bit.

"A week ago, I watched the young woman before me triumph over our greatest fear. Today, she stands before us to receive the blessing of the Sins and become the next Queen. Ahnika, what say you?"

The Sin of Sloth stepped forward, her light green skin beautiful against the black floor-length number she wore. She came to stand before me and pass her judgement. "I was the last Sin to meet you, Ruby. The last to leave my mark. I have watched you grow from a petulant young girl to a true leader. You are many things, girl, but indolent isn't one of them."

I nodded my thanks to her and we hugged. This was a slight deviation to the ceremony I was supposed to have. Tradition said they would brand me, but me being what I was, I didn't want it. I already had enough power at my fingertips that I needed to master, and unlike my Seelie magic, nothing else came with an ancient rune that could teach me every aspect in a matter of days.

Ahnika stepped back and said, "Saraphine, what say you?"

I'd known this she-demon as an old woman named Martha in my time on Earth, but here in Hell she was known as the fiercest of the Sins. Her long blonde hair trailed in the breeze as she stepped forward. "You are the daughter I always wanted. Those years I got to watch you grow in the plastic seat of a dingy diner have been the greatest of my very long life, child. You are kind, but you don't let people walk all over you. You stand up for what is right, even when it is not easy. You've given up everything to become what we needed you to be. My girl, you are many wonderful things, and you hold no greed in your heart."

When I hugged her, it felt like home. Black coffee and bacon, the scent of fresh asphalt and baked apple pie. I clutched her slim shoulders tight as tears pricked the corners of my eyes. Saraphine was crying when she stepped away and said with a heavy voice, "Merula, what say you?"

Merula had been like a mother to me once upon a time. She was as strict as they come, but in her heart she truly loved children. I had always believed she truly loved me in her own way. "I was the first Sin to be allowed the privilege of raising you, and for ten years I did just that. I watched you grow from a babe to a scruffy-faced tomboy, into the beautiful woman you are today." She smiled and there was a sadness there. "Envy is not something we could easily test you on, but I watched you with Iona when you first came to Hell. I watched how she envied and pushed and took from you. But you never succumbed to the same jealousy I myself cannot always control, just as you never coveted what others had on Earth. You are many things, my child, but envious is not one of them."

I hugged her and I meant it, even though she'd sent Iona to me. While my heart was hardened and the darkness within had not abated, I'd found ways to not let it control me. To not let the ways I'd changed dictate my own happiness. Some days were better than others—but I was trying—and that's what mattered.

She stepped away and said, "Lamia, what say you?"

I'd known her as Sadie in my old life. She had been the house mother at the orphanage I spent most of my teen years in, and while she hadn't been nearly as hands-on as Merula or Hela, she'd let me grow from afar. I met her toe-to-toe. "I watched you experience many hardships while you were with me. Both of you," she said and glanced to Moira. "Neither of you believed you had any power, and you were content. You did not covet your neighbor. You did not take more than you needed of anything in life. Even here today, you reject the ceremony to take our brands because you do not want the power it would bring you. Ruby Morningstar, you are many things, but you are not a glutton."

I hugged Lamia knowing without a shadow of doubt that she saw more than she ever said back then. Our connection was brief before she was stepping away and said in a steady voice, "Hela, what say you?"

My blood fizzled with nerves as she stepped forward to stand in front of me. "Blue, I wish I could say that wrath was not a sin you are afflicted with, but it would be a lie." I inhaled sharply and half the room took a collective gasp before she smiled. "You have a fire inside you that burns. I saw it when you were younger, and over the past few months it has only grown. If you let it, this fire would consume you—and us." She paused, her index finger guided my chin upwards to look her straight in the eyes. "But, as you well know, it is not the great power itself that matters, but what you *do* with it. You've used that strength to become a woman that I myself wish I could be. Ruby, my friend, you have wrath, but you are not a slave to it."

I couldn't hold in the tears as they dotted the corner of my eyes. My heart had split apart in pain and been forged back together by fire, but never had I wept from happiness. I let her go and wiped my tears with the palm of my hand, turning to face the beast. She was the final decider.

Without being told, she stepped up and took the spot Hela had vacated. In her hands was a crown of glittering black metal with sapphire gemstones. She held it between us and I placed my hands over hers. "I made this crown for you myself, in the hope that I might one day wear it with you." There was a sadness in her voice that was unmistakable, but there was hope too. She was becoming more...human. I wondered if she realized it. "We will be united again. Our soul will heal, but in the meantime, you rise, and you will rule. There is no other as worthy as you." She lifted the crown and I took the cue to drop to my knees before her. The crown was heavy on my head, but not crushing. I no longer felt constricted or confined. I chose this.

"Rise, Ruby Morningstar, Queen of Hell," she declared.

I pushed back on the balls of my feet and turned to face the people—my people. Sinumpa's words came to mind as I looked out to them, and I knew deep down that I'd found what and who I was always meant to be. A queen that would serve first and rule second. A leader that would change this world.

"Long live the Queen!" the beast projected. Every voice in the room and the hallway beyond and the streets below heard her as a rallying cry rang out so loud that even Heaven might have heard it.

"Long live the Queen!"

In my heart of hearts, I knew then that this wasn't just the end of an age. It was the beginning. My beginning, and theirs.

Life was a gift and I had no intention of wasting it.

As I looked down at each of my Horsemen, I whispered those three little words in their minds. When I said them now, it was because I wanted to—because I meant it—because the best was yet to come.

** MOIRA **

Three months later...

I let out a yawn that ruffled the pages of the ancient text. I'd already read the damn thing three times, but whatever answers the Sins had claimed it held didn't seem to be there.

My hand slammed the book shut and I pushed back in my chair, standing to head for the door. I strode down the aisle and out of the library, the heavy doors closing behind me. The night air was cool, almost chilled. This high in the clouds it was always that way, though. I stuffed my hands in the pockets of my leather jacket and took a walk.

I wandered aimlessly for a bit, nodding to the blood Fae and demons that also inhabited this city with me. In my time here, I'd grown to have quite the name. I rather liked it, if I was being honest.

But the loneliness could be crushing at times.

I'd seen Ruby only just last week for spring equinox. We'd celebrated in Inferna but stayed in Lamia's mansion this time instead. Months had passed and the reconstruction was still underway at Hela's palace. Which was fine by us since Lamia did indeed host the best parties. Ruby and the Horsemen had come out in full glory, looking far better than when I'd last seen her. I knew she was happy. I felt it, even though phantom whispers of destruction still dwelled within her. The beast and those mates of hers balanced my best friend well, as did the bloody raccoon.

I scrubbed a hand over my face and let out a whistle into the wind.

The people of the floating city heard my call and moved as the giant three-headed dog barreled down the streets. Behind her, three little monsters squealed in delight.

They had three heads like my Fate, but their faces were fucking raccoons. It wasn't enough that he'd impregnated my damn dog. No, he'd given her three mutant trash pandas that never left me the fuck alone. Ruby thought they were so adorable with their little faces and blue fur.

Terrors. They were devil-damned terrors.

Fate came rolling up to me and planted a slobbering kiss on my face, her three brats nipping at her heels. I was looking forward to the day I could pass them onto Ruby. As it was, Fate still had to feed them, and they were doing wonders for the kids here. Lilith's youngest daughter was a three-year-old half-banshee who was fearful of most things—except three-headed dogs, apparently. Having the monster-babies around was helping her and some of the other kids. Enough so that I let Ruby talk me into keeping them a little longer...but at twelve weeks, these bad boys were going to her.

I grasped a handful of Fate's fur and swung myself onto her back. I could just fly if I felt like it, but this was more comfortable for both the Cerberus and me. Here on a floating city, thousands of feet above with nothing but wind, we took all the comfort in each other we could.

She let out a howl and took off down the steps, her spawn trailed behind us as we traveled half the city before Fate came to a stop. One her heads lolled, giving me the biggest puppy eyes. I groaned, pinching the bridge of my nose.

"Fine." I threw my hands up in the air. "You can come, but the ugly trash pandas gotta stay outside. Got it?" The middle head let out a whine and I groaned, looking to the night sky above me. I would pray, but given my best friend was the very deity these people prayed to, that wasn't going to do me much good. Her other familiar was the reason I had this problem to begin with. "Ugh, whatever. Just keep them quiet, will ya?" The third head nodded while she wagged her tail. I leaned in to scratch her between the shoulder blades, then turned to walk into the bar. The swinging shutters hit the walls with a wild bang. Fate and the three stooges came in behind me and went to curl up in the corner of the lounge.

Demon bars on Earth had been downright normal compared to the ones in Hell. They let literally anything in, because you never knew who or what was a familiar. Mine were regulars and well acquainted with the massive dog bed in the corner. A generous contribution from an "anonymous" donor, i.e. Ruby. She was worried I spent too much time alone and thought having dog beds put in wherever I frequented most was the best way to encourage me to get out.

I didn't have the heart to tell her that I had no desire to enter a relationship just yet. While it was lonely at times, I still hadn't left that place of fight or flight. I wasn't ready for anything serious right now. That's alright, though. I had Burt the bartender, and for tonight he would be enough.

"Evening, Moira. What'll it be?"

"The usual," I said, pushing the sound waves forward for my voice to carry. He smiled as I sat down at the counter and slid an oversized frosted mug of amber liquid to me. This shit was brewed from fermented white lotus and tasted like perfection. I inhaled deeply and took a long sip, exhaling on a happier note.

Sometimes it was good being me. A cold night in a pub with an open tab and Fae beer to drink was always one of those times.

My immortality had only just begun and I planned to enjoy every second of it.

EPILOGUE

"ALRIGHT, EVERYBODY," THE GREEN ONE SAID. "Tonight is the night we crown the King of Fools!" Then the other ones with opposable thumbs began grunting and stomping their feet.

"Pffft. And they say I'm the animal," Bandit huffed. He rolled his eyes, settling against Fate while the banshee went on. Not far, Ruby sat with their pups.

"Moira doesn't care for the babes," Fate said.

Bandit knew from his time with her that the green one was prickly. She would need to be persuaded. While Fate adored her familiar, Ruby was a far better bond mate. She enjoyed feeding him sardines and thought it was adorable when the little ones had flaming burps. Yes, she was a better bond mate.

"Have you tried having them groom her?" Even the green one shouldn't be able to resist that affection.

"She complains about 'spit'."

"What is spit?" he asked. She licked him behind the ear and he let out a purr.

"I'm not sure. It comes from licking."

Bandit narrowed his eyes at the green one. Ruby's four mates were standing on chairs, along with other demons. They were all covered in food.

"My person likes to be licked," Bandit said, recalling all the times her mates seemed to groom her. It was a bit excessive, though, even for him.

"Maybe she'd like it more if they were cleaning her all together," Fate mused. Bandit lifted an eyebrow and listened as Fate told him her idea. Bandit liked it. He liked it very much.

Rising up on all four paws, he stretched languidly before shrinking. He needed to blend in for this. Weaving through the crowd of drunken persons wasn't hard. Neither was finding a bucket of delicious vegetables. He was very tempted to eat some of them...maybe just a nibble.

Bandit snatched an orange off the top, stuffing it into his mouth before anyone noticed. A sly glance at Ruby said she was still preoccupied by the triplets. Good.

He grew a little in size, just enough to snatch the handle of the pail with his teeth and disappear before anyone saw him. Sneakily, Bandit dashed up the stairs to the second floor. His bucket clanked against the wooden steps, but no one paid any mind with all the cheering going on.

It only took him a moment to climb over the railing and heave the bucket onto the rafter right above the green one. Perfect. He clapped his paws together and let out a chitter. Taking great care, he grabbed a giant tomato that squished in his paws. Balancing right over her, he held the tomato out and dropped.

"What the—" she said. He grabbed an egg and tossed it.

"RUBY!" she roared. The rafters swayed a little with her annoyance. Bandit wasn't worried though. He dug through the fruits and veggies to find the litters' favorite.

Kiwi.

He threw the little green fruits off the rafters, cackling as they pelted the fuming demon. The babes followed the scent of food and left Ruby to chase the green one. They quickly caught up, despite her running, and pounced. Licking at all the delicious fruit splattered on her.

"What in the world..." Ruby frowned, looking up to where the food had come from. She spotted him and Bandit backed away slowly, hoping she wouldn't notice... "Bandit! Get down here," she called.

Welp. Fate's rumbly laugh hit his ears as he quickly scaled down the rafters and bolted through the crowd, outside and onto the street beyond. Fate came after him, followed by the triplets, and they ran through the alleys under the pale moonlit in a land that was finally at peace.

"Moira's not happy with you," Fate told him as one of the young ones hopped on her back, grabbing at the first head's ears.

Bandit let out a raucous laugh that lit the sky with blue flame while the green one's cries about *that devil-damned trash panda* followed him.

It seemed that the more things changed, the more they stayed the same.

At least where Bandit was concerned.

He was but a simple raccoon, after all. One that now had an eternity of trouble to look forward to—and with Rysten and Moira to terrorize for many years to come...

Bandit grinned into the dark shadows of the night, ready for wherever life might take him, so long as he had Ruby.

And sardines. He couldn't forget those.

The End.

—This is the end of Ruby's story. If you loved this series and want to check out more from me, join my reader's group Kel's Krew for all the latest book news, or flip the page to check out my newest series.—

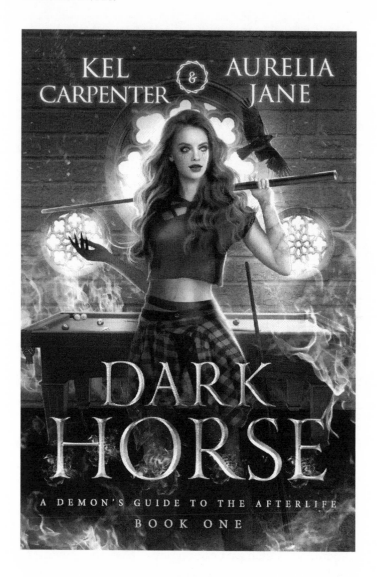

My husband killed me.

Instead of spending my immortal Afterlife pissed off and angry, I moved on. I became someone.
Sure, that someone was a demon with the highest track record of reform, AKA punishment, in Hell. But who's bragging?

I'm right on my way to retirement behind the pearly gates. Everything was going fine . . . until the Risk Witches saw a terrible vision.

Three men. Each scarred in their own way, born with powers that haven't been seen in eons.
Upper Management sent the best to correct their path. Angels. Poltergeists. Nothing worked.

These men were too stubborn. Too bad. Too untamed...

So they sent me.

Roman. Ezra. Dorian.
Combined, they have enough power to end the world—and they will.
Unless I find a way to stop them first.

Breaking people is my job. But this time...my job might break me.

—Get the Book Now!!!—

"Dinner time, Huck," I called out, tapping my fingers next to the bowl.

A forty-year-old-man came around the corner on all fours. His naked skin hung flaccid, and his knees stuck to the crappy linoleum floor. The tags on the dog collar around his neck tinkled.

Hate-filled, shit-brown eyes stared up at me. I grinned.

"You call that dinner—" he started.

I grabbed his face by the jaw and squeezed tight. "No talking back. Bad dog."

Indecision warred on his face. He wanted to hit me. Kill me, if he could. But he was thinking back to the last time he had made those attempts. It didn't end well.

For him, at least.

A moment passed, and he lowered his eyes. I

dropped my hand away and patted his head mockingly. "Good mutt," I said without any of the positive inflection I'd use on a real dog.

I left Huck McKinley to his dinner of dog food covered in hot sauce, not feeling the least bit bad. Some would say I was more than a little fucked up. Cruel.

They were right, of course.

But I was a demon by trade. It was sort of in the job description.

A hundred years ago, I died. More accurately, I was murdered—by my ex-husband, to be exact. He was a piece of shit too, but that was a whole other can of worms I didn't often like to open.

The point was I died and came to the Afterlife.

Because I wasn't in the bottom forty percent of humans that had to serve punishments for their transgressions on Earth, and I wasn't in the top one percent that automatically went through the proverbial pearly gates, I had to get a job. That's how I became a demon.

My time in the realm of the living had mostly held pain. It was what I knew. What I was good at. I took that pain and I turned it on assholes like Huck McKinley. He had also died, except he was a wife beater, and he ran dog fighting rings that had killed hundreds of animals.

That was how he ended up here under my tender loving care.

Where is here? Hell.

Huck took a bite of food and gagged. He spat it out

all over the floor, grasping at his throat. Murder shimmered in his eyes.

How cute.

"You bitch—"

"Ah-ah." I wagged my finger back and forth. "We talked about this. Dogs don't speak—"

He let out a growl that might have scared me a hundred years ago. Now?

I cracked my knuckles and grinned. He launched off the floor, saliva dripping from his lips, hot sauce mingled with bits of dog food staining his chest.

As he came up, so did my knee. I struck him square in the face. A crack echoed in the room. He flew through the air, crashing into the wall with a loud bang. He dropped to the floor, an indent of his disgusting body left in the drywall.

I tsk'd.

"Now you've done it, Huck." I walked over and picked him up by the back of his neck. My demonic strength was a godsend in moments like this. I tossed him in a wire metal crate and latched the door.

He groaned.

I hummed under my breath as I lifted my Apple watch to my face. "Play 'Baby' by Justin Bieber."

Huck let out a slew of profanities that were drowned out by the tween's obnoxious singing. I bobbed my head along to the music as I started for the front door.

"Wait—wait!" he yelled out for me. I paused at the

exit. "You can't leave me like this. Please—" He cut off when I grinned manically.

"Should have thought about that before you were a bad dog."

With that, I stepped outside and closed the door.

All along the street sat ordinary cookie-cutter houses. They spanned miles. Every house was actually a prison containing a bad soul that had fallen into that lower forty percent of the human race that needed to be punished. How long each person served before being recycled and sent back to the realm of the living differed, but the houses didn't. The only thing separating each of them was the number on the door. Each one was special to the soul inside it. I was currently in charge of a dozen or so. People that ranged from pedophiles, to Huck McKinley, to emotionally manipulative twats that stole from their kids.

Each of their crimes were different in act and severity, but the outcome was not. They'd landed themselves in Hell, and it was my responsibility to punish and rehabilitate them before they were wiped clean of all memories and sent back to try again.

Two houses down, Malachi the Dreaded stepped out of a door. He let out a low sigh of exhaustion and straightened his blood-soaked tie.

"Long session?" I asked.

He took one look at me and wrinkled his nose in distaste. I knew what he saw. A twenty-something-year-old body with leather pants and a black corset. I wore knee-high black boots with a chunky heel. My red hair hung loose around my shoulders and not a weapon or speck of blood was in sight.

"Very," he said after a pregnant pause. "You?"

"Not terribly so. I'm enjoying this case. I've already got another fifty years planned out for this guy." I hooked my thumb toward the door behind me, and Malachi's eyebrows inched up in barely discreet incredulity.

"Hmm."

I had to give it to him. He didn't say what he was clearly thinking. Must have learned from that asswipe, Karen. It wasn't exactly a secret that my methods of punishment were unusual. On the contrary, it made me an oddity for a demon.

It also made me the best at our job.

Anyone could hammer nails in a kneecap or shove bamboo under someone's nails. I was a true master of torture. A connoisseur, of sorts.

Not every demon saw it that way, though. Our profession generally attracted people that barely came in just above the forty percent. Shitheads that liked the idea of taking out their daddy issues on other people. People like Karen the Horrible.

A couple of decades back, I got assigned a case she wanted. Thinking she could get it back, she had openly challenged me to a duel. She and the others like her assumed I chose the punishments I did because I was weak. How wrong she was.

Malachi must have been there, or at least heard the stories. Then again, almost every demon had. The open snipes stopped after that day, even if the wandering eyes didn't. Oh, I heard the whispers through the grapevine, and over the years, several of the newbies had started to wonder. New demons always had something to prove. A bone to pick. It came with the territory. The demon guild was one of the most cutthroat in the Afterlife, and they had a tendency to judge or maim first and think later.

In that lay the problem. That behavior had broken way too many souls before their punishment was up. They weren't fully healed, and then those souls went back to the living realm to make the same shitty life choices that led them right back to Hell. Talk about a broken system.

Malachi idled warily, as if waiting for me to decide what I wanted. He likely didn't want to seem openly rude and run the risk of winding up on the other end of my legendary temper. Taking pity, or rather tired of my own mind games for the day, I waved at him and hit the home button on my watch.

My body de-materialized as I teleported into the demon dorms.

Several people took notice. I walked past the reception area where Diego the Dastardly was on duty. He gave me a wink and a sexy smirk, flirting shamelessly despite me having turned him down twice now. Still, I smiled back and inclined my head toward the gawking new girl next to him.

"Fury," she said in a low whisper.

"In the spirit," I chimed as I went by. Diego chuckled, his deep voice following after me.

Some of the oomph left me as I climbed two flights of stairs, but I kept my shoulders back as people passed me in the hallway. Some idolized me, like the girl downstairs. Usually that worshipping phase wore off after they had a few years to settle in. Right about the time the punishing and their new reality finally got to them. She was as green as they came, but that wouldn't be the case for long, and when life after death became the new norm, it wasn't so easy for most.

There was a reason over seventy percent of our new recruits dropped out in the first six months and transferred to a new guild. Everyone was earning their way toward one of two things: retirement, or the chance to be recycled. Most wanted to be recycled.

In the Afterlife, everything was what you made of it.

On Earth, you get what you get by happenstance, but either way—you get it.

Money. Opportunities. Race. Ethnicity. When you were recycled, your circumstances and start to life were all completely random, and it was utter bullshit.

One thing I learned in dying was that most people preferred the bullshit. They'd rather play the lottery and hope they got an easy ticket in the next life, and maybe an easy ticket into heaven.

I was never one for believing in chance. Whenever fate had a choice, it fucked me over. So, I opted to take the hard route.

Become a demon. Earn my spot.

My own little piece of heaven.

Literally.

I sighed at that thought as I opened the door. A full-size bed, half kitchen, and tiny bathroom. Everything I needed was in these four walls. By this point in my career, I could have left the dorms. Moved into my own little place in one of the lower circles of the Afterlife. Settled down with another demon and lived in . . . boring blah.

I refused. Instead, I was biding my time, saving every single second I earned for the big ticket. A place behind the golden gates.

On Earth, I'd been no one, but here—here I would be someone. Here, I already was.

Sort of.

It was an ongoing process.

I started for the bathroom, ready to strip out of my badass (and uncomfortable) outfit, run a nice hot bath, and drink a few beers.

Maybe whiskey instead.

It could really go either way after dealing with Huck all day.

I was just reaching for the buttons on my corset when my watch started to ring.

Incoming call from . . . Jake.

I threw my head back and groaned. Why? What could Jake from Afterlife Resources possibly want?

I weighed the merits of ignoring his call till tomorrow, but my curiosity got the better of me. I wanted to know what reason my resources officer would have for calling me this late in the evening.

My thumb hit accept before I could think it over more, but instead of a voice picking up on the other line, my body de-materialized once more.

I had only just registered that I was teleporting when I appeared in the hallway outside his office. His personal assistant, Francine, blinked in surprise.

"I'm sorry, but Jake is not available right now—"

"Well, I hate to break it to you, Francine, but I didn't come here by choice." I motioned to myself, happy I hadn't stripped first. I was so not feeling an orgy tonight.

Francine adjusted her glasses and picked up the phone on her desk. "Let me just call and see," she muttered, dialing his extension. Never mind that she could have just knocked on the door, or yelled, or better yet—Jake could have just given either of us a heads-up. I leaned against her desk and tapped my fingernails impatiently on the shiny veneer surface. "Your name is . . ." She left it open-ended, waiting for me to answer.

I gave her a hard look. You'd think I hadn't seen her once a month for the last thirty years.

"Fury."

She sighed. "Which Fury? Fury the Great? The Awful? Oh, I know—"

"*Just* Fury," I said, pinching the area between my brows and closing my eyes. A hundred years ago, I'd been an angry, murdered dead girl when I chose my name and profession.

How was I to know that Fury was essentially the 'Jessica' of the Afterlife?

"Ooookay," she drawled passive aggressively. We both waited for Jake to pick up. When he did, Francine said, "I have a 'Fury' here for you. She said you summoned her."

"Which Fury?" I heard him ask.

If my eyes could shoot fire, I would have melted the phone. I leaned forward over the edge of the desk and said into the receiver, "*The* Fury. The one you called after—"

The line went dead, and my lips parted.

Why that piece of—

His door opened. Jake stood there, wearing a wrinkled suit and chipper smile that always made me a little stabby.

"Hey Fury, why don't you come in and take a seat?"

I shook my head, heading into his office. The door

closed behind me right as I sat in the metal-framed chair. Outside, the second sun was setting.

"Why did you summon me?" I asked, cutting to the chase. He hummed to himself the whole way to his chair, and then took his sweet time sitting down. I waited expectantly.

Finally, Jake said the last thing I ever expected to hear.

"I want to send you back to Earth."

—Get It Now—

Ongoing Series:

—Adult Urban Fantasy—

Demons of New Chicago:

Touched by Fire (Book One)

Haunted by Shadows (Book Two)

Blood be Damned (Book Three)

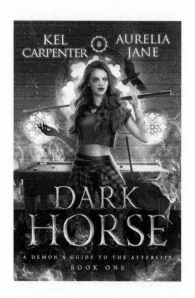

—Adult Reverse Harem Paranormal Romance—

A Demon's Guide to the Afterlife:

Dark Horse (Book One)

Completed Series:

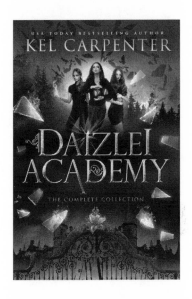

—Young Adult +/New Adult Urban Fantasy—

The Daizlei Academy Series:

Completed Series Boxset

—Adult Reverse Harem Urban Fantasy—

Queen of the Damned Series:

Complete Series Boxset

—New Adult Urban Fantasy—

The Grimm Brotherhood Series:

Complete Series Boxset

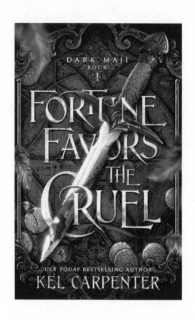

—Adult Dark Fantasy—

The Dark Maji Series:

Fortune Favors the Cruel (Book One)

Blessed be the Wicked (Book Two)

Twisted is the Crown (Book Three)

For King and Corruption (Book Four)

Long Live the Soulless (Book Five)

ABOUT THE AUTHOR

Kel Carpenter is a master of werdz. When she's not reading or writing, she's traveling the world, lovingly pestering her editor, and spending time with her husband and fur-babies. She is always on the search for good tacos and the best pizza. She resides in Maryland and desperately tries to avoid the traffic.

Join Kel's Readers Group!